HOT DEMON IN THE CITY

LATTER DAY DEMONS SERIES, BOOK ONE

CONNIE SUTTLE

To Walter, Joe, Larry, Lee, Dianne, Sarah and Mark.
Thank you.

ACKNOWLEDGMENTS

As always, this book is the result of collaboration. If it weren't for the support of my editor, my cover artist and my beta readers, it would be less than it is. All mistakes, as usual, are mine and no other's.

About the Author:
Connie Suttle lives in Oklahoma with her husband and a conglomerate of cats. They have finally banded together to make their demands, which has proven disconcerting to all humans involved.

You may find Connie in the following ways:
Facebook: Connie Suttle Author
Twitter: @subtledemon
Website and Blog: subtledemon.com

High Demon Series:

Demon Lost

Demon Revealed

Demon's King

Demon's Quest

Demon's Revenge

Demon's Dream

God Wars Series:

Blood Double

Blood Trouble

Blood Revolution

Blood Love

Blood Finale

Saa Thalarr Series:

Hope and Vengeance

Wyvern and Company

Observe and Protect*

First Ordinance Series:

Finder

Keeper

BlackWing

SpellBreaker

WhiteWing

R-D Series:

Cloud Dust

Cloud Invasion

Cloud Rebel

Latter Day Demons Series:

Hot Demon in the City

A Demon's Work is Never Done

A Demon's Due

Seattle Elementals Series:

Your Money's Worth

Worth Your While*

BlackWing Pirates Series

MindSighted

MindMage

MindRogue

MindMaster*

Black Rose Sorceress Series

The Rose Mark

Rose and Thorn

Black Rose Queen

Queen of Thorns and Roses

Future Wars Series

Buffer Zone

Black Zone*

Other Titles from SubtleDemon Publishing:

Malefactor

Transgressor

Underhanded*

by Joe Scholes

*Forthcoming

CHAPTER 1

exsi

    San Francisco in the past wasn't anything like Avendor. I'd been there for a month, with barely an excuse for a vehicle in the garage of Aunt Bree's house and still hadn't learned all there was to know about the place.

I realized I was a captive in this place and time—I could skip back to Avendor, but it wouldn't be the Avendor I came from. That meant I had to adjust to living in San Francisco.

Actually, I didn't live in the city—I lived across the bay in a very large (for one person) home overlooking San Rafael Bay. Aunt Bree had given permission for me to live in her house as long as I wanted, with one stipulation—I had to find a job.

It wasn't any job, either. It had to be with Rome Enterprises. I had no idea why, but when Aunt Bree spoke, people tended to listen and obey.

I couldn't—and wouldn't—hazard a guess as to whom (or what) she really was. What I did know is this; I'd had an arranged marriage waiting for me back home, with a man I hadn't even met.

No way would I settle for that. I wanted to pick my own man— when I was ready and not before. After all, I was barely twenty-three

1

and hadn't lived on my own anywhere. I wanted that experience. Wanted to know what freedom felt like.

Kordevik Weth could screw himself, for all I cared.

Yes, that was his name. I didn't want to know anything else about him. Tapping the keyboard of the archaic computer system people from Earth still used, I searched through the job listings at Rome Enterprises.

Until now, I'd only seen janitorial positions or jobs for assistants of assistants. My eyes locked on a new one—*Investigative Reporter*. I filled out a job application immediately.

~

"Miss Silver? Lexsi Silver?" the female voice on the other end of the cell-phone conversation asked.

"Yes?"

"This is Anita Grant from Human Resources at Rome Enterprises. I have the application and photograph you sent, and I'd like to schedule an interview for you with Mr. Andrews."

"All right," I agreed, attempting to stop the flutter in my stomach. I'd never gotten a job on my own, before. *What if they hired me?*

What if they didn't hire me?

Panic threatened; I shoved it back. Aunt Bree said I'd have what I needed to get the job, but I knew nothing about being a reporter. Yes, I had an education—in Alliance Policy and Politics. That would likely be useless on Earth.

"Is tomorrow at three a good time?"

"Three is perfect."

"Mr. Andrews' office is on the tenth floor of the Rome Building. You know where that is?"

"I do."

"Good. We look forward to meeting you, Miss Silver."

I barely remembered to thank the woman before ending the call and covering my face with a shaking hand.

I look so much like my mother, I told myself as I gazed in the mirror the following day. Silver-blonde hair fell down my back and nearly to my waist. I'd thought about putting it up, but decided I'd be more comfortable with it down. I had my father's blue eyes, however, and I was taller than Mom.

She stood barely above five feet, in Earth measurements. I was seven inches taller. Pushing thoughts of my parents away, I concentrated on my image in the mirror, hoping that Aunt Bree hadn't set me up to fail in an interview.

An hour later, I opened a glass door to enter the Rome Building and headed for the elevator. Squaring my shoulders and releasing a sigh, I decided to hold my head up, no matter what happened.

Mr. Andrews was round and shorter than I was. In fact, if he'd been painted red, blue, yellow and white, he'd be a beach ball. Squashing that image, I leveled my gaze on him as he searched through a stack of papers on his desk.

The top one was my application form. The rest—I had no idea what they were. "Your college credentials are quite good, Miss Silver," Mr. Andrews blinked at me through thick glasses. "We don't usually offer jobs to those who've attended such small schools, but we may make an exception in your case."

I gaped at him for a moment, before looking down and clearing my throat to cover my shock. "Thank you," I lifted my chin again. Mr. Andrews thought my surprise was due to the fact that Rome Publications would consider me because of my small-school credentials.

I was actually surprised that I had credentials in the first place. "If you're hired," Mr. Andrews went on, "you'll be working as an assistant for one of our best field reporters, Vann Jacobs. Do you know who he is?"

"I've seen his work—and his broadcasts," I nodded. "I appreciated the update he did last week on the congressional probe into bribery and fraud." I mentally thanked my instructor in foreign diplomacy for that answer—Vann Jacobs was more concerned about how he looked on camera than exposing crimes committed by politicians.

"We're proud of that piece, too," Mr. Andrews nodded. "You understand that Vann employs two assistants, who do preliminary interviews and gather information for him? One of them got married and left the company two weeks ago."

I was young and not from Earth, but I recognized politics anywhere. What Mr. Andrews was telling me is that Vann Jacobs let others do the work, then stood in front of a camera, appropriately dressed for the venue and spilled out what others had given him.

"I can handle the work, Mr. Andrews," I assured my interviewer.

"I have no doubt of it," he smiled. "Let me take you to Mr. Jacob's office; he'll finish the interview."

On the way home, I stopped at a Starbucks and asked for a frappé. The day was cool but the mists had cleared away for my drive home, convincing me it was warm enough for a cold drink. The young man at the drive-through window grinned at my vehicle and stretched downward to hand the drink to me. Yes, it's a TinyCar. Yes, it's cause for hilarity almost everywhere.

Maybe I ought to get something else to drive. Let's face it—most people don't drive a vehicle you could easily navigate down a sidewalk.

Mr. Andrews said they'd call tomorrow about the job—that they had two more interviews to do before a decision was made. A part of me hoped they'd turn me down.

A part of me hoped they wouldn't.

Vann Jacobs wouldn't be easy to work with—he was demanding, pig-headed and, well, a pig. He'd stared at me from one end to the other, making me wish I'd worn anything but the drop-waisted black dress with tiny pleats in the skirt and a short, white jacket over that.

He'd even studied my shoes, which were fine enough; short, black heels that were comfortable and good for walking. The questions he'd asked were common-sense questions, but after a while, I got the idea he wasn't paying attention to my answers.

That's why a part of me hoped I wouldn't get the job. I didn't want to knee my first boss in the groin to discourage unwanted advances. After all, getting away from a male was the reason I was looking for a job to start with.

Kordevik

I'd lived in the condo for six months and had finally gotten used to San Francisco people, traffic and food. Yes, I understood I was trapped in Earth's past. My marriage was supposed to take place in the future, but six months earlier in Earth time, my intended ran away from me without a backward glance.

I admit to getting drunk and destroying a bar on Kifirin after receiving the news.

I barely remember being sentenced to five years on Earth as punishment. A job awaited so I could support myself—one that came with a warning that if I fucked it up, my sentence would be doubled.

After learning to talk (and curse) like the locals in a short amount of time, I realized that didn't bode well for my future. It made me want to get the hell away from Earth as soon as possible.

My job was working as a driver for Rome Enterprises, a local news conglomerate with offices in San Francisco and Los Angeles. I ferried reporters and news crews from the studio to locations and back again.

I had a commercial chauffeur's license, in order to do my job.

The thing is—I'd never taken the test; someone had handled the license for me, as well as the job.

I still wondered how that had happened.

I'd started rising early so I could get to the gym—I missed sparring with my friends in the military back home. Krav Maga lessons were a substitute for bladework—I didn't anticipate finding anyone who would spar with blades. Earth had given those up for guns, knives and other, more portable weapons.

Hauling my gym bag over a shoulder, I grabbed the keys to my Jeep and strode out the door. If I timed it right, I could grab coffee at Starbucks before I had to be at work.

Lexsi

"The job is yours," Anita Grant had a smile in her voice as she delivered the news. "If you can, come in to fill out paperwork this afternoon; Vann wants you on the job tomorrow morning. You'll be going out with one of his other assistants to investigate the murder-suicide in Sausalito."

I'd heard early news on the murder-suicide in question—wealthy, philandering husband with pretty, socialite wife. The mistress was being blamed for their murder, after which she'd offed herself—in the formal dining room.

Open and shut—in most people's minds.

Something about it bothered me, though. I was hoping I'd get to speak with witnesses—I would know whether they were telling the truth.

"I'll be there this afternoon," I told Anita. "Anything special I should bring with me?"

"Two forms of ID," she replied. "Do you have a passport, by any chance?"

"I do have a passport. Why?"

"In case Vann wants to travel out of the country—he does on occasion."

"I understand," I said. "Will I see you this afternoon?"

"Sure. Drop by my desk; I'll have the papers ready for you."

Anita had lovely, latte-tinted skin, dark green eyes that shone with intelligence and a beautiful smile as she handed a sheaf of papers to me. I knew about Earth taxes, Social Security and a mountain of other things most people take for granted—as long as they were born on Earth. I'd had to learn everything, but I'd found information waiting on the kitchen island the day I first landed in Aunt Bree's house.

Anita Grant didn't know that, but I liked her immediately. It would be nice to find a friend to trust—someday. Anita was added as the first candidate on that list.

~

Kordevik

"Kory, drop me off at the front door," Fiona Hall directed. Traffic in front of the Rome building was a bitch; I had to inch the limo toward the curb rather than asking Fiona to walk ten extra feet to get to the sidewalk.

Fiona was an aging princess of a journalist, who did a syndicated talk show adored by ten fans (maybe) across the nation.

Sleeping with an executive ensured that she kept her job, which is why I was delivering her to the Rome building instead of the studio across the bay.

I figured the only reason the executive was still sleeping with her was because he was married and Fiona could ruin him.

After cursing mentally at traffic and Fiona for ten minutes, I pulled up to the curb and got out of the car to open Ms. Hall's door for her.

That's when I saw *her*.

The one responsible for my five-year sentence on Earth.

Yes, I recognized her—I'd seen photographs of her.

She, on the other hand, had never seen me—which made it all the worse to leave me empty-handed on our wedding day. She didn't even know me—didn't bother to get to know me. That was a stinging blow, because I'd had to apologize to wedding guests, my friends and everyone else who seemed determined to make this my fault instead of hers.

I gaped as she stopped for a moment on the sidewalk, platinum hair blowing across her face as she waited for the traffic light.

"Kory," Fiona's petulant whine brought me back to the present.

"Ms. Hall," I took her hand and helped her from the car.

"That's all for today," she said.

"Thank you, Ms. Hall." I still had another trip to make to the studio before my workday was over, but at least I wouldn't have to deliver Fiona to anyone else's doorstep today.

By the time Fiona walked past me, the bitch I was supposed to marry had already gotten away.

Probably just as well—I wanted to shove her against a wall and let her know exactly what she'd given up without a second thought.

Lexsi

I now understood what women who worked a high profile job went through on most days.

I had to pick an outfit.

One I could comfortably wear all day without fighting it or fidgeting in it.

One that looked professional enough to those around me.

One I didn't hate.

Clothes were strewn across my bed before I was able to walk out of my bedroom fully dressed. All my fussing ensured that I barely had time for coffee before sliding behind the wheel of the TinyCar and driving toward the studio in Sausalito.

Within ten minutes of arriving at work, I discovered that Vann Jacob's first assistant was almost as insufferable as he was. "Make sure the crew is ready," Mike Ellis commanded, waving an arm. "Make sure the satellite and sound gear is packed. We may need the generator truck—make sure it's on standby for Vann."

I learned quickly that most of Mike's sentences began with *make sure*. The one thing I was most sure of, however, was that Mike was great at ordering other people around while doing very little himself.

He'd also used the term satellite, when everything used by Rome Enterprises was cellular. The old term was still in use, though, because technology changed frequently while people didn't.

My day started with me not knowing where anything was. By the time we'd arrived on the street where the murder-suicide had taken place, I knew where half the things in the studio were and had spoken to most of the people. Some were nice, others not so much, as my paternal grandmother would say.

"I'll do the talking," Mike tapped his chest as if that made him more important when we stepped out of the news van and walked up the steps to the first witness' house.

Gerta Britt, forty-ish and a bottle blonde, answered the door, dressed in her finest with makeup caked on. She wanted to be on television, no doubt. "I thought Vann was coming," she said after looking Mike over and finding him inadequate.

"Vann will be here later," Mike said, attempting to placate her. He was offended that she didn't find him suitable, too, but I wasn't about to say anything. After all, Mike was younger and handsome enough, but Vann's name was the one everybody heard as it was touted often by *News Seventy-Four of the Bay Area*, a wholly owned subsidiary of Rome Enterprises.

I listened as Gerta explained what she knew to Mike, who held a microphone pointed at her chin. She made it sound as if she knew more than she did, and knew the victims better than she did. She only strayed a short distance from the truth, though—likely worried that she'd be caught in her lies and shamed in public.

After all, public shaming was a coup in the journalistic realm.

"When did you see them last?" Mike asked.

That question—and the answer—drew my attention.

"I saw them six days ago—they were dressed up to go somewhere, so I just waved from my driveway," Gerta sighed. "They looked so nice together."

"Do you know where they were going?" Mike asked.

"No—sorry."

Mike didn't think that question would lead to any real information —two rich people going out to dinner or whatever. It stood out to me, although I couldn't really say why. Mike wasn't interested, but I intended to follow up on that lead. Somebody, somewhere, knew where they'd gone.

"What about the family—have you spoken to them?" Mike asked next.

"I saw both of their daughters—the police met them at the house yesterday, but I didn't get a chance to talk to them."

I was beginning to think that Gerta had only seen what she'd seen through her front windows—I doubted she went outside much to do her snooping.

"Did you hear the gunshots?"

"No. I heard dogs barking, but that's it—my house keeps most sounds out," Gerta claimed.

"So you believe a neighbor's dogs heard the shooting?"

"Yes. It was the right time—I was about to go to bed but didn't think much about it—those dogs are usually let out to do their business before they're brought back in for the night. They bark at anything—cats, squirrels, whatever," Gerta waved an arm.

"Do you know which house?" Mike perked up. "Where the dogs are?"

"Oh, down the block," she shrugged. Gerta wanted her fifteen minutes of fame and didn't want to be upstaged by the owners of barking dogs.

"What about any servants?" Mike persisted.

"All gone home for the evening; I don't think Donna liked having them in the house after hours."

"Do you know why that was?"

"I never asked her about it." She sounded defensive.

Translation—*Donna Raven didn't like talking to Gerta.*

"Did you ever see Reece Channing before?" Mike turned to the mistress.

"No," Gerta shook her head. "Never. I had no idea Abe was having an affair. He and Donna seemed so close."

That statement interested me immediately—in Gerta's mind, it was absolute truth. Information about Reece, the murderer and supposed mistress, was still coming in, but she was the unlikeliest candidate to commit murder or suicide, in my opinion. She'd just moved to the Bay area; she'd rented a house and started a new job—working as a nanny for a wealthy family in the city.

Before that, word was that she'd lived in a suburb of Los Angeles—Whittier, actually. My questions—if I could ask them—were whether Abe Raven traveled often. He'd have to, in order to engage in a long-term affair with Reece.

If not, then I suspected a setup. I just didn't know how to go about getting the information I wanted.

After Mike was satisfied he'd gotten everything he could from Gerta, including a signed waiver to use her image on television, we went looking for the neighbors with the dogs. Both Rottweilers came to the door with the maid, who answered our knock.

The lady of the house wasn't home; her husband was out of the country on business, she informed us.

Mike attempted to ask her questions, but she cut him off, saying she wasn't there the night of the murders. The door was shut in Mike's face—it was a good thing, actually. Both dogs looked as if they'd like a chunk of him.

We found two other neighbors home, but neither were very helpful. Vann and Mike were going in the wrong direction. I hoped the police were doing a better job—the more I thought about it, the more the case nagged at me.

"Worthless," Mike strode toward our van, the cameraman and sound girl trotting behind him. He shoved the microphone at the girl, who almost dropped the shoulder case she carried in an effort to balance everything. I stopped to help; she nodded her thanks as I took the case, she unzipped it, placed the mic in its cover and zipped it up again.

"He's just as ruthless as Vann if he doesn't get what he wants," she mumbled as we started walking again.

"Does the station have a society editor?" I asked.

"No, but the online newspaper does," she replied. "I'm Jessie. I'd shake hands but," she did her best to shrug beneath the load she carried.

"Do you know who it is?" I asked.

"No, but if you call the main number at the office downtown, they'll give you the information. Why do you want it? Are you getting married?"

"Nooo," I shook my head with more emphasis than I should have. "I was just wondering if the Ravens had gone to a fancy function the night Gerta was talking about—the last time she saw them."

"I just assumed they'd gone to dinner," Jessie sighed. "If you find anything out, let me know. That sounds like a good lead."

"Sure," I agreed. "It's probably nothing."

The rest of the day was spent in the editing booth, watching the interviews we'd gotten with Gerta and two other neighbors, all of which (in my mind) was completely worthless.

Vann showed up in the booth sometime after three to see what we had. The interview had been whittled down to two minutes—it was all the six o'clock producer was willing to give us.

Vann did a voice-over on some of Mike's questions, while only Gerta's image was recorded answering questions. The finished product looked (and sounded) as if Vann had done the interview with Gerta instead of Mike.

"I'll take a quick drive back to the neighborhood and do my part now," Vann announced after watching the images. He'd called it footage, which was another archaic term. Everything was digital now, in a world that had once been film and then video tape.

"You," Vann pointed at me. "You'll come with me. I have a driver waiting outside."

This was what I worried about—and it looked as if Vann would get my knee in his crotch sooner than I imagined.

When I was five, Daddy and Uncle Sal started teaching me self-defense. I was good at it now, although Sal would always be the ideal for me. He moved so swiftly at times it was difficult to keep my eyes on him.

Whenever I said I wanted to be like him when I grew up, he'd grin and tell me I could be if I wanted.

Those skills might be needed before the day was over, and I imagined myself hunting for another job the following morning.

Kordevik

I waited in the limo for an hour before Vann Jacobs walked out the back door of the news station. That wasn't unusual.

What *was* unusual was the person who followed right behind him, between the sound girl and the cameraman.

My ex.

I stiffened. *What the hell was she doing here?*

"Don't just stand there, Kory, open the trunk," Vann snapped.

I hated driving Vann. More than I hated driving Fiona, even. Little Miss Lexsi was the foul tasting frosting on top of that nasty cake for me.

"I'll help," Lexsi offered, taking the heavy equipment bag off Jessie's shoulders. It was placed carefully in the trunk once I got it open. Then, Lexsi held the camera while Chet stuffed his equipment in, too.

All right—so she could play nice. I didn't trust that for even half a second.

If Chet weren't gay, he'd be following her like a puppy. Vann was watching too closely; her looks were probably his reason for hiring her in the first place.

Not my problem, I reminded myself. I had to remind myself of that at least six more times during the trip, and again when Vann asked her if she'd have a drink with him after the eleven o'clock news.

She politely refused.

That wouldn't stop Vann for a minute. He'd see her as a challenge; one he intended to conquer.

I was so pissed by the time I got off work that I headed straight for a bar. I'd been practicing holding my temper—I could now hold back from breathing smoke whenever I was mad enough to crack heads, so that was definitely a step in the right direction.

I'd chosen my regular hangout for a reason—if there were a place I'd feel more at home on Earth, it was at a bar where the vamps and werewolves hung out. Sure, shifters came in, too, but everybody was civilized—for the most part.

Once in a while, a human wandered in. The vamps always sent him (or her) out the door pretty quick. They didn't know exactly what I was; all they knew was that I wasn't human.

That was enough to let me stay since I drank at the bar, didn't raise a fuss and tipped well.

The *L* in Clawdia's was out in the neon sign as I opened the door to go inside. It wasn't a recent development—the letter had been dark for as long as I'd been coming here.

"Jamison's. Double. On the rocks," I said, sliding onto a worn-leather barstool.

"Well, well. Mr. Kory's back." Watson, the werewolf bartender, offered a wry grin and hauled the bottle of Jamison's off the shelf.

"This is Mr. Kory's front," I tapped my chest.

"You think that's funny, man?" he asked.

"Is it just you without a sense of humor?" I shot back as he poured my drink.

"Is it just you who can't tell a decent joke?"

Country music played softly overhead—at least they kept the volume down. It likely had to do with the fact that werewolves and vampires have sensitive ears.

"You're in a sour mood tonight," I pointed out.

"You try living without your woman."

"Hmmph," I snorted and tipped the glass of whiskey to my lips. I had a story I could tell him about missing women and what that had cost me.

"Besides, I'm not in a sour mood. I'm morose."

"Morose? Now there's a word," I muttered, thumping my glass on the bar and silently asking for a refill.

"Dude, we got trouble," Watson whispered as the door opened behind me. I turned to see what Watson considered trouble.

He hadn't exaggerated.

Lexsi

"Anybody who's anybody will be on the guest list," the tall, slender woman pushed a paper list across her desk.

As it turned out, all I had to do was ask Anita who the society editor was, and I'd been sent to the proper office on the fifteenth floor.

"This is the only event happing in town that night?" I asked, lifting my eyes from the list and gazing at the woman.

"As far as I know. Mr. and Mrs. James Rome, Junior, celebrating their thirty-fifth wedding anniversary. Names on the list are in alpha order."

Going back to the list, I searched for Abraham and Donna Raven.

Not there. I felt it unlikely that the Ravens knew the Romes, but it had been worth a try. "Thanks for your help," I pushed the list back with a sigh.

"Didn't find what you wanted?"

"No. It was just a hunch, and a bad one at that."

"Anytime," she offered a smile.

Lifting my jacket off the chair, I waved and walked out of her office.

Kordevik

"A gun's not much help against a vamp," I hissed as Watson slowly reached beneath the bar. "There are three here. They'll have you shredded before you can pull the trigger."

Neither Watson nor I could take our eyes off the scene before us. Three older vamps held a younger one between them, and he'd already been cut and beaten.

"Why the hell are they bringing that in here?" Watson hissed. This was something that should have been played out in a back alley somewhere.

Actually, the younger vamp should have already died, if I read things correctly.

The reason appeared thirty seconds later, when two more vamps hauled the human woman into the bar.

You double-cross your rich vamp boyfriend with a younger, not-rich but better-looking vampire and you both get it.

In paranormal public, I suppose.

CHAPTER 2

*K*ordevik Watson eased the rifle out of its hiding place. This was no shotgun; it was a semiautomatic that looked as if it belonged in a SWAT team's arsenal instead of a nook below the bar.

"Are you suicidal?" I hissed at Watson. I was waiting for the vamps to hear either of us and come running. While Watson might be fast if he changed to wolf, he still couldn't outrun a determined vamp.

"They're gonna kill him and the girl," Watson said. "We have to do something."

"You need to get down behind the bar," I said. "And forget the Rin-Tin-Tin shit."

I had half a second to close my eyes in disbelief when Watson pointed the rifle at the vamps.

Bloody hell.

"You're fucking lucky I didn't burn down the bar," I slapped a bag of frozen peas onto the kitchen counter in front of Watson, whose left eye was turning purple.

"What the hell are you, man?" Watson held the bag against his eye and winced at the contact.

"Hmmph," I snorted while a curl of smoke drifted from my nostrils.

"How is he?" Watson asked, turning toward the vampire who lay unconscious on my leather sofa.

"He's still breathing," I muttered, jerking a bottle of Crown off the top of the fridge and filling a glass. "That means he'll be all right. At least we got the girl to the hospital. If Klancy hadn't shown up to help with that," I shook my head.

Klancy was a vamp—a regular who showed up at Clawdia's just for the company. He'd been a professional at martial arts in his human life. He was deadly, as it turned out, since becoming vampire.

I was grateful he was on our side. He was the one to get the girl to the hospital, too, while I hauled Watson and the vamp out of there, each tucked beneath my smaller Thifilathi's arms.

The werewolf bar manager had shown up to take over while I hauled Watson out of there before the police showed up to ask questions. He'd asked me to take the wounded vamp, too.

Questions would be asked; I understood that—about the building on the opposite side of the street and why there were holes in the brick, now.

After I'd tossed vamps through the façade, the place looked as if somebody drove a tank into it.

Clawdia's had no security cameras—for obvious reasons.

I couldn't express how happy I was about that.

"This is a nice place," Watson looked around with his right eye; his left was still covered by the bag of peas.

"Hmmph," I snorted again. Grabbing a second glass, I dumped it in front of the werewolf and poured a generous serving of Crown. At least he wasn't whining about his girlfriend or scratching at the door to be let out.

~

Lexsi

"Wear nice jeans. Black is better, but as long as you have a dressier top and jacket," Farin Armstrong, the morning weathergirl, informed me. "For now, Vann and Mike will hog the camera. Count on it."

I'd worn a skirt to work, only to discover that Mike and I were being sent to the Presidio, where several dead seals had washed up on a rocky shore. For now, we were pointed away from the murder/suicide investigation.

Our driver—the same one who'd ferried Vann and me the evening before, waited for us, looking as if he'd had maybe an hour's sleep before coming to work. "You all right?" I asked as he opened the door for Jessie and me.

"I'm fine," he growled, his words clipped and evasive. The door was shut the moment I was inside the car; Kory got Chet's camera bag into the trunk and slid into the driver's seat a few seconds later.

In the rearview mirror, I saw his eyes glance in my direction twice on the way to the location, but they were dark and unreadable from where I sat. Maybe he had a hangover. I sure didn't want to push him to find out.

An investigative team from Marine Animal Sanctuary met us at the shore where the seals had been found. Mike poked a microphone in the lead investigator's face and started asking questions.

"We sometimes see them die from bullet wounds," the man shrugged. "That was the first thing we looked for."

"Did you find anything?" Mike asked.

"No bullet wounds. We found they'd been killed by some sort of predator. We suspected sharks, of course, but the teeth marks aren't those of a shark."

"Do you know what kind of predator it was, then?"

"We're still investigating," the man replied.

"You have to know something," Mike responded.

"Cut off the camera, this is off the record," the investigator said.

Mike made a motion with his free hand, indicating to Chet to shut off the camera. Chet lowered it with a nod.

With the mic held loosely in his right hand, which rested near his hip, Mike nodded for the investigator to continue.

"The teeth marks are sharp and deep," the man shrugged. "But the size of the mouth is roughly the size of a human's. Now, I don't know about you, but I've never seen something that could place a bite like that. It didn't look as if a meal were what the predator was looking for, either."

"Will you contact us if you get more information?" Mike asked.

"If I can hand you proof," the man shrugged.

"Do you have photographs of the dead animals—that are safe to show on the news?"

"I'll send something this afternoon."

"Gerta Britt is on the phone for Vann," a production assistant informed Mike the moment we walked inside the station. "The e-mail from Marine Animal Sanctuary is here, too."

"Silver, take the old biddy's call. I'll check the images in the e-mail," Mike barked. "Make sure she knows not to bother us with inconsequential shit."

I blinked at Mike twice before hunching my shoulders and heading toward my cubicle to take the call.

"Line three," the PA called out.

"Ms. Britt?" I answered the phone. "This is Lexsi Silver. How can I help you?"

"I found them on my camera footage," Gerta crowed. "The night I saw them leave."

"The last time you saw the Ravens?" I asked.

"Yes. I didn't think my security camera was pointed in that direction, but I caught Donna getting into the car after Abe backed out of the garage."

"So you only saw Donna. Not Abe."

"No, I saw both of them, but the camera only recorded Donna."

"I see," I said. "Is it possible to get a copy of the recording?"

"I don't know how to do that," Gerta said. "All this electronic stuff just goes right past me. Can you come back to the house and take a look?"

"Let me check my schedule for this afternoon, Ms. Britt. Hold, please."

It took two minutes to find Mike and attempt to tell him what Gerta found. "Check on it," he waved a hand. He was busy sorting through photographs in the e-mail sent by Marine Animal Sanctuary.

That meant I had to find a ride, or drive myself in my TinyCar.

After considering the bad mood Kory was in, I opted for the TinyCar.

"You have mud and sand on your heels," Kory pointed out as I walked past him in the parking garage to get to my TinyCar.

"Damn." I lifted a foot to look.

He was right.

"I have a pair of athletic shoes in the car," I mumbled. "I'll change."

"Which one's yours?" he asked as I started walking again.

"The blue TinyCar," I muttered without turning.

"A TinyCar?" His laugh grated on my nerves.

"Yeah. It belongs to my aunt," I said and kept walking.

Kordevik

A TinyCar. I didn't consider them cars. They were glorified skateboards in my opinion. She said it belonged to her aunt. As far as I knew, she only had one aunt—her father's half-sister—and that one had never visited this planet.

Didn't make any sense to me.

"Hey, where are you going?" I trotted after her. She was climbing into the TinyCar when I caught up with her.

"Back to Gerta Britt's," she said. "Claims she found the Ravens on her security camera recording. Has no idea how to transfer the images, so I'm off to take a look."

"Are you sure that's safe?" I asked.

"Gerta Britt isn't dangerous," she said, her blue eyes raking over me, haggard face and all.

"I meant in this thing that isn't a car," I said, suddenly defensive. "A stiff breeze will blow you to Chicago."

"Awesome. I've never been to Chicago." She started the car and put it in gear.

"I can drive you," I offered.

Wait. What kind of difik was I? I hated her.

"Get in your excessively large car, Kory Wilson, and take a nap. I think you need it," she snapped and drove away.

I cursed as she drove away—not only had she pissed me off—she was right.

❧

Lexsi

Gerta was right—electronics went right past her. I had to search the recorder for the images again—she'd managed to lose them. After nearly half an hour of her leaning over my shoulder while I watched a small monitor in a closet devoted to her security system, I found the images she'd reported.

"See, that's Donna getting in the car. Normally she'd get in while it was parked in the garage. Maybe she forgot something."

Donna was dressed in a gown and diamonds, I could see that. Gerta had a decent security camera, at least. Donna's evening dress had a bolero jacket dripping in glittery fringe and her hair was swept up in an impressive French pleat, with a comb that matched the glittery fringe.

A lot of money had been spent on that dress—it had *designer exclusive* written all over it.

Before I left Gerta's house, I had a copy of the images on a flash drive to take back to the station. Wherever the Ravens had gone that night, I'd bet it wasn't just to dinner.

~

Kordevik

Things had changed when I got home from work; Watson was asleep, the vampire wide awake.

I was surprised Watson trusted the vamp well enough to take a nap on the sofa.

"Name's Mason," he extended his hand. "Thanks for last night. The wolf says you changed into something, but he wasn't sure what it was. Doesn't matter—you saved my ass."

"I only saved it last night," I said, hanging my jacket on the hall tree and studying the vamp who occupied the easy chair in my living room. "You still have to worry about those vamps who wanted to kill you."

"Yeah." He wallowed in gloom and self-pity for a moment. "I was only trying to get her away—she was scared. I can't blame her—Granger tends to murder what he has no use for."

"Granger?"

"Old." Mason shrugged. "Has a bunch of local vamps under his thumb. Figure the law would like to ask him a few questions about missing people."

"You—you were a cop, I'm guessing. Before you developed a taste for blood."

"Good guess," Mason rose and stretched. "Only on the job five years when I got shot in Sacramento. Somebody took pity on me and made the turn."

"Is that what convinced Watson to fall asleep in your presence?"

"Yeah. He remembers the huge flap in Sacramento six years ago when a cop disappeared. Haven't been seen, since," he shrugged.

"You mean Granger didn't bother to place compulsion?" That surprised me.

"Hmmph."

I held back from asking the next question that tickled my brain. It could get both of us in trouble.

"Did it take all five of those vamps to bring you down?" I asked instead.

"Six. One of 'em didn't get back up after I put him down. I hear you took out the rest."

"We won't discuss that," I held up a hand.

"Sounds fine. Wish I could ask for a beer, but it wouldn't do any good. I have bagged blood in the fridge at my place. Better get goin'."

"I think you ought to stay here—at least for now," I said.

"I need to eat," he said. Simple. Direct.

"Great. There's a bar around the corner. Want to satisfy both cravings at once?"

"I don't bite women," he growled. "I hate biting guys."

"Men in kilts, then? As a compromise?"

"You know—that almost made me laugh. Come on, we'll find somebody who's had a bath and didn't drown in cologne afterward."

I understood something as I followed Mason out the door—I figured he'd been in his twenties when he joined the Sacramento Police Department. Five years as a cop, followed by six as a vamp had given him wisdom beyond his age.

~

Lexsi

"Hey, want to get a drink after work?"

Anita called me first—I figured I'd have to call her if I wanted to make friends.

"That sounds great," I said. "I just have to get this flash drive downloaded for Vann and I'm done for today," I said. "Where?"

"I'm headed in your direction," she said. "There's a place off 101 in Sausalito that serves food, so we can eat and drink."

"Sounds really good, I'm starved," I admitted. She gave me the name and address and said she'd be there in half an hour. I was grateful for her invitation the moment Vann stuck his head inside my cubicle to ask me if I were free for dinner.

"Canada," Anita shrugged when I asked her where she was from. "I have citizenship here, now. Applied right after I got my degree from UCLA."

"What the heck are you doing working in HR, then?" I asked.

"I don't know if you've noticed, but there aren't a lot of people of color—black or otherwise—working for Rome Enterprises. No offense," she held up a hand.

"None taken, and yes, I have noticed."

"So," she toyed with the saltshaker for a moment, as if she were deciding whether she could trust me or not, "I went to work in a low-level job so I can write an article on Rome's hiring practices. If I'm lucky, I can sell it to a New York newspaper or magazine."

"Sounds good to me," I said. "Can you include womanizing bosses in your article?"

"Vann giving you problems already?"

"He's asked me out twice, and I've only been on the job two days."

"Yeah—his last assistant of the female persuasion got engaged and married in self-defense, I think."

"How long have you worked for Rome Enterprises?"

"Nearly a year. You should see the stuff I have on my computer," she laughed.

"Aren't you worried that you'll be found out?"

"No—I sort of want them to fire me," she said.

"Well, that could cut into our budding friendship," I said. "Have you gotten any directives from someone above you—to only hire certain people?"

"No, but that doesn't mean it can't happen. Besides, look at me. You think they'd tell me to do that?"

"Well, no," I admitted. I knew little about discrimination on Earth; the Reth and Campiaan Alliances were naturally integrated, as each had more than five hundred member planets. I also wondered why Rome Enterprises hadn't been called to account for its hiring practices already.

"It wasn't always like this," Anita said, dropping her eyes for a moment. "I've done research. It all started when Rome Senior died and Jayson Rome and his mother sold their interests in the company to the oldest son and his wife."

"So the current owners are the reason?"

"I think so. I just need some undeniable proof that they're directly involved in the hiring process."

"That's sort of scary—to think they're watching over every decision," I frowned. "I thought they gave underlings some sort of autonomy."

"I heard Laurel fired somebody just because she didn't like the way they looked," Anita whispered. "I got wind of that while I was still at UCLA."

"Have you talked to that person? Do you know who it was?"

"I'm still working on that."

My gran always said that if you couldn't prove something, it didn't happen. Anita might have a strong basis for her article, but she was right—she didn't have sufficient proof. I could tell which of her words were truth and which were uncertain—she'd only heard rumors about Laurel Rome firing somebody. I felt she was on the fence about her article, too, but didn't want to dig too deeply into that mystery.

"I think you should tread carefully, and hand somebody a backup of all your information," I suggested instead. "Or put it in a safe place so someone you trust can find it. Just in case."

"I sent it already," she said. "To my cousin in LA. She works in a law office."

"Good. Here comes the waiter—what are we going to eat?" I opened my menu to read the selections.

~

Anita's car was parked two down from mine in the minuscule parking lot surrounding the restaurant. At least she'd turned to workplace gossip after dropping her initial bomb on me.

Yes, the attack took me by surprise. I promised myself I'd never let that happen again.

They were after Anita, that much was certain, but in their eyes, I presented little problem. Three of them came for us, with knives. I felt like giggling hysterically as something my gran always said ran through my mind.

You don't bring a gun to a vampire fight.

I'd been trained to protect myself at a very early age.

No, I wasn't vampire. I could hold my own against these, though. The first man who rushed me learned quickly; I had his knife in my hand and thumped him on the back of the neck with the thick handle, dropping him to the pavement in two blinks.

Anita faced the other two, who were poised to lunge at her.

I discovered she wasn't human, either.

She changed. Her clothing, torn to shreds with the transformation, puddled about her feet.

Something amphibious hissed at both men, who'd taken a step backward.

Don't kill them, I sent hasty mindspeech, hoping she'd hear me. We didn't need human spaghetti left on the pavement surrounding a popular nightspot—somebody was bound to notice.

My worries were alleviated the moment both men turned and ran.

"Get up," Anita's alter ego jerked the third man off the ground; he was beginning to wake from the blow I'd delivered. "Tell your boss," she swung him around and locked eyes with his as the power in her voice dripped from scaly lips, "Tell your boss," she repeated, "that he should think twice before sending someone after me again. Now get the hell away from us, and never bother us again."

Anita and I watched him run as fast as he could down a dark street.

"Fuck," Anita snapped, toeing the ripped clothes at her feet. "I really liked that dress."

~

"This is all I have." I shoved clothes through the bathroom door. Anita had ridden home with me in my TinyCar, her other self barely fitting onto the passenger seat. Her neck may have had a crick in it by the time I pulled into my garage.

She'd waited until I showed her the nearest bathroom to change back to her human-looking self. The only things I found in my closet that might fit her were sweatpants and a T-shirt.

"These will do," she said and shut the door. I shuffled into the kitchen, attempting to decide whether I wanted wine or tea.

I opted for tea.

"So, I guess you have questions," she said, sliding onto a barstool at the kitchen island and accepting a cup of hot water with a tea bag.

"Probably less than you think," I said, sipping Earl Grey from my cup. "The things I want to ask most are—what the hell are you doing here, and have you bitten any seals, lately?"

~

"See," I showed Anita what I'd gotten from Vann—he'd copied Mike and me on the images sent by Marine Animal Sanctuary. One of them showed the bite marks clearly.

"Biting seals sounds repugnant," Anita huffed. "Plus, I hate cold water. Whoever did that," she tapped my computer screen, "has to be nuts."

"But you think it's one of your race?" I turned off the computer.

"It could be," Anita shrugged. "I still can't believe you're okay with all this."

"I'm not okay with three men coming after you with knives in the parking lot," I retorted. "Why would they do that?"

"No idea," she shrugged.

"Lie," I said.

"Fuck. Please tell me you're not one of those lie detectors."

"I won't tell you, but it won't change the truth of it."

"If you were human, you'd have run away screaming when you saw me change," Anita pointed a finger in my direction. "So, what are you? Shapeshifter? I hear some of those can move fast enough to snatch a knife away like that."

"Stop digging," I held up a hand. "Drink your tea. We have to decide whether it's safe for you to go home."

"I'm going home," she said, her voice flat. "You don't need those assholes showing up outside your house."

"You don't need them showing up at your place, either," I snapped.

"Look—if they knew where I lived, they'd have waited until I got home to attack, instead of following me to a restaurant. Besides, the address on file at work is a decoy. It's an empty building."

"Well, aren't you Miss Ingenuous," I said.

"I knew the minute I saw you that we'd be friends. Come on, I need to go home. You have to drive me back to the restaurant so I can get my car."

"Right. At least you'll fit in my car this time. Without getting a crick in your neck."

"At least I have sweats at home that actually fit. People with tiny butts should be outlawed."

"I don't have a tiny butt."

"Right. And I'm the Queen of England."

"Lie."

Anita laughed.

I should have known better. Really.

I learned two lessons that night—to always keep my guard up and to leave the car in the parking lot until daylight.

This time, six tried to jump us in an otherwise empty lot. It was a tougher fight this time, and I was blindsided by one man while fighting off two of his partners. My left eye started swelling immediately after he punched me. I returned the favor by knocking him into Anita's car.

Left a dent in it, too.

I thought Anita was going to shred the three she fought—one had an arm half torn off before he turned tail to run. When the other two got a good look at her teeth, they took off, too.

My three—well, they lay scattered across the pavement, in various stages of unconsciousness.

"I say we call the police," I said.

"I don't want to."

"We're gonna," I pulled my cell from a pocket of my jeans and dialed 9-1-1.

An hour later, we watched as three attackers were loaded into a cruiser while a concerned officer offered to take us to a hospital. My black eye by that time had almost swollen shut.

"I have ice at home," I waved him off. I really didn't want anybody drawing my blood in any emergency room—they might find a few things they didn't expect and I wasn't in the mood to make explanations or hasty exits.

"Any idea why they attacked you?"

"None," Anita shook her head. She was wrapped in a blanket supplied by the police—she'd lied once already, telling the officer that our attackers had ripped her clothing off.

"I figure it was attempted rape, but we'll get back to that after we question them downtown. I'm sure they're trying to remember their lawyer's phone number about now. It's a good thing you've had a self-defense course," he nodded at me.

It was another partial lie—I'd been trained to protect myself most of my life. One self-defense course wouldn't cover what I could do. I considered buying a knife to hide in a boot or a thigh sheath—that would be the first thing my mother would have done.

"I'll have someone escort both of you home," the officer said.

Fine with me. I had to get up in four hours and go to work.

CHAPTER 3

*K**ordevik*

"What the hell happened to you?" I demanded. Lexsi ignored me as she climbed into the van the following morning. Mike had another appointment with the Marine Animal Sanctuary people, in their downtown San Francisco office.

Lexsi looked as if she'd come out the loser in a bar fight. Her left eye was swelled shut and turning a deep shade of purple—even Watson's hadn't been that bad. Mike should have sent her home first thing—instead, she was chasing after his ass.

"I got attacked in a restaurant parking lot last night," she sighed. "You should see the other guys."

"Guys? As in more than one?"

"Three. And I called the police afterward," she said. "They're in jail. Do you have any aspirin? I've used up all I had already."

"Were they trying to rob you?" I demanded.

"Police think they had rape on their minds."

That's when my vision went red. Red as in *I was ready to turn and kill somebody* red.

Think happy thoughts. Think happy thoughts.

"They're in jail?" I asked when I could speak without growling or breathing smoke.

"Yes. Unless they got out on bail. I didn't check."

"You didn't know who they were?"

"Never saw them before in my life."

"Hurry it up," Mike snapped. "You can talk later."

Adding Mike to the line of people I wanted to beat into pulp and then make paper, I shut Lexsi's door and climbed into the driver's seat. Half an hour later, we were at a street-level charitable foundation downtown.

Lexsi

"Here." Kory handed me a small packet of ibuprofen and a bottle of water while I watched Mike record a second interview with the Marine Animal Sanctuary folks. I wanted to tell the marine biologist what had actually bitten his seals, but as I didn't have that particular person/creature's name, I held back.

Chances are, he wouldn't believe me anyway and Anita might be pissed if I gave her race away.

"Found an ABC Store close by," Kory said when I turned my good eye on him.

"Thank you," I mumbled. He took the packet and opened it for me —I took all four tablets and downed them before he could tell me it was too many to take at once.

It wasn't—not for my kind. I sure didn't want to tell him that; he was being nice today, and I didn't want to mess that up.

"How much do I owe you?" I asked after drinking half the bottle of water.

"Nothing. Just—put some ice on that when we get back to the station, all right?"

"Yeah."

"I mean it."

"I do, too."

A frown marred his features, and I suppose it was then I realized he had a nice mouth. "Stop frowning—you look better when you smile," I said.

"I suggest that your vision is skewed at the moment."

"Maybe, but I've seen you with both eyes before."

"And my heart stops," he placed his right hand over his chest.

"Difik," I muttered.

"What did you say?"

"Nothing. Look—Mike's wrapping up. I have to help Jessie."

I wanted to tune Mike out on the drive back to the studio, but he needed an audience, so I listened. Nothing new had cropped up on dead seals, although several more had washed up. I figured somebody was killing them for fun; the race in question preferred raw fish in their alternate state, not pinnipeds.

It made me think that Anita probably loved sashimi.

"What happened?" Farin demanded as I trailed Mike through the studio.

"Three guys in the parking lot of a restaurant," I said. "They got hauled to jail last night."

"I'll get ice," she said and disappeared into the employee break room. After she brought ice wrapped in a clean towel and fresh coffee for me, Farin the weather girl was added to my tentative-but-tiny friends list.

"I wanted to work in Texas or Oklahoma," she told me as I sipped coffee and tried to keep the ice pack on my eye at the same time. "I'm a weather geek," she added. "Wanted to go where the weather is more volatile, but Mom and Dad live here, so here I am. Dad's the one who got Rick and me interested in weather—Rick's my brother and he's the chief meteorologist for News Eighty-Two."

"I understand about the family thing," I nodded, then wished I'd kept my head still. The ibuprofen was wearing off already. It made me wish for Uncle Kevis, who was a physician, but I couldn't call any family members or they'd know where I was.

Better to let the bruises heal on their own, or I could get hauled back home and dragged to a marriage ceremony on Kifirin. That was the reason I was working a job on Earth now—because I didn't want to be married to someone who felt entitled to be my husband.

"Silver," Vann barked, making me jump. I turned to look—his head was stuck in the break room doorway. "We have another tip—police investigated a bar fight the other night and they're still scratching their heads over what caused it. Haul Mike away from his desk and go check it out."

My head throbbed as I stood up; Farin handed me a glass of water and her personal bottle of aspirin. I took more than was polite, determined to buy her another bottle to replace what I'd taken.

I wasn't looking forward to spending the afternoon with Mike, but I didn't have a choice. At least Mike wouldn't press me to have dinner with him afterward.

~

Kordevik

I managed to hide the smoke I'd breathed after Mike informed me we were going to Clawdia's. Somebody, somewhere, had leaked information on the bar fight.

Fuck.

Watson wasn't scheduled for duty until eight, so he'd be left out of the initial investigation. I worried about Lexsi, though. Didn't give a damn about Mike—he was just as much a slave driver as Vann was. My worry was that whoever was on duty would make note of who'd come to ask questions, and then notify one of the vamps, who'd then attempt to place compulsion.

Lexsi, unless I missed my guess, wouldn't be fazed by any of that.

That, in the vamp world, spelled trouble. Maybe she could fend off three human attackers in a parking lot, but vamps?

That was another story.

Claudia Platt, who owned Clawdia's, was a werewolf, but she'd been around the block a few times. Had vamp lovers in the past, too, if gossip were to be believed. Nobody spread that around in her bar, though, unless they wanted to be removed and banned from the premises—until the end of time.

At least Watson and Mason were still holed up in my condo. I didn't think Mason would live long if he went back to his place. I figured Granger had marked him for a takedown.

The last I heard, Granger's mistress was still in the hospital and still alive, but I didn't think she had long to live once she left. If she had any sense, she'd get the hell out of the states during daylight hours and travel to a foreign country to disappear.

If we were lucky, Mike wouldn't think the story worth pursuing. Plus, if any regulars saw me driving the nosy reporters around, I could be added to the list of unwelcome customers. I slowed down to round a corner; we were getting closer to Clawdia's and my worry ramped up with every inch we traveled toward it.

Lexsi

"What the hell caused that?" Mike zoned in on the brick building across the street from Clawdia's—the bar in question. Brick had been knocked off the underlying concrete, and in some places, even the concrete was gouged out, as if someone had repeatedly driven a vehicle into it.

I'd seen that kind of damage before; it spelled vampires to me. I wasn't about to say that, though. Mike was blissfully unaware of the existence of supernatural creatures. It needed to stay that way, too.

Kory was slow to get out of the car; Mike was already snapping at Chet to get images of the damaged brick wall.

"Are you sure that was part of the bar fight?" I asked.

"Sure as hell is—I read the police report," Mike said. He hadn't bothered to pass that information to the rest of us, so we were following him in the dark.

"Were they driving their car into the building?" Jessie asked.

"Nobody would say anything about how that happened," Mike grinned. "That's why we're here—to find out."

Mike smelled a story; I worried that he was sticking his nose into something he shouldn't. Vamps on Earth weren't happy about being outed on the six o'clock news, and everything I'd seen so far spelled exactly that.

Of course, he was looking at this from a purely human perspective, because that's all he knew. My headache, as a result, was threatening to return. My concern ramped up, too, because I felt we had eyes on us.

Unfriendly eyes. I wanted to shiver, I felt so uncomfortable.

Kory also appeared uncomfortable, pacing back and forth as Chet readied his camera and Jessie fussed with the sound equipment.

Mike was already seeing this as a coup—he wanted to upstage Vann and this was a way to do it. I couldn't imagine anyone not being curious as to how large chunks and gouges had mysteriously appeared in a building across the street, during and after a bar fight.

It was all caught on camera—Mike being tossed out of Clawdia's Bar after attempting to ask the bartender and patrons about the night in question.

The fact that Mike was thrown out of the bar only raised more questions with Vann, who was now determined to get to the bottom of this story. My headache worsened while Mike and I were subjected to Vann's rant—that *he* was important and if *they* refused to answer *his* questions, they'd be sorry, blah, blah, blah.

It made me wonder, in a less painful moment, whether those who'd attacked Anita and me had anything to do with the bar fight at Clawdia's. Fights were rather prominent lately; I'd been involved in two, after all.

The rant ended with Vann informing us that a second visit to

Clawdia's was planned the following day—with him leading the charge while the rest of us followed as backup.

I wasn't looking forward to driving home in Aunt Bree's TinyCar after my workday ended. I just wanted to be home, in bed, after taking half a bottle of painkiller. I found Kory leaning against the TinyCar and dwarfing it with his height. Arms were crossed over his chest, too, as if he disapproved of everything about me.

"I hope you're going straight home," he huffed, taking my key fob away and opening the driver's side door.

"I wish I was there now," I breathed, rubbing my forehead and hoping for the thousandth time that I could get rid of the headache.

"Call in sick tomorrow," he said as I sat wearily behind the wheel.

"I can't. Vann has already decreed that we're going back to that bar to demand answers, just like the idiot he is."

"You're joking?" Kory's hand stopped halfway to mine; he'd intended to give the key fob back.

"Not kidding. If you don't want to go back there, I wouldn't blame you for calling in sick," I said. "I think he's messing with stuff he shouldn't, because he wants to throw his weight around."

"That's Vann, full to the hairline with his own self-importance," Kory placed the fob in my hand. "The bar management doesn't have to answer his questions; they've already talked to the police," he added. "Mike had the police report."

"Yeah," I acknowledged. I was exhausted from fighting the headache and listening to Mike and Vann all day. Closing my eyes and leaning my head on the wheel for a few minutes was more than tempting.

"Look, you should go home," Kory said. "Get some rest and get rid of that headache. It's hard enough to see you so bruised up as it is. A headache on top of that just makes it worse."

"Well, you go home and think up your excuse to call in sick tomorrow," I replied, feeling somewhat embarrassed by genuine sympathy from him. "This will be a debacle, no matter how you look at it. Save yourself." I allowed him to close the door before I started the car.

The drive home was going to be torture.

Kordevik

I stood there, watching her drive away and cursing myself for not taking her home. She probably had a mild concussion after the attack and had spent the day at work, because Vann and Mike couldn't pick up after themselves without an audience.

I had to contact Watson, too, to let him know about Vann's intentions. I had no idea what he'd do about it, but he needed the warning. Watson could go to Claudia with the information if he wanted—he was scheduled to work the late shift at the bar tonight.

Jerking keys from my pocket, I headed for my Jeep. Time to go home and do damage control.

"You look pissed." Watson pulled a beer from my fridge and flipped the top off before handing it to me.

"I have a message for you, and you can take it to your boss if you want," I said before tipping the bottle back and draining half of it.

"What message?" Watson went still.

"Vann Jacobs is set to show up at the bar tomorrow and attempt to force his way in while recording it all for the news." I emptied the bottle and tossed it in the recycle bin before going to the fridge for another. "He wants to get personally involved in this, and you know what kind of trouble that will cause."

"I'll call Claudia now," Watson had his cell phone in a hand and punching a button almost before I stopped talking.

"Claudia, this is Watson," he said. "You know Kory Wilson—who works for News Seventy-Four? He says Vann Jacobs plans to show up at the bar tomorrow and record us throwing him out after refusing to answer questions."

"Son-of-a-bitch," I heard Claudia's voice clearly. "Tell Kory thanks —I know this could jeopardize his job," she added. "Let me think about this and get back to you."

"Will do," Watson replied. "I'll see you at eight." Watson ended the call before turning to me. "I almost want to ask you to come with me tonight, but that would land you in more hot water if Vann or somebody else shows up early."

"I hear that," I said before pulling on my second beer. "Still," I said after swallowing, "if something looks like it's about to go down, call me. I doubt they'll recognize the other me—if it's needed."

"You still haven't told me," he began.

"Need to know," I held up my free hand. "Need to know only, bro. Need to know."

"What's going on?" Mason shuffled into the kitchen and walked between Watson and me to pull a unit of blood from the fridge. Watson and I watched as he snipped the top off the bag neatly with a sharp claw before sipping blood like a child would sip juice from a box.

"I'm glad we're not the squeamish type," Watson pointed out dryly.

"Hmmph." Mason walked out of the kitchen while flipping both of us off with his free hand.

"I'll bet he was grumpy after waking when he was human, too," Watson observed.

"Save your philosophy—it's wasted on both of us," I grinned. "Go— if you leave now, you'll actually be on time for work."

"Why should I spoil my record?" Watson chuckled. "Look, man, if I need you, or Claudia makes a decision, I'll let you know." He held his cell phone in the air with one hand and flipped me off, just as Mason did, with the other. I laughed as he headed for the door to go to work.

Lexsi

I should have bought stock in the company making my brand of ibuprofen; I'd gone through enough of it during the day from hell. I lay on the sofa, a cool, wet cloth over my eyes when my cell phone rang.

It was Farin.

"Lexsi, I need your help," she begged before I could say anything other than hello. "My brother, Rick, is good friends with Mike—they used to work together at News Eighty-Two. Mike went to that bar again tonight and was thrown out again. He called Rick and now they're both going back down there. I have a bad feeling about this. Will you call Mike and tell him that Vann has an emergency or something, just to get him and Rick out of there?"

"What the hell are they thinking?" I snapped, sitting up and causing my head to pound from the sudden movement. "Do you know if they're already there?"

"According to the app on my cell phone, they are. They're just not answering."

"Fuck," I said. "Look, keep trying to call. If the app shows they've moved, call me. I'll see what I can do from here."

"Thank you." Farin was crying, now.

Fuck. Fuck, fuck, fuck.

I hadn't used my ability to skip in a while. Sending mindspeech to Anita to let her know where I was going, I skipped to Clawdia's Bar.

Kordevik

"Dude, that guy you drove to the bar is back again, for the second time tonight," Watson reported. "This time, he brought the weatherman from channel Eighty-Two with him."

"Then get him out of there," I said.

"That's not all," Watson hissed. "Some of Granger's vamps just showed up. They overheard the humans asking questions. Now, maybe you don't know much about Granger, but he gets real paranoid when humans start asking about vamp fights. I'm not sure these two will be found alive if they walk out the door."

I swore in my native language, which left Watson completely baffled and asking for an explanation.

"I'll be there in a minute," I snapped and ended the call.

Lexsi

I didn't expect Anita to be waiting outside the bar for me, but she was. I shouldn't be surprised—her kind could fold space.

"This is a supe bar," she whispered when I appeared.

Supe—supernatural. I wasn't surprised at all.

"I'm glad you're here," I straightened my tee and smoothed my hair back. "We may need your mojo to get these guys away from here."

"I'd be happy to make that suggestion," she nodded. "Let's go get 'em."

The bouncer at the door knew we weren't human when we walked in—the loud breath he drew was a telling indication. Uncle Sal taught me that years ago—to read the signs. This one was a werewolf; he didn't have a vamp vibe.

Except for the music, the bar hushed when Anita and I walked in. Everyone started talking again the moment we stood beside Mike and Rick's table, frowning down at them.

"Who gave you the shiner?" Rick drawled.

"You know, I like your sister a helluva lot more than you," I snapped. "We have to get you out of here," I added.

"You'll come," Anita worked her mojo. Both men stood up, which drew the attention of everyone in the bar, including the vamps in the corner.

How did I know they were vamps?

They all had full beer glasses in front of them. They weren't even pretending to drink.

Read the signs.

"Come on," I grabbed Mike's arm while Anita took Rick's. *We have eyes on us*, I sent to Anita. *Vamps in the corner booth*, I added.

Then let's go out the back way, she suggested. *Through the ladies' room.*

Yeah. I think you're right. The vamps had stood the moment it looked as if we were about to haul both human men out of the bar.

One of them hissed when we herded our charges down the hall toward the restrooms. I figured we had minutes at best before the fanged and clawed came after us. I regretted not buying the knife I'd considered after the attack in the parking lot.

"Why are we going in here?" Mike asked when I hauled him through the ladies' room door.

"Shut up," Anita hissed while dragging Rick farther in. I wanted to laugh—there was a baby changing station folded up on one wall. It must have been part of state law or something—I couldn't imagine anybody in a supe bar needed a changing station.

"I'll get us out of here," Anita began before the restroom door hit the adjoining wall so hard it cracked.

Six vamps attempted to crowd in while Anita folded space, dragging all of us with her.

Kordevik

Mason insisted on coming with me; I was forced to skip with him tucked under an arm—for the second time. He didn't remember the first time, actually; he'd been unconscious during that trip.

By the time we walked into the bar, it was to find six angry vamps headed toward the front door. That's when they saw Mason. Their attention shifted from their first targets (I could only assume they were Mike and Rick), to Mason and me in the space of a heartbeat.

None of their hearts were beating; I could only count nanoseconds between the beats of mine. Those had ratcheted up to an alarming rate the second the vamps settled on us as a suitable second objective.

"Well, well." The six separated into groups of three to allow a seventh vampire through.

Granger.

No, I'd never seen him before, but I could put one and one together, just like most people could. The way he eyed Mason, too, spelled doom for the vampire at my back if I didn't do something quick.

"Clear the bar," Watson shouted behind the counter, before blasting the ceiling with the rifle he kept within easy reach below the bar.

Granger didn't blink while everyone else ran past our little standoff and out the door.

"You on their side?" Granger turned to Watson, then.

"Yeah."

"Then get over here," Granger sounded magnanimous. He and six other vamps intended to make mincemeat out of us—in short order.

Watson left his rifle on the bar and walked past several tables to get to my side. "You ready, bro?" He gave me a dark look.

"Oh, yeah," I agreed. I skipped Mason and Watson six blocks away, landing on the sidewalk just in time to hear the explosion and watch the fireball from Clawdia's bloom upward into the foggy night sky.

"Didn't kill a single one of the vamps," Watson reported the following morning. "That means Granger will be more determined than ever to wipe the floor with what's left of us after his goons are done. They ran away when we disappeared, so they weren't caught in the blast. What I'm worried about," he hesitated, "what I'm worried about is the news guys. They went toward the restrooms with two women just before you came along. I expected the vamps to have blood on their claws after coming back down the hall, but they didn't. I have no idea why that is, or why there weren't any bodies found in the restroom area."

"This was Clawdia's plan? To blow the place up? While there were humans inside?" I shook my head at Watson.

"Yeah," he shrugged. "Humans getting too close; she gets rid of her problems and still owns the ground the bar stood on. It'll sell for quite a bit. She has plans to rebuild the bar somewhere else."

"Insurance?"

"Werewolf-owned company," Watson shrugged and went to find something for breakfast.

"They didn't find a finger or anything else?" I pursued the human aspect of Watson's story.

"Nothing. That's what Claudia called to tell me a few minutes ago. According to the police, fire and everybody else at the scene, the place was empty when it blew."

"Then how the hell did they escape? Through a window?"

"Not unless they made one," Watson replied. "Want eggs?"

"I guess I'll know for sure if Mike doesn't show up for work today," I growled.

"Well, you won't have to worry about Vann sticking his nose into werewolf business, now," Watson snickered.

"You," I pointed at him, "are a piece of work. Or shit. Take your pick. What about the women who came in?"

"Both lookers, but the one with long, platinum hair and a black eye made everybody sit up and take notice, if you know what I mean."

"What the hell?" Smoke escaped my nostrils as I went for Watson's throat.

"Dude, stop choking me," he managed to get out as I bent him over the island and breathed clouds of smoke in his face.

"Look like this, did she?" I jerked my cell phone off the counter with one hand and scrolled through my recent photos until I got to the one I'd secretly taken of Lexsi.

"That's her," Watson coughed as I let him go. "Who is she?"

"None of your business. If I find out she got hurt or killed last night, I'll kill you and Claudia for keeping that bomb shit to yourselves."

"You're serious?"

"Hell, yes."

"Damn. Do you have a way to reach her? I need to know whether I ought to start running or not."

I had the news station on the phone in seconds. "She's here—with Mike, the weather guy from Eighty-Two and somebody else from the downtown office," the intern at the night desk informed me. "Mike looks like he's been through hell and keeps yelling that his car was blown up."

"Thank the Mighty," I muttered. "Look, I can come get them if you think they need a ride."

"Mike and the other guy for sure," the intern said. "I'll have to ask Lexsi."

"I'll be there in half an hour," I said. "Tell them not to go anywhere," I added. "I'll drive them home."

Lexsi

Kory showed up in less than half an hour, checked out one of the station's vans and herded us into it. Anita didn't like it—she'd intended to fold space to get us away from Mike, who was still yelling about his car.

My headache still hadn't gone away; that meant I wanted to yell right back at Mike, telling him he was damn lucky to be alive instead of blown up or drained vampire bait. Those six vamps would have been all over him and Rick, with the bodies hidden so well afterward nobody would have found them.

"We're gonna talk," Kory growled as he held the van's back door open for me to climb inside.

"About what?" I rubbed my forehead.

"Fuck," he muttered before shutting my door and stalking toward the driver's side door.

He dropped Rick, Mike and Anita off at their homes, leaving me for last.

"Get in the front seat," Kory barked after Anita walked into her building.

I was too weary and in too much pain from the perpetual headache to argue with him. He buckled me in after I fumbled the seat belt. He waited until he'd pulled away and headed for the bridge to start talking.

"What the hell were you doing at that bar," he demanded.

"Farin," I whispered. "Rick is her brother. She was worried that he and Mike would get hurt at the bar. She begged me to convince him to leave. I had to ask Anita to go with me, because I sure as hell didn't want to go by myself."

"Why didn't you call him?" Kory still wasn't happy with my explanation.

"We tried. He wasn't answering."

"Fuck."

"Yeah. I hear that, all right." I closed my eyes, hoping that would help with the pounding inside my skull. "If Vann hears that Mike tried to go around him to get the bar story," I didn't finish.

"Maybe Vann needs to hear exactly that. Mike could have gotten you killed, tonight."

"Mike could have gotten himself killed, and Rick, too."

"I don't give a damn about Mike or Rick."

Silence fell after that statement, and somewhere between the Golden Gate Bridge and Aunt Bree's house, I fell asleep.

I dreamed about Kory carrying me into the house, while someone else opened the back door for him.

Everything was hazy, after that. I just remembered falling into a deeper sleep when the pain went away.

CHAPTER 4

Kordevik

I worried that Li'Neruh Rath would be angry that I sent mindspeech, or that he'd ignore me altogether, but he didn't. After I carried Lexsi to her bedroom, he took away her headache with gentle fingers.

They hit her harder than she thought, he sent afterward. *It's taken care of. Go home. She doesn't need to find you here in the morning.*

I know. I hung my head. Things were supposed to be so different, yet here we were.

Woo her. Carefully. You're not a caveman, you know.

Li'Neruh disappeared. That's when I figured out why he'd placed me on Earth to start with. So I could win my intended, instead of expecting her to be handed to me outright.

I was still so angry with her about going to that fucking bar, though, while she was injured and in pain. I almost touched her, too, while she slept. I only wanted to run a finger down her cheek; I knew her skin would be velvety soft beneath my hand. Tearing myself away from that thought, I walked back through the house and made sure everything was locked up before driving the van back to the station. Little Miss Lexsi occupied my thoughts the entire time.

~

Lexsi

The headache was gloriously absent when I woke, and upon my examination of the bruises and black eye in the bathroom mirror, I found both looked fainter and my eye had actually opened all the way.

Still, feeling as if six more hours of sleep would be the greatest gift ever, I showered, dressed, filled a mug with coffee and shut myself in the TinyCar to drive to work.

Farin wore a guilty expression when I walked in. She wanted to say something and worried I was upset with her. "I'm not mad at you," I said, heading for my tiny cubicle. "Is Mike coming to work today?"

"Oh, uh," Farin looked extremely uncomfortable for a moment.

"Mike's looking for a new job," Vann snapped as he walked along the hall toward Farin and me. I'd known Vann was a camera hog, but firing Mike because he'd acted foolishly and was nearly killed for his efforts sounded a bit extreme to me.

"I have something for you," Farin took my arm and led me away from Vann, who was headed for the coffee machine.

"What's that?" I asked, once we'd reached my cubicle.

"Rick says thanks," she whispered. "He doesn't remember much, just that you and Anita got them out of the bar before things went boom."

"What will Mike do?" I asked.

"I think Rick will put in a word with his station; Mike won't be unemployed long. Everybody knows how difficult Vann can be to work for."

"Farin, I don't want you to take this the wrong way, but you should tell your brother to stay away from that bar if it happens to pop up somewhere else. Let the police handle this, all right? It's dangerous."

"I think he got the message last night, but I'll tell him." She started to walk away, then turned back to me. "He likes you. He says you're gorgeous, even with a black eye."

"Oh. Uh, tell him thanks, I guess. You ought to thank Kory, too, for driving them home last night."

"That ought to be fun," she grimaced.

"Maybe I'll send him a bottle of something," I said. "He had to be awake most of the night to get all of us back where we should be."

"I owe you," Farin said. "Dinner, sometime, at my place? I'm a decent cook."

"That sounds like a deal," I said. "Thanks."

"Silver," Vann appeared as Farin walked away, "I want to go back to what's left of that bar. I intend to get to the bottom of this, if it takes the rest of my life to do it."

Kordevik

The look on Lexsi's face as she followed Vann and his crew out of the station told me exactly where we were going—to the burned remains of a bar, where a mysterious explosion happened the night before.

She was pissed about it; Jessie and Chet weren't looking forward to it, either. It made me want to turn my smaller Thifilathi loose on Vann, but that couldn't happen. Instead, I drove us to Clawdia's—or what remained of it.

Lexsi

Vann waved his copy of the police report from the explosion the night before, and referred to the bar fight before that. "While the police say it is too early to link these two incidents, it certainly looks suspicious," he preened before the camera.

"Our requests for an interview with the bar owner have been refused; her assistant referred us to the police investigation unit, and gave their phone number. When we pointed out that we'd already spoken to them, he hung up."

Half a block away, Kory stood with his cell phone in his hand, texting someone. At least he could walk away and not pay attention to Vann; his job was to drive us and nothing else.

I held Vann's notes and brushed hair from my face—a breeze was blowing off the bay, stirring ash in the bombed building behind us. We'd had to set up across the street; crime scene tape was still strung up everywhere and a grumpy security guard eyed us with a mixture of disgust and malevolence from his nearby post.

At least the owner had thought to protect what remained of the bar; looters would probably be all over it if she hadn't.

Besides, it was probably hazardous to walk through the rubble without thick boots on—broken glass from liquor bottles was everywhere.

"How long is he going to babble?" Kory appeared at my elbow.

"As long as he wants—he's the boss."

"Gee, that's too bad," Kory rumbled.

"What do you like to drink?" I asked. "I'll buy a bottle to say thanks for getting all of us home last night."

"Crown works."

"All right. I'll see what I can do."

"Do you drink?" he asked.

"Not often. A glass of wine with dinner, sometimes."

"Wimp."

"I fought three guys in a parking lot. You think that's wimpy?" My temper was beginning to rise.

"Not that way," he held up a hand. "Just in your drinking habits."

"I'll get your bottle of Crown," I said and stalked away from him.

Kordevik

Way to go, Weth, I chastised myself as she walked away. I needed to remind myself of how young she was. Yes, she was extremely mature, which likely prompted my lack of propriety.

Or maybe I'd just been hanging around males too long. My father would be ashamed of me. My mother, too.

"Look, I didn't mean it that way," I strode after her. "I think I've just had too much male company for a while, and tossing back a few drinks is what we do."

"Should I buy them a bottle, too?" She turned to look at me. Her eyes betrayed her anger; her words merely conveyed sarcasm.

"Really. I didn't mean it," I repeated.

"Fine." I watched as her shoulders slumped. At that moment, she appeared lost. Alone.

As she was. I wondered if any of her family knew where and when she'd landed. I hadn't taken the time to consider what Lexsi's disappearance had done to them—or to Kifirin's reigning King and Queen.

Lexsi was related to royalty, after all. I didn't even want to consider her paternal grandmother, who was also a Queen, Or one of her uncles, who was a King. Another uncle was the founder of the Campiaan Alliance, for fuck's sake.

Damn. I'd just been so angry I'd burned down a bar and was sent here as punishment by Li'Neruh Rath.

Fuck. He'd sent me here to protect her, and I was too stupid to see it.

Except she didn't want my protection—as far as I could see.

Well, she didn't know who I was. If she did, she'd get away from me as fast as she could. I had to work around that and—according to Li'Neruh Rath—woo her at the same time.

He'd planned my punishment perfectly, by placing me in a situation I had no idea how to deal with. The biggest problem I faced, of course, was that Miss Lexsi didn't want protection. I'd seen that firsthand when she'd waltzed into a supe bar to haul two humans out of it.

That's when it hit me. I had a temporarily out-of-work werewolf and a vamp staying at my house. Lexsi had a house far too big for only one person; Mason and Watson could help protect her. There had to be a solution she'd accept, I merely hadn't thought of it, yet.

Lexsi

By the time Vann wound down, cut the recording and waited for us to pack the equipment in the van, I was ready to strangle him. For some reason, Kory chose to make things worse by calling me a wimp.

For not drinking.

Go figure.

I knew Vann could still draw unwanted attention with the interest he was paying to this; he'd referred to it in his monologue as a cover-up—by the police and the bar's owner.

Difik.

If he'd bothered to talk to Mike before arbitrarily firing him, he'd at least be forewarned about some of the dangers related to the bar and its destruction.

While we were on our way back to the station, Vann got a call from Lee, his producer. Someone had already hired Mike. Not only had they hired him, he was doing the noon news, describing what he recalled from the evening before—and the bar's subsequent destruction.

He even showed images of his car, which had been parked close-by. It looked as if it had been hurled into a building by an angry giant.

Vann had been upstaged by his former employee and he wasn't happy about that. I didn't intend to tell Vann that Anita and I'd pulled Mike and Rick out of the bar to save their lives; he was too busy cursing Mike and threatening to ruin him at the same time.

Farin looked guilty when we trooped into the station; I knew then that Mike was working at Eighty-Two. Rick had likely gone to a producer there, who'd listened to his and Mike's story and hired Mike on the spot to report on it. After all, they got their scoop in first, leaving Vann to do cleanup.

Vann was furious as he stomped toward the editing room. He was determined to make his report better than the one Mike had hastily put together for a rival station.

To me, none of that mattered. What did matter was the fact that they were making the bar fight and subsequent explosion into a turf war, and I worried that the vamps involved would certainly take notice.

Unwelcome notice.

"Farin," I grabbed her arm and led her toward the ladies' room.

"I didn't know this was going to happen," she began the moment the restroom door was shut and we'd checked for anyone else inside.

"Farin, you need to warn your brother—and Mike if you can. I know this is turning into a testosterone war, but there are bigger things out there that may not like the attention."

"I don't know what you're talking about," she muttered, struggling not to cry.

"Hey," I pulled her into a hug. "It's not worth your tears. Mike should be the one needing tissues. If Anita and I hadn't pulled his ass out of that bar—Rick's too—they could be toast right now instead of fighting with Vann from another news station."

"But people deserve the truth," she leaned away from me.

"Trust me on this one," I begged. "Somebody doesn't want this truth told, and they'll do whatever it takes to make sure of it."

How could I tell her that Mike and Rick could end up dead or under compulsion? Vann, too, for that matter. They'd investigated a simple bar fight and taken it much too far. Vamps and werewolves were still hidden and didn't take kindly to threats of exposure.

I wasn't even including the others that belonged to Anita's race, or what they were capable of doing. The dead seals in the bay could attest to their playful fetishes.

An intern found me after Farin and I left the restroom. I had a message from Gerta Britt. She wanted to know what, if anything, we were doing with the information she'd given. She was also asking why Mike now worked for News Eighty-Two.

I wanted to curse—I held it back.

"Tell her I'll call back when I have more information," I said. "I have to ask Vann if he's planning a follow-up on that story."

"I will." He grinned and loped toward the intern's shared cubicle.

"Farin?" I turned back to her.

"What?"

"Where's the nearest sporting goods store?"

~

I ended up buying three hunting knives; I couldn't decide which might be best to defend my life if it became necessary. A gym might be the next item on my list—I really hadn't exercised since my arrival, so that needed to be rectified. Sure—sleeping later in the morning was a gift—and one I'd have to give up, it appeared.

Uncle Sal would be disappointed in me for letting things go for so long. The threat against Mike's life in a supe bar, as Anita called it, brought that home in a hurry. Those vamps had seen Mike and Rick, I knew that much. Vamps also had long memories. They'd know who I was if they ever saw—or scented—me again.

Yes, I could fight off three human men. Six vamps? Likely another story. For a moment, I wished for my mother's talent, before squashing that thought. It had never manifested in me—or any of my sisters.

That's why I had to rely on my lifelong training with Dad, Uncle Sal and a few others; they'd taught me how to protect myself from mundane attacks. It made me wish I'd brought my swords with me; I knew how to fight with twin blades. Swords were considered archaic weapons on Earth, so I hadn't brought them.

I wanted to kick myself, now, for leaving them behind.

Anita called just before I walked through the back door, after parking the TinyCar in Aunt Bree's overly large garage.

"Hey," I said.

"Problem," she replied.

"What's that?"

"Mike's missing. Never made it to his friend's house after he got off work."

Another line on my cell phone buzzed while Anita's words ran through my mind. "Wait," I said, "I have another call."

"Hello?" I said after switching to the other line.

"Rick's about to go crazy," Farin wept. "We can't find Mike anywhere."

"Where are you?" I asked.

"At Rick's." She rattled off the downtown address.

"I'll be there in a few," I said, before going back to Anita. "That was Farin," I said. "She and her brother are about to have a meltdown because they can't find Mike. I told Farin I'd be at her brother's house in a little while. Want to come?"

"Sure, although I believe you're aware that either the wolves or the vamps probably have him by now—it's dark outside."

"Yeah. That has crossed my mind," I agreed. "Want to come here, first?"

"Nah. Give me the address. I don't like getting my car out unless I have to."

"Agreed. I'll meet you at Rick's place," I said and ended the call. If Farin hadn't asked, I'd probably leave Mike to his fate.

Or not.

Stuffing one of my new knives into a boot after I changed clothes, I skipped to Rick's downtown loft. Anita was in the hall outside his door, waiting for me when I arrived.

"Want dinner after?" I asked her.

"Sure. Weather apparently pays good," she jerked her head at Rick's door. It was an upscale condo building, with plenty of space, which was unusual for the area. Houses and buildings tended to be narrow and tall.

"Yeah." I pressed the doorbell. Farin answered the door and hugged me immediately.

"I'm really sorry to bother you like this," her brother, Rick, stood behind Farin. "It's just—you got us away from that bar last night, and I still don't understand how that happened. We need to find Mike," he added, sounding a bit lost.

"Did he say he was going to make any stops on the way home?" Anita walked past us and set her purse on the glass coffee table next to a stylish, chocolate-brown sofa.

"He said he was going to pick up pizza, after getting a rental car since his was destroyed," Rick said, motioning me farther into his apartment. "Pizza from Cecille's, our favorite place. I called—they know us there. They said he never came in."

"What about the parking lot?" I asked. "Is that a good place for somebody to grab him? Do you know what his rental looked like?"

"That parking lot does get dark at night, especially if it's foggy," Rick conceded. "But this was still daytime and not much fog. He said the rental was a black Lexus."

"Let's go take a look," Anita pulled her purse over a shoulder. "We can look for the car, at least."

"I didn't think of that," Rick muttered before grabbing a jacket off a chair. "Farin, do you want to stay here, in case he comes back?"

"I guess," she agreed. "Let me know if you find anything."

"You know I will," he said. Anita and I exchanged glances as we followed Rick out of the apartment.

It took half an hour to get to the restaurant, which had a small, partially lit parking lot. Parking spaces at the side were illuminated; spaces behind the building weren't, except for one weak bulb by the back door. A Dumpster close to the door could have hidden an attacker, if he intended to grab somebody.

That's where we found Mike's Lexus—empty and locked. "We really ought to call the police," I turned to Rick. "This is their job, now. We shouldn't muck up the crime scene."

"All right," he mumbled and hauled out his cell phone.

It was while he was dialing 9-1-1 that the horrible feeling of panic hit me.

Dad always said that his mother—my grandmother—had some sort of sixth sense when somebody was in trouble that she cared about.

Farin was in trouble.

No, don't ask me to explain it—I couldn't explain it to myself. "I have to help Farin," I shouted at Anita before skipping back to Rick's apartment.

~

Kordevik

"I don't have good news," Watson said the minute he walked in the door. He hadn't left a note and I hadn't been able to reach him by phone, so I wasn't the happiest person to see him at the moment.

"What?" I demanded. Mason, who'd somehow snagged more bagged blood, was drinking his dinner beside an open refrigerator door when Watson hesitated to answer.

"You know Claudia wasn't happy with that news guy after he made his accusations on the noon broadcast," Watson began.

"So?"

"So, uh, she made a deal with Granger."

"What the bloody hell are you talking about?" I hissed.

"Two of her wolves picked up the news guy at a pizza place. Kept him locked up until Granger's vamps could collect him after nightfall."

"What are they going to do with him?" My temper was on edge, suddenly.

"Probably just lay compulsion," Watson shrugged.

"And if they don't? He'll be shredded and the pieces buried where nobody will find them," I snapped. "This guy is a public figure. Somebody will go looking for him if he isn't found, and that will raise even more suspicions."

"Look, I tried to tell Claudia that, but that jerk going on about the explosion being suspicious and possibly involving the owner? Claudia doesn't take that very well."

"What, she can't handle the truth?" I raked fingers through my hair in frustration. "You said yourself she planned this."

"Just to get everybody off her tail," Watson hung his head. "She's done it before—just not for a while."

"Well, I'll bet things weren't as high tech when she did it before," I said. "People could be paid off, too. Nowadays, it's harder to do that."

"Yeah."

"Somebody breaking the law?" Mason asked after draining his bag of blood. "Sorry," he shrugged. "Habit," he explained. Watson and I watched as he rinsed the bag in the sink, then shredded it and tossed the remains in the recycle bin.

"I have a plan," Mason went on.

"No," I snapped.

"What is it?" Watson asked at the same time.

"I was going to offer myself in exchange for nosy news guy," Mason said. "If you two go along, maybe we can nab news guy and get the hell out of there."

"Too dangerous," Watson shook his head. "You could be toast the second they show up, and news guy could still be just as dead. Also, stop using alliteration. It's annoying."

"I didn't think a werewolf would even know what alliteration was," Mason grinned, showing a bit of fang.

"I have a question," I turned to Watson. "Does Claudia or anybody else know that you're staying here, and that Mason is also here?"

~

Lexsi

I almost couldn't believe my eyes after folding into Rick's apartment. A man was there, backed against Farin, who was, in turn, backed against the wall.

He was protecting her from two vampires, who were ready to kill.

Or rape first, then kill.

"Tell us where your brother is," one attempted to lay compulsion.

Even I could see he was too far away from Farin for the compulsion to work. I also saw that the vamp had scratches on his face.

Well done, stranger guy, I thought as I turned back to Farin and the man protecting her.

That's when the vamps noticed me and jumped; I must have moved or made a noise. They hadn't expected anyone to magically appear inside the apartment.

"We're leaving," I said, pulling the brand-new knife from my boot and pointing it at them. When one of them snarled and came at me, I skipped to Farin's side, hauled her and the man into my arms and then skipped to my house before the vamps, in their attempt to grab all of us, hit the wall at Farin's back.

I have Farin and someone else at my house; we found vamps in Rick's condo, threatening Farin because they wanted to know where Rick was, I sent to Anita. Are the police there, yet?

They're here, she confirmed. *Rick is answering questions for them.*

I hope they haul Mike's rental in for testing, I said. *You need to get Rick away the minute you can and bring him here. We'll decide where to take him afterward.*

Will do, she responded. *This is becoming a mess,* she added.

I hear you.

I turned back to Farin and the man I'd brought to the house; she was still in shock after the unusual method I'd employed to transport her across the bay. The man—I still didn't know who he was but he was muscled enough to be a prizefighter—attempted to console her.

"Tiburon," he held out his hand. I shook with him. The word rolled easily off his tongue—Spanish was his native language.

"Shark?" I asked.

"My father," he shrugged and turned back to Farin.

"How?" Farin croaked at me.

"That's a story for later, okay? I had to get you away from those men."

"Vampires," Tiburon muttered. I went still. He knew what they were.

"Hmmph," he said. "If they come hunting you, you'd better know what they are."

"Have I seen you before?" Farin blinked at Tiburon.

"Middleweight boxer," he grinned. "Because I was born in Mexico, they almost didn't let me buy a condo in the building where your brother lives."

"Snark Demonio," Farin breathed. "Rick said you were in the building."

"Snark?" It was my turn to blink at him.

"It was supposed to be Shark—the English word for my name. People started calling me Snark when I spoke my mind about opponents."

"I loved it when you called Frankie the Flail, Frankie the Fail," a slow smile lifted the corners of Farin's mouth.

"I'm surprised someone else didn't do it first," Tiburon shrugged. "I put him down in four."

"Where's Rick?" Farin asked. "Is he safe?"

"He and Anita are talking to the police," I said.

"Do you think more of those—vampires—have Mike?" She shuddered as she said the word vampire.

"It is possible, chica," Snark responded before I could. "Why else would they be looking for Rick, too? I believe this happened after Mike spoke so harshly about that bar."

"What's so special about that bar?" Farin demanded. She slid off the barstool that Tiburon had placed her on and wrapped arms about herself.

"Beautiful Farin, that bar is frequented by the supernatural community," Tiburon explained.

No, I wouldn't have said a word about it, but Tiburon was right—if vampires are hunting you, it's best you know what they are—and that they exist.

"Supernatural? Ghosts?" Farin didn't understand.

"No, vampires. Werewolves. Shapeshifters and other things. They go to that bar, to be with others of their kind. Mike has poked his nose into an angry hornet's nest, and I worry that he may pay dearly for his persistence and curiosity."

"Farin," I sighed, "Anita and I got Mike and Rick out of that bar last night, right under the noses of six vamps. They're still pissed—that much is obvious. If Mike hadn't done his stint on the noon news, it may have blown over. It's a vendetta, now."

"What about Vann, then? He's doing his exposé on the eleven o'clock news," Farin whispered.

"You know, I'd like to say I don't care about Vann, but he may end up wherever Mike is."

"Not good," Tiburon sighed. "Humans," he added.

"What are you talking about?" Farin demanded. Tiburon took a step back, but was interrupted in whatever he was about to say by the doorbell ringing.

"Maybe that's Anita and Rick," I said, trotting toward the front door.

I was expecting Anita and Rick. Instead, I found Kory and two other men standing on my doorstep, gym bags in hand.

"What?" I snapped.

"We need a place to crash," Kory stated flatly. "Until we find something else that's more suitable," he added.

"But," I attempted to argue.

"Lexsi, please do this," Kory begged. "Let us in. These two," he jerked his head toward his companions, "they're in the same boat Mike is in, I think."

"How do you know about Mike?" I asked.

"Word gets around," he said. "Can we come in?"

"Yeah, I guess," I stepped aside to let them walk through the door.

Kory went still when he saw Farin and Tiburon in my kitchen. The two men with him almost ran into each other after his abrupt stop. He hadn't bothered to introduce either of them, although they were watching me closely.

"I know you," Kory pointed at Tiburon. "Farin, why are you here?" he asked.

"Because two vampires decided they wanted her to answer questions about Rick's whereabouts," Tiburon answered.

One of Kory's companions went still.

The doorbell rang a second time. I hoped it was Anita and not vampires.

Kordevik

"Where the hell is Mike?" I hissed at Watson. I'd dragged him into an empty bedroom before I started asking questions. "They're looking for Farin's brother, now. We need to stop this before it goes too far."

Not least among my fears was that Lexsi would figure out who I was, and that could ruin everything.

In other words, I'd have to lie to get her—and everybody else—off my back. Meanwhile, we needed to find Mike, if for no other reason than to let them know they couldn't just grab people on a whim.

"You don't know where Granger's house is?" Watson muttered, backing away from me. Yes, I was breathing smoke by that time. After I'd almost strangled him at my place, he knew to get away from me when my breath turned cloudy.

"No. Please tell me," I flung out a hand.

"On Nob Hill," he said, dropping his eyes.

"Well why didn't you say that to begin with?" I demanded.

"It's a big house," he added.

"Great. Where will they have Mike—if he's still alive?"

"Probably in the basement." He rattled off an intersection in Nob Hill.

"How big is this house?"

"Five levels. Nearly nineteen thousand square feet. Good luck getting past all the vamps to find one human."

"Really? I'll burn the fucking building down if I have to," I snapped. "Vampires don't do well against fire, you know that?" I added and skipped to Nob Hill.

It wasn't difficult to locate Granger's house; it was the one with all the windows blacked out to prevent the intrusion of sunlight during the day. As Watson said, it was huge.

I was about to go through Granger's front door. If anybody stood in my way, they'd get their fingers burned at the very least. Turning to my smaller Thifilathi, I took off at a run.

CHAPTER 5

"The police are checking the area for evidence," Rick accepted the cup of decaf I handed him. "I don't think they'll find anything in Mike's rental, but they're hauling it in, too."

"You?" I lifted a cup at Kory's friend—the one who wasn't locked up in one of my bedrooms with Kory.

"Black," he shrugged. I think that's when I understood he was vampire. I resolved to sort that out later.

He's a vamp, Anita's mindspeech echoed in my head.

I get that, I agreed. Automatically I shoved a coffee pod in the brewer before pulling a box of tea from a cabinet to make a cup of chamomile for Anita and me.

"Have anything to eat?" Kory's friend from the bedroom now walked into the kitchen.

"Where's Kory?" I asked.

"In the bathroom," the man ran fingers through dark hair, mussing it up.

"All right. I have stuff for sandwiches, or I can throw pasta together, but that's all I have right now," I said.

"Pasta? I'm Watson, by the way," he held out a hand.

"Nice to meet you," I said as we shook.

"This is Mason," he pointed a finger at his vampire companion. "In case he hasn't told you. He's pretty close-mouthed."

"Mason," I nodded to the vamp. He offered a lopsided grin and lifted his coffee cup in a salute. "I'm Lexsi," I introduced myself. "This is Rick," I pointed in the proper direction. "Anita, Farin and Tiburon," I finished the introductions.

"I know Tiburon—from his boxing matches," Mason nodded. "Damn good fighter."

"Thanks, man," Tiburon said. "I guess I ought to check in with my manager, in case he gets worried." He pulled a cell phone from a pocket and walked toward the living area to make his call in private.

"Farin," Anita turned toward her, "I hope you understand that you can't talk about vampires outside present company," she laid the obsession. "You, too, Rick. No talking about vampires. You'll die if you do—they're sort of murderous that way."

"Werewolves, too," Mason pointed out. Anita laid a second obsession, covering werewolves and shapeshifters.

"Not all vamps are bad," Mason said. He didn't understand what Anita had done, but as Farin and Rick had nodded like bobble-heads both times, he felt it safer to speak, now. "It's like anything else—a few bad apples ruin it for the rest."

"Do you know how scary that is? Vampires," Farin shivered again at the word.

"Most of 'em—you won't even know," Watson observed. "It's the bad ones who show you what they are—just before they uh, well."

"Nice work, fur-butt," Mason muttered.

~

Kordevik

I'd already punched four vamps in the face, knocking them through ordinary walls as I raced through Granger's house. Sure, their skin was smoking from the brief contact with my fists, but I didn't really care.

If Granger thought he was at the top of the food chain, it was time for him to learn better. Somewhere along my way to the lowest level of the house, the vamps started shooting. At least one bullet ricocheted off my left horn.

It barely slowed me down.

Then, when they learned they couldn't shoot me with normal weapons—well, they could but it didn't pierce my scales—they attempted to swarm me.

I don't know how many of Granger's vamps died that night, but it was quite a few. Vamps burn fast when a High Demon turns up the heat. By the time I got to the basement, however, I found Mike—and Vann—both bleeding profusely from numerous cuts.

The vamps thought to have fun with them before killing them outright.

This was also where I'd be vulnerable for a few seconds; I heard more vamps running when I turned off my heat, snatched up Vann and Mike and skipped to the nearest emergency room.

Mike, who was limping, had to drag an unresponsive Vann through the sliding doors; I stepped away from the light long enough to ensure they made it into the ER entrance before skipping back to Lexsi's place. I took a cold shower to remove blood residue, then dressed in the clothing I'd left behind in the bedroom.

Lexsi

I was called to the station roughly half an hour after Kory walked out of the bedroom; he drove me, instead of allowing me to drive myself. A microphone and copy was shoved into my hand and I ended up reporting that Vann Jacobs died at the emergency room while Mike Ellis was in critical condition after being kidnapped and tortured the evening before. The other news I reported was that a large, expensive home in Nob Hill had burned to the ground, but that was secondary to the information on Vann and Mike.

News Seventy-Four had been hit and hit hard; everything now

pointed toward Clawdia's Bar and the events there that Mike and Vann had investigated.

I was surprised to find Kory waiting to drive me home around noon the following day; the day crew had taken over and everybody was either in mourning for Vann or pretending to be.

Farin and Anita had gone to work; they weren't at the house when we arrived. Mason was asleep, as any vampire would be during the day, Watson held a cup of coffee in his hand as he wandered silently through the house and Tiburon had called a cab to go home.

Rick was about to leave—he still had a job to do, too, although the area weather wasn't set to change much in the coming days.

"Need to talk, man," Watson told Kory. I didn't care that they needed to talk; I needed a bed and was heading toward mine as fast as I could go. The station manager said he'd call if they needed me to come in for the night news, so I intended to sleep until then.

"Help yourselves to whatever's in the house, I'm going to sleep for a while," I waved an arm in their direction and headed toward my bedroom.

~

Kordevik

"Granger's still out there and he's put a price on your head," Watson hissed the second he heard Lexsi's bedroom door close. "He doesn't know what you are, but there's a description out, with a hefty reward."

"He may be running low on vamps at the moment," I yawned and raked fingers through my hair. I wanted sleep, too. I couldn't deny that I wanted to snuggle next to Lexsi and sleep with her.

"I guess it's good that Mike doesn't recall who saved him," Watson mumbled. "If Claudia finds out I told you anything," he didn't finish.

"Then don't let her know. I'm not about to tell her," I said. "Look, put all your concerns together and I'll deal with them when I wake up. Later. Much later."

I ended up in a bedroom across the hall from Lexsi's; I didn't want to be thrown out of the house by sneaking into hers, just so she could wake up next to me.

~

Lexsi

I was called in to do the eleven o'clock evening news. Vann's producer, Lee Patrick, said he was already getting calls from the Bay Area, telling him they liked the girl who'd reported the news earlier and they'd asked if I were going to become a regular.

I didn't know how to react to that; a part of me felt good about it. Another part felt guilt about taking Vann's spot, while a third part was scared as hell about being shoved in front of a camera. I thought I'd be doing research and chasing after Vann and Mike for a long time.

All that had changed in less than forty-eight hours.

Condolences were pouring in by the thousands regarding Vann's death, many of them asking if there were going to be a memorial broadcast for him. Lee said it was already in the works and he and the editors were in the process of selecting parts of Vann's best pieces, in addition to some of his quirky outtakes to air.

"We're waiting on some things from the Romes—they knew Vann pretty well," Lee added. "They want to send a few photographs they have of them together."

"I'll make that announcement on the news," I said.

"Perfect. Thanks for stepping in so quickly," Lee offered a weary grin. I could see he had mixed feelings, too, about Vann's passing, and part of that was anger at Vann for having the temerity to die at the height of his popularity.

My anger was directed toward those who'd killed him—or injured him so badly he couldn't survive. Lee had no idea that vampires were involved and I wasn't about to tell him.

After getting some rest earlier, I'd had time to consider how Kory knew a vampire and a werewolf, but that would have to wait. I worried that Rick and Farin could still be targeted, and had no idea what to do about it.

Both were at work, but I was concerned about what could happen when they went home. Mike was under police guard at the hospital, but that wouldn't help him after nightfall when the vamps, all of whom could place compulsion, would still be hunting him.

He wouldn't be hard to find, either. All local news stations had done interviews with doctors at the hospital, asking for updates on his condition.

For now, he was asleep most of the time, with doctors warning visitors away. Again, that would last all of ten seconds if a vamp showed up.

It was a relief to put the news to bed that night; I finally had time to go back to my cubicle and check e-mails. I had sixteen messages from Gerta Britt, asking for information on Vann's funeral, where she could send flowers and dozens of other questions about his death.

I sent her a link to the obituary section of Rome Enterprise's online newspaper, telling her that the information she requested would have to be supplied by Vann's family.

He did have family, as it turned out. A brother and two sisters, all of whom were married. Vann was the one who couldn't settle down. He had no children and three ex-wives to prove it.

Lee peered over my cubicle wall as I was mulling the conundrum of Vann's life. "I want you to stay on top of that story—the one Vann and Mike were looking into," he said. "Talk to the police to see what you can get from them, and try to track down the owner of that bar. I want her on camera if at all possible."

My breath stopped for a moment. How could I tell Lee that what he was suggesting could be a death sentence? It had been for Vann, and still could be for Mike. "I have Vann's password, too, so you can follow up on his other leads," Lee added. "We still have calls coming in about dead seals in the bay."

"Of course," I stuttered.

"Do it tomorrow," he said. "Go home and get some decent sleep for now; you've earned it."

"All right." I pushed my chair away from the desk, feeling numb.

~

"Mason is at the hospital," Kory said when I slid onto the passenger seat of the van. He'd waited for me—again.

"But why?" I began as Kory put the van in gear and headed for the parking garage entrance.

"He's watching for other vamps to show up—ones who may not be so friendly."

"Oh." I sat with my hands in my lap for several minutes, watching the reflecting highway lines rush past. It was foggy again, so only three lines at a time were visible in the van's headlights.

"How do you happen to know a vamp and a werewolf?" I worked up the courage to ask.

"Accident," he shrugged, turning onto the highway. "Met both at a bar. Kept them from getting into a fight."

"Oh." He'd answered with mostly the truth—so I let that go.

"I could ask you a similar question," he turned dark eyes on me. They glittered in the dim interior light of the van, expressing his curiosity. "How do you know about vamps and weres?"

That was a tricky question, which required an even trickier answer. "My grandmother told me," I said. That part was true. Mom and Dad told me about High Demons, which constituted much of my heritage.

The rest—my grandmother had given me plenty of stories and introduced me to all sorts of people; vampires, werewolves, shapeshifters and dozens of other races. Anita's race was a long tale all on its own. I didn't want Kory to know about that—it could place him in danger.

"What will Mason do if other vamps show up?" I asked.

"He's pretty talented, plus he took a portable flame-thrower with him."

"What?" The word expressed my level of shock.

"I bought it for him," Kory shrugged again.

"Oh, my gosh," I rubbed my forehead. "I really, really don't want to hear that someone burned the hospital down in the middle of the night."

"Yeah, you'd just have to report on it," Kory turned briefly and grinned at me.

"Lee wants me to continue the investigation into the bar fire and what led up to it," I blurted.

"What?" It was Kory's turn to be shocked. "You know that's the most dangerous assignment he could hand anybody, and to hand it to the rookie," he broke off, realizing that he'd likely offended me.

"No, you're right, I am the rookie," I admitted. "I think he ought to just leave this thing alone, unless he wants to watch the bodies pile up. I understand that I might be at the bottom of that pile, too."

"Fuck that," Kory growled.

"It's investigate it or I'll likely lose my job," I muttered.

"Then find another job," he snapped.

"That's really not an option," I retorted. Aunt Bree had been quite specific. I *had* to work for Rome Enterprises. I worried she'd haul me back to Avendor if I quit, and an unwelcome marriage would commence shortly after.

"Then tread carefully and call me if there's trouble," he said. I stole a glance at his face as he concentrated on driving the van; his mouth was set in a thin, disapproving line, his brow furrowed with restrained anger.

"Fine."

"It better be fine. Vann lost his life because of this, and Mike's fate is still on the line. I've already warned Rick and Farin; they know where those two live, you understand."

"Yeah. I understand." I hesitated for a moment. "Lee wants me to track down the bar owner and get her on camera."

"No." Kory smacked the steering wheel to emphasize his command.

"You think I want to?" I tapped my chest. "That's suicide, in my opinion."

"Then hold Lee off," he said. "Tell him you can't find her."

"I need to find out what the other stations are planning to do about this," I closed my eyes in resignation.

"Rick can ask at his place," Kory pointed out. "That's actually a good idea—let them take the fall."

"Did that just come out of your mouth?" I stared at him in disgust. "You want somebody else to die?"

"Better them than you," he said.

"My grandmother would call you a piece of work," I informed him. "That's not a compliment, either."

"I know what that means," he shot back. "I don't give a shit about who else is investigating this. If they want to take a crack at that bar owner, more power to them."

"Look, I don't want to lie to Lee about this," I mumbled. Well, that wasn't true. I did. I wanted to tell Lee that the bar owner was in Mexico having margaritas on a beach and couldn't be reached for comment.

That was the cowardly thing to do, and it was so very tempting for me to do it. People would die if the investigation continued—I'd have bet my salary for the next hundred years on it. Whether it was the bar owner or her vampire business associates, somebody didn't want this story told.

"So, you think Claudia Platt is a vampire or werewolf?" I asked, naming the bar's owner.

Kory's head jerked in my direction for a moment before turning back to the road. "Can't say," he replied.

Well, that was one way to skirt my truth meter; his ambiguous words pinged in the truth category.

"Whatever she is, she's involved somehow with the not-so-nice vampires of San Francisco."

"I suppose that's obvious," Kory agreed. "Here we are—chateau de Lexsi." He shoved the gearshift into park and shut off the engine.

"It's chateau d'Aunt Bree," I sighed. "She's letting me live here. I wouldn't make enough to buy this in a thousand years."

"As long as it's big enough to hold all of us," he said, pulling a duffle from the back seat of the van.

"Hey," I objected. He'd invited himself to stay?

"Look, it's for the best, really. I'll explain sometime soon. For now, we need to keep Mason and Watson safe."

"In my house?" I squeaked.

"In your Aunt's house," he countered with a grin. "Besides, Mason says that pasta you put together for him was better than most restaurants make."

"You want me to cook, clean and pick up after you, too?" I was really pissed, suddenly.

"No, that's not what I said," he began.

"Yes it is," I said. "It's exactly what you said."

"We can pick up after ourselves," he defended himself. "But if you'd cook now and then, we'll pay for the groceries and booze."

"This is impossible," I whispered, shaking my head.

"Come on, you need sleep. Tell me that's not true."

"I'd like to throw stuff at you," I huffed.

"You're too tired. You'd just miss."

"Jerk."

"Prissy pants."

"What did you call me?" I stopped halfway to the front door and rounded on Kory.

"If you get to call me jerk, which I'm not," he tapped his chest, "then I get to call you prissy pants, which you're not."

"Is that how it works?" I demanded.

"Works well enough for me."

"Fine. Get your jerky ass in the house. I'm tired and I want to go to bed."

"Why didn't you say so?"

"I'm saying so now."

"Fine. Get your prissy pants in the house, too. I'm tired and I want to go to bed."

"Why didn't you say so?"

"I'm saying so now."

Mason opened the door at that moment—of course he'd be awake, he was vampire. Watson and Anita were asleep, he informed us as we walked through the door.

"I'm running a boarding house," I mumbled, striding away from Mason and Kory. My bed waited, and I only wanted to get inside my room, lock the door and fall face-first on the mattress before I passed out.

∼

Kordevik

"Watson got a call from Claudia," Mason said as I watched Lexsi disappear down the hall. "The new bar is being set up in Oakland and she wants him there tomorrow to order bar supplies and stock the place."

"She already has a building?"

"I get the idea that Granger had a hand in this, in exchange for her cooperation. Klancy took the second shift at the hospital—he's appointed himself as guardian over the girl and Mike."

"So Granger has someone else set against him, and it's not just you," I blew out a breath.

"Yeah, but two vamps against Granger's stable isn't much resistance. How's the girl doing?"

"Better, but she doesn't remember much. Previous compulsion kicking in, no doubt. Police don't have any more information than what they started out with."

"Have you ever seen the supernatural community at such odds, or coming so close to outing themselves before?" I asked.

"I talked to my sire—he says no. I'm surprised the Council and the Grand Master haven't weighed in on this."

"Maybe they have and we just don't know," I shrugged. "Look, I'm beat. I need to sleep because I have an early morning gig. Picking somebody up at the airport, I think."

"Then get to it. I'll be on guard the rest of the night."

"Thanks, man." I took off toward the dim hallway, where my borrowed bedroom was located. If I were lucky, I'd get five hours of sleep before I had to get up and go to work.

~

Lexsi

Kory was already gone when I convinced my weary body to get out of bed at eight the following morning. Anita and Watson were also at work, while Mason was asleep for the day.

That meant I had the house—and the kitchen—to myself. I wanted eggs the way my mother cooked them, so I went through the fridge to check for ingredients.

People on Earth would call what I'd made Eggs Benedict, but it was a variation on the usual recipe that my mother perfected and I loved it. It was one of the first things she'd taught me to make.

A part of me liked the silence of an empty house. Another part missed the conversation and the comfort of having others there. It's the way I grew up—the house was always occupied by many.

At least Aunt Bree's house could hold all of us. I fantasized, then, about the raise I might get for taking the nighttime field anchor spot, and wondered if it would cover all the bills. I didn't lie to myself— more money would be very welcome and I wouldn't feel like such a freeloader if I could pay utilities, upkeep and any other expenses that came along.

A new car would be nice, too.

That's when I reminded myself that all this was happening as a result of Vann's death and Mike's firing. It felt wrong to profit from it. I also didn't want to toss karma into the mix for Vann firing Mike— that was between them and I didn't want to get into it.

Sighing, I shoved my dishes into the washer and went to get a shower.

~

Kordevik

I received a call from Anita as I waited at the airport terminal for my passenger. The call surprised me, although it shouldn't have.

"I want to tell you this first," Anita said. "Lee almost handed Vann's job to Lexsi yesterday, because people in the area liked her so much. The Romes have taken matters into their own hands and are sending Hannah Tilton from LA to take Vann's place. I don't think this looks good for Lexsi—Hannah doesn't treat her female coworkers very well, especially if they're pretty. If Lexsi ends up as her assistant," Anita left the sentence hanging.

"I get it," I said. "Fuck."

"I said the same thing. Look, I have to get back to work—I just processed Hannah's paperwork, so it's a done deal."

"Got it," I said. "Oh, shit." I watched as Hannah Tilton and two young, male assistants walked out of the airport. "Tilton's the one I'm picking up at the airport."

"Lucky you," Anita said and ended the call.

～

Lexsi

I could tell something was wrong when I walked toward my cubicle. At least three knots of people, consisting of production assistants, researchers and news assistants were whispering together until I appeared.

Lee poked his head out of an office down the hall. "Silver, I need to see you," he said. He didn't sound happy. "We have to view the footage of the rough cut of Vann's memorial video, too," he added.

"On my way," I said, tossing my jacket and purse onto the desk before heading in his direction.

"Sit down," Lee pointed me to one of two guest chairs inside his office. He shut the door, leaving us alone. Whatever this was, it had been the subject of conversation before I'd arrived at work.

"I spoke out of turn yesterday," Lee began. "The Romes pointed out that you're still a rookie and haven't earned a reporter spot, yet. They've sent Hannah Tilton from our sister station in LA to take Vann's place. She'll be your new boss."

"I understand," I said, while inwardly, my new hopes crumbled. I did understand, and had allowed my own wishes to get in the way of

75

good sense. The way he'd said Hannah's name troubled me, though. Something was wrong and he wasn't telling me.

While I pondered Lee's announcement, his phone rang. "She's here," he said. "Come on, we're going to watch the rough draft of the memorial video, so she can take notes and make suggestions. I'll introduce you afterward."

Dutifully I followed Lee toward the screening room at the back of the station. Editors and directors would be there, to make suggestions for the final product before it aired the following evening.

I assumed that Hannah would narrate, since she was well known throughout the news community. After all, who was left to do the honors? I'd been slapped down; at least that's how I felt. Yes, my reaction wasn't rational, but emotions rarely are.

I didn't get the opportunity to have Lee introduce us; Hannah waited at the screening room door, a double latte in her hand and looking so shiny and well-groomed she could have been peeled off a magazine cover.

"Well, little assistant bitch," she handed her half-empty cup to me, "warm that up and get it back to me before the footage rolls."

I ran. Not just from her, but from what they'd done to me.

Lee knew.

Hell, the entire office knew, and nobody thought to warn me.

I made it back to the screening room with barely two seconds to spare. I ended up taking a seat at the back of the small theater, too. Not just because I didn't want to sit anywhere near Hannah Tilton, but both chairs around her were taken up with young male assistants she'd brought with her from LA.

Throughout the video, I fumed.

Until the last two minutes.

That's when the photograph was shown of Vann at the Rome's anniversary party. Yes, someone said he was friends with the Romes. That wasn't what drew my attention. There Vann was, standing between the Romes, his arm around Laurel Rome's shoulders.

No—that wasn't it. I leaned forward. Yes. There it was. The unmistakable, glittery fringe of Donna Raven's designer jacket.

Donna stood with her back to Vann and the Romes, but I recognized her outfit from Gerta Britt's security recording.

The Ravens had gone to the Rome party, but hadn't been on the guest list.

Not only did I now have the boss from hell, I also had a deepening mystery on my hands.

CHAPTER 6

*L*exsi

My first day in hell consisted of getting coffee for Ms. Horrible, followed by doing research for Ms. Horrible, making phone calls for Ms. Horrible and issuing invitations for a dinner party she was planning for the weekend.

If I'd thought Vann the worst, it was only because I hadn't met Hannah the Horrible, yet.

Perhaps the worst part of my day was when she ordered me to find the name of the company driver who'd picked her up at the airport—she wanted him at her party, too, and offered to rent his tux if he didn't have one.

Only one driver fit the description she'd given me—Kory. I wrote his name down for her and said I'd take care of the invitation. I watched as she tapped a red, manicured nail on Kory's name.

"Kory Wilson. Do you know if he has an education? What his work background is?"

"I'm sorry, Ms. Tilton, I don't," I replied while refusing to grit my teeth. "I believe HR may be able to help with that."

I walked away before she could ask me to call HR for her. Kory was about to be next on her list of the most fuckable men she'd met that she hadn't yet fucked, and I wanted no part of that.

Half her words were lies, too, but I also didn't want to get into that. If Aunt Bree hadn't been specific about the job I had to take, I'd have turned in my notice and went to work peeling potatoes at a restaurant somewhere.

I had plenty of experience at that sort of thing—in between my schooling, I'd worked with Mom and Uncle Fes at their restaurants in Targis. I'd been paid, too, for the hours I'd worked.

It was worth it just to see the working kitchens in the two best restaurants on the planet of Tulgalan. I already knew how to cook pretty well before I was allowed into either kitchen, and I'd learned even more working with my family.

I was a decent cook, even if I were still a rookie journalist.

I kept telling myself that on the drive home in the TinyCar; that Hannah the Horrible probably couldn't boil an egg without ruining it.

For the first time, too, I missed my family. Mom, Dad, Gran, my uncles and aunts. Shoving those thoughts away, I reminded myself of why I'd left them behind—an arranged marriage with a man I'd never met.

If this were the universe's way of forcing me to see the unvarnished real worlds, then perhaps I deserved it, Hannah the Horrible and all.

Kordevik

Hannah wants you at her dinner party this weekend, Lexsi's text said, and included the time and address. *She wants to rent a tux for you, and I doubt she wants you to park cars for guests.*

Do I detect a note of jealousy? I texted back.

You detect nothing except the performance of my duties, she snipped. *Ms. Tilton is expecting an RSVP. The sooner you reply, the sooner she gets off my back about it.*

Then I'll send a gracious and respectful NO, I tapped. *Ms. Tilton doesn't belong in my universe.*

Mine, either, she responded. *Yet here we are.*

I recognized the truth behind her statement. Neither of us belonged on Earth in the past and she'd let that knowledge slip through, never thinking I'd understand exactly what she meant.

Ms. Tilton was not only Lexsi's new boss, but she wanted to lay claim to me, too. I wanted no part of her diva attitude. Hannah's kind of pretty came with a streak of meanness that left broken souls and destroyed lives in its wake. I'd read that in her when she ordered her two male assistants around as if they were worthless slaves.

From an outside point of view, she was the spider luring her prey into a web they couldn't escape—their future in the business ensured it.

She wants you in that web with her, I reminded myself. The prospect was grim; accept her invitation and be trapped, refuse and wait for her to find fault so I'd be fired or relocated.

That's how her kind worked. I'd seen it before—in men and women. All of them power hungry and deep down, somewhat insecure. Most of them I'd met during my six-hundred-year stint in Kifirin's military.

I'd only met a handful since my arrival on Earth. Hannah Tilton wasn't the worst of the lot—I reserved that slot for Granger and his ilk —the vamp who killed or attempted to kill anyone he didn't like. As far as I knew, Hannah had only managed to make enemies of just about everyone, because she treated them like shit.

Claudia—the jury was still out on her, but recent activity didn't paint her in a flattering light. I wondered that Watson was still willing to work for her. He didn't seem the type to put up with her sort of bullshit.

What worried me most about Hannah was the trouble she could cause Lexsi and me. I was slowly working my way into Lexsi's life, yet Hannah threatened to sever that tenuous bond.

I wasn't much on parties, either, and hoped I wouldn't be forced to go to Hannah's. That would only lead to trouble. Tapping Hannah's number into my phone, I sent her a text, explaining that Lexsi had delivered my invitation, but that I'd already made plans for the weekend.

I hoped it would stave off the inevitable; she'd see me as an elusive conquest, which could serve to make me a bigger target.

One way or another, I would end up regretting any association with the woman.

Lexsi

My cell phone rang the second I walked in the house after the long drive home. Farin was on the other end of the conversation. "Rick is staying with me," she said.

"That sounds good—the vamps found the other place," I acknowledged while setting my purse on the kitchen counter.

"He still goes back there to pick up his clothes and stuff, but that's not really what I called about," she said. "Tiburon texted me—he invited me to dinner."

"So?" I didn't want to tell Farin that I should be the last person to offer dating advice; I didn't have much experience in that area. "Do you like him?" I added.

"Yeah. I really like him," she confided. "I just don't want to be all starry-eyed and forget to eat, or worse, drop food on my clothes or something."

"I don't think he'll care if any of that stuff happens," I said. "I think he likes you, too."

"I just don't want to mess this up," she wailed.

"You won't. If it's meant to be, it's meant to be," I attempted to calm her down. She'd called me, needing help, when I wanted nothing more than a friend I could confide in concerning Hannah the Horrible and the awful, looming future I faced as her least-appreciated assistant.

"When is the date?" I asked, attempting to hide the sudden weariness that enveloped me.

"Friday night."

"That's tomorrow," I pointed out.

"What should I wear?" She was back to wailing.

"Wear pink—you look awesome in that sweater set."

"I hope he likes pink," she sniffed.

"Farin, it won't matter how you're dressed. He'll be thinking that he's out with the sexiest weather girl ever, the whole time you're together. Trust me."

"I hope you're right."

Why are Earth women so insecure about everything? I wondered, as Farin went on about the jewelry she might wear, and the shoes that would go with her outfit. Perhaps it was the culture they'd been raised in, I surmised as I listened and responded now and then with what I hoped was useful advice.

"You'll be great, I promise," I told her when she wound down. "Stop worrying, laugh when he says something funny and enjoy the company."

"I'll let you know how it goes," she promised. "See ya," she ended the call.

I was on my way to the bedroom when my cell phone rang again. Anita, this time.

"You could send mindspeech," I reminded her. Yes, I sounded grumpy. "Sorry," I apologized. "I had the day from hell," I explained.

"No doubt," her words were dry. "Nobody in the company likes Hannah, except the Romes. They liked Vann better, but Hannah is number two on their list."

"I need to talk to you sometime—in private," I muttered. "No phone conversations, either."

"You got something?" She perked right up.

"Maybe, but it doesn't make much sense."

"All right. How about tomorrow after work? I'll come by your place and bring a bottle of something with me."

"Sounds great. Hannah wants her claws in Kory already," I added.

"That's not what's bothering you so much?"

"I just don't want her forcing him into something he doesn't want," I sputtered.

"Riiight."

"Look, save it for tomorrow, I want to lie down and get rid of my Hannah headache."

"I doubt you're the only one with that particular problem tonight," Anita said. "I hear she's already made an enemy of Lee, and he can get along with anybody. Looks like he's looking for another job already."

"How do you know that?" I asked.

"Somebody called for references this afternoon."

"You're kidding? Who called?"

"Same station that hired Mike, that's who. It won't matter—just about anybody would take Lee if he applied with them. He has great experience and a reputation for working with even the worst in egotistical anchors."

"Wow. I never thought about that, but Vann wasn't easy to work with, I know that much."

"Maybe it's time Lee thought of himself, then. I wouldn't work with Hannah if I had a choice. Oops—sorry."

"Yeah. Rub it in," I mumbled. "It's probably a matter of time before she gets me fired."

"She's the jealous type," Anita said. "So she doesn't want to work with any woman who can put her to shame in the looks department. Plus, you're young. She's getting crow's feet. That pisses her off, too."

"Thanks for eliminating my job before she does," I snapped. "My life is complicated enough already, you know."

"I'm just giving you the real reasons she'll want to get rid of you— no matter what the paperwork says at the end."

"You've looked into her records, haven't you?" I accused.

"Yep. She's fired every female assistant she ever had. I'm adding her to my list of investigations into Rome hiring practices. No woman has ever lasted more than three months, working with Hannah."

"Great. More good news," I sighed.

"I think you should apply for a job elsewhere, especially if Lee gets the job he applied for, hint-hint."

"Right. That's great in theory, but not so great in practice," I said. I couldn't tell Anita why I was working for Rome Enterprises to begin with—it would only raise questions about relatives I couldn't explain or produce on demand.

"I guess the clock's ticking, then," I said.

"It's always better to turn in a notice than wait to be fired; that way you won't have to put that on your next job application."

While I pondered that bit of advice, it occurred to me that perhaps this was Aunt Bree's way of telling me I shouldn't have run away in the first place. It was diabolical in its simplicity; force me into a situation where I couldn't meet the terms of our agreement, and I'd be homeward bound for a wedding I didn't want.

"I'm going to be the best female assistant Hannah the Horrible has ever had," I announced.

"What?" Anita's voice betrayed her shock.

"Just what I said. She won't be able to get rid of me because I'll be that good."

"On your head be it," Anita huffed. "She'll make you wish you were dead; believe me."

"Oh, that may already be," I retorted. "I just intend to be the perfect assistant when that inevitability arrives."

"Then stay two steps ahead of her," Anita responded. "Read her mind and anticipate."

"I'll see what I can do," I said.

"Three months, tops," Anita reminded me.

"Yeah."

~

Kordevik

"That's simply not acceptable," Hannah informed me. "Plans can be changed—this is important for your future career," she added.

How the hell was I to know she wouldn't take no for an answer? And the veiled threat at the end?

Genius. On her part, at least. It didn't bode well for me in the least. She was telling me that my future as a Rome Enterprises employee depended on my showing up at her party on Saturday night.

Fuck her, and not in any traditional sense.

"I'm engaged," I blurted.

"What? I have no record of that," she purred.

"I am," I insisted.

Well, I had been, at least. I still considered myself engaged, no matter what Lexsi thought.

"To whom? Bring her with you. I'll make an exception this time."

She intended to break us up. Well, break my phantom fiancée and me up.

Fuck.

Triple fuck.

Now what?

I needed a fiancée in two days.

Holy, fucking hell.

"I'll see if I can pry her away from her plans," I sighed.

"Please do. I look forward to meeting her."

Visions of Hannah, with a knife held behind her back invaded my thoughts.

"Of course," I responded. "Thank you for inviting us."

"It's nothing, darling. See you Saturday."

I was never so glad to end a call in my life. Hannah Tilton, as predicted, was going to complicate my life terribly.

I dialed Lexsi's number, then, to ask if she wanted me to grab pizza for dinner on my way to her house.

Lexsi

Anita came up with the solution I needed, and it surprised me that we hadn't thought of it before. Anita planned to lay her obsession whammy on Hannah the Horrible, and things would work out for everybody.

At least I hoped they would. We only had to get Anita within speaking range of Hannah, and that looked to be a problem.

Until Kory came home, loaded down with pizza boxes. He

announced that he needed a fiancée by Saturday night, to keep Hannah at arm's length.

I was on the phone with Anita in three seconds. She agreed to go to Hannah's party with Kory, but we needed a suitable engagement ring. "You know I can't do much—just tell her not to fire you," Anita pointed out. "Too much of a change and people will get suspicious."

"Wow. So I still get to live in hell, but have job security?" I asked.

"That about sums it up. Tell handsome hunk to buy an engagement ring and I'll get gussied up for Saturday at Hannah's."

"I'll let him know," I said.

"I heard," Kory lifted his second slice of pepperoni from a box and gave me a grin. "I'll find something for her to wear."

"Why aren't you asking about Anita's special talent?" I studied the sides of boxes, looking for the sausage and mushroom pizza.

"Hmmph," he said and continued chewing an overly large bite. I took that to mean he wasn't surprised in the least. Well, he knew vampires and werewolves. Why wouldn't he recognize a Sirenali, too?

Setting his half-eaten slice of pizza on a paper plate, he pulled out the box I wanted without looking at it and handed it to me. I made a face at him before opening it and extracting a wedge for myself.

He tapped his plate and kept eating. I placed another wedge of sausage and mushroom in front of him, then went looking for a glass of wine. After the day I'd had, I needed it.

"Don't let that bitch upset you," Kory said emptying half his glass of beer. "Deep down, she's paranoid and insecure."

"That doesn't help when she calls me her little assistant bitch," I pouted.

"I realize that's worthy of getting her arm ripped off," Kory looked away for a moment. "Try to hold yourself back."

"Why—and how—would I do that?" I huffed.

"You took care of three guys in a parking lot. Your eye looks almost normal," he added.

"I heal fast," I said and bit into my pizza.

"Just—try not to take that shit personally. If it weren't you, she'd treat the next woman exactly the same."

"Yeah. That's what Anita says. I've just never been talked to like that."

"I know. Ignore it and think whatever you like about her. That's what everybody else does."

"It sounds easy, the way you say it. Not so easy in reality," I said.

"I know—I'm just trying to make you feel better right now. This is life, little onion. People will dump shit on you all the time. You just have to find a way to use what you can and slough off the rest. Don't ever let them rule your life with their own fallibilities."

"Yeah." I pulled out a barstool and sat across from him. I was certainly learning about life the hard way. I hadn't realized how privileged I'd been before running away from home.

"Don't let depression rule your life, either," Kory rumbled before emptying his beer bottle. "If you let that witch upset you, she wins. Don't let her win. Let your actions define who you are, not hers."

"You sound like my uncle Sal."

"Then Uncle Sal must be a wise man," he said.

"His best friend is even wiser," I sighed and dropped pizza crust onto my plate. "I only talked to him a couple of times, though."

"Then you'll have to make do with me," he offered a wry smile. "Come on, onion, let's go find an engagement ring that'll fit Anita."

I'm sure Anita didn't appreciate the multiple images I sent her from the jewelry store, but we finally found something she liked in her size. Kory made sure to ask about the return policy before he handed the clerk his credit card.

The clerk, who frowned the whole time we looked at rings, was no doubt wondering why Kory brought another woman with him to pick out the engagement ring for his fiancée, while keeping her on the phone to make a final decision.

It wouldn't have made any sense to me, either, so I gave the poor man a pass. The ring wasn't expensive by some standards, but looked like something Kory could afford on his salary.

None of this would be happening if Hannah the Horrible hadn't filled Vann's spot on the evening news.

That brought back the images of Donna Raven's dress in the image of Vann at the Romes' party. I considered telling Kory of my discovery, but held back—it held no interest for him. Anita was the one with whom I needed to discuss my findings and speculation.

"Anything new on the vamps chasing Mike?" I asked when we were inside Kory's Jeep and driving toward the house.

"Nothing yet, although Watson hasn't checked in," Kory said. "I'm hoping he'll have something. Mason should be awake when we get back, but as he's been asleep all day, unless he's gotten a recent message on his phone, he has nothing, either."

"I worry about Farin and Rick," I said.

"They were only trying to find Mike, trust me," Kory observed. "Farin and Rick were just bystanders who got caught up in the frenzy."

I watched Kory's face as he drove—there was something else he wasn't telling me. Leaning back in my seat, I closed my eyes. He'd either tell me or he wouldn't; I was too tired to pursue it.

Kordevik

I considered telling Lexsi about the price Granger had on my head, then thought better of it. She was concerned enough as it was, and my story would only make things worse.

On the plus side, Granger only knew first-hand what I looked like in my humanoid form. He had to rely on witness accounts of my smaller Thifilathi. It made me wonder how much Granger had offered for information.

Worse yet, what he was offering for my death.

I'd never had a price on my head before. It wasn't a pleasant experience. High Demons could hold their own in most fights, unless the fight became overwhelming in his opponent's favor.

If Claudia were in bed with San Francisco's controlling vampire, figuratively and (in all probability) literally, then she could also be out for my blood.

No, I didn't regret saving Mike and what little was left of Vann— but that situation should have been handled differently. Something had set the supernaturals off in the city, and I wondered what it was.

If they'd employed common sense, they'd realize they were in danger of outing themselves to the human population. The last I'd heard, neither the Vampire Council nor the Werewolf Grand Master wanted that.

"Park in the garage," Lexsi said, interrupting my thoughts. I realized we'd reached her house while too many things occupied my mind.

"Remote?" I asked.

Lifting a small fob on her key ring, she pressed the button to lift the door. The TinyCar barely took up any space. I maneuvered my Jeep in beside it and shut off the engine.

"I need more wine," she announced and opened the passenger-side door.

Lexsi

Day two in Hannah hell went much like the first, until it was time for me to leave. Hell became worse in a hurry. "I want you to be at the party, just to make sure the caterers are doing their jobs," Hannah swept up to my desk after a meeting with the station's General Manager. "Dress appropriately. If you don't have one of those server jackets, I'm sure they can lend you one. They arrive two hours before the party, so you need to be there, too."

I was no stranger to a cook's or server's jacket, but her intention was to embarrass and humiliate me in front of everyone else.

"Yes, ma'am," I gave her a bright, completely false smile. If she thought I'd fail miserably at managing a catering gig, then she should think again. If I'd been my mother, I'd have stared her down.

I wasn't my mother, sadly enough.

I was determined to do a good job, however, no matter what the assignment.

"One more thing," Hannah turned back after walking a few steps away. "The Romes will be at the party. Make a good impression, little bitch."

~

"I got a copy from one of the assistant editors," I shoved the thumb drive into my laptop at home so I could show Anita what I'd found. "See—that's Donna Raven's back. I recognized her jacket from images I found on her neighbor's security system."

"Do you have those, too?" She asked.

"I do." I'd already saved those, so I pulled up Gerta Britt's security recording and placed a frozen image of Donna Raven standing in her driveway next to the photograph from the Romes' anniversary party. Vann and the Romes were so close to Donna Raven's back in the photograph that they could have touched her.

"That's the same jacket, all right," Anita narrowed her eyes and peered at the image. "Anything new on those murders?"

"No. I checked during lunch, today. The police think it's a done deal—that the poor woman who offed herself at their house did it and that's the end of it."

"But you don't think so."

"No, there's something going on, here. I feel it. The Ravens weren't on the guest list submitted by the Romes' assistant. Why would they do that? Wouldn't they be looking to draw viewers in by saying they were among the last to see the Ravens alive? It makes no sense to me."

"You could be right," she said and tapped the image of Vann on the screen. "I talked to Mason last night. He says a vampire named Granger is responsible for Vann's death."

"For real?" I blinked at her.

"Yeah. There's something else, too. Lee turned in his two-weeks' notice today. He got the other job." Anita sighed and leaned back in her seat.

"That's too bad. I like him. Everybody else is avoiding me like I have a contagious disease, now," I said.

"They're just waiting for Hannah to fire you," Anita shrugged.

"Right. Meanwhile, I have to dress up like a servant and make sure her dinner party goes without a hitch."

"Watch out for her—she could be looking for an excuse to fire you before the party gets started. I can't help you if that happens."

"True. Wow. I didn't think of that," I said. "She really is a witch, isn't she?"

"That's the word I got. Gives actual witches a bad rap, too."

"I hear that," I agreed. "And call them Wiccans. They're not in the same category as Hannah the Horrible, nor would they want to be."

"Yeah. Look, just hold on until Kory and I can get there. We'll handle it from there."

"Thanks," I said. "You don't know how much I appreciate this."

"Oh, you're gonna cook some of that pasta for me. I barely got a taste before Watson ate it all."

"Hmmph, that was nothing," I flung out a hand. "You should taste some of the other stuff I cook. Stuff that takes longer," I amended.

"I'll be waiting," she grinned. "What are you wearing to go with your server's jacket and humble pie?"

"Black slacks, flats and a white button-down," I replied promptly.

Kordevik

"Where the hell have you been, man? I haven't heard from you for two days." I glared at Watson as he climbed into my Jeep.

"Claudia's on a tear, man. Get off my case," he muttered. "She wanted the bar stocked completely. Something about important visitors Saturday night. At least somebody else is running the bar; I'm bushed and I have another full day tomorrow before she opens."

"Important visitors? Who?"

"She wouldn't say. I've been all over the place, getting stock for the bar. Whoever's coming likes martinis with French vodka and imported olives."

"That means nothing to me," I pointed out.

"Me, either, and I'd have remembered somebody like that. This is somebody I don't know, and since vamps don't care what their drinks taste like, then Claudia's guests are either human, werewolf or shifter. Bet on it."

"She happen to mention me—or the other me?" I asked.

"No. Granger didn't come up, either."

"So she either doesn't want to talk in front of you, or she's letting Granger handle the vendetta."

"I'd say the latter," Watson frowned. "Can you make a food stop on the way home? Better yet, you think Lexsi's cooking something?"

"I can ask," I said. "Hit her number and put it through the truck's Bluetooth."

"Hello?" Lexsi answered her phone.

"Are you cooking, or do you want us to pick something up?" I said.

"I can cook," she replied. "What do you want?"

"Steak," Watson said immediately.

"Then stop and pick up what you want. Get the best cuts you can find. I'll grill them. I have stuff to go with them."

"Your wish, my command," Watson sounded as happy as I'd ever heard him.

"I'll get started on the sauce, now," Lexsi said and hung up.

"I get steak," Watson grinned. "My wolf is happy."

Lexsi

"Seared on the outside, raw on the inside. As ordered," I placed the huge T-bone in front of Watson. "Try the sauce, it's incredible."

I watched as he tentatively put a tiny amount of sauce on the chunk of steak he cut and placed it in his mouth. His eyes grew wide and his smile wider.

He attacked his steak afterward, but not before he'd dumped all the sauce I'd given him on it first.

Kory's steak came next; he wanted medium-rare, then Anita's and mine, because we liked ours medium. Every drop of sauce I'd made disappeared, along with the salad and sautéed asparagus.

"Damn, that was good," Watson growled and rubbed his belly.

"Want some coffee or something else to drink?" I asked.

"Nah. Let me savor this. I don't get meals this good very often."

"That was outstanding," Kory pushed his chair back. "Thank you for cooking. I'll do the dishes; it's only fair."

"I'll help," Watson scooted his chair back.

Anita blinked as both men went to work, stuffing plates, pans and flatware into the dishwasher.

Have you ever seen anything like that before? She sent.

Only in a few guys, I responded. *I like it.*

Who taught you to cook?

Mom and Gran.

They must be magnificent cooks.

They are.

CHAPTER 7

Lexsi

I wasn't looking forward to dealing with Hannah and her dinner party. I didn't doubt my ability to handle caterers; I did doubt my ability to handle it if she continued to call me little bitch.

I wanted to punch her in the face for that insult—it pissed me off every time she said it. That was my thought as I gazed at my image in the mirror before leaving the house. The step backward was involuntary when the curl of smoke left my nostrils.

What. The. Bloody. Hell?

Only two High Demon females had ever breathed smoke—or turned Thifilatha. *What the hell was happening to me?*

Regardless, I couldn't let it slip out again; people would be watching. I didn't need that scrutiny. Shoving down my shock and anger, I straightened the cuffs on my long-sleeved button down and headed for the bedroom door. The sooner I got on the job, the faster it would go.

Kordevik

I'd learned from Lexsi during dinner the night before that the Romes were coming to Hannah's party. What it meant was that Anita and I would be forced to stay engaged for a while—to make it appear authentic.

I wasn't her type, though, and she was comfortable with the fact that she wasn't mine, either. This could save my job as well as Lexsi's. I felt I owed Anita a favor, however, for doing this for us.

Lexsi had already left the house; she had to be there early to watch over Hannah's caterers. I couldn't imagine that any caterer would need that much supervision. *Unless*, I allowed a bit of smoke to curl from my nostrils.

This was a setup. I should have recognized it for what it was; Hannah's excuse for firing Lexsi, because she wouldn't be able to handle what she didn't have any experience with.

Except she did. I knew where Lexsi got her talent in the kitchen. I'd eaten at Dee's and Desh's in Targis. You couldn't get better food in either Alliance. "Fuck you, Hannah Tilton," I muttered, straightening the bowtie on my tux. "Lexsi Silver can make mincemeat of you—and make you taste good with the perfect sauce and wine to go with your sour ass."

Lexsi

It would have been better if Hannah had informed me that all food would be cooked on the premises, in her overly large, Sausalito mansion. She'd failed to mention that one vital piece of information.

The head cook had also failed to show up.

Whether there was a legitimate excuse or it was by design remained to be seen.

The caterer had sent a group of relatively inexperienced staff to help the head cook, which left me in something of a bind. Hannah wanted sashimi. She wanted salads. She wanted a multitude of other items, paired with appropriate wines and drinks.

She fluttered in and out while I rounded up the troops I'd been allotted. Somebody cooked rice. Another two chopped vegetables. Someone else was set to carefully slice tuna, Kobe beef and other delicacies. He appeared to have the most experience in the group; nevertheless, I watched carefully until I was sure he knew what he was doing.

"We have twenty pounds of fresh shrimp in the van," a young woman informed me.

"Then bring it in," I said. "We'll make pasta with seafood sauce. I assume you have cream and spices with you? I'll need some of the crab, too. Can you do that for me?"

"Yes," she bobbed her head.

"Good. Gather everything for me and we'll get started. Time is running out for everything except the sushi and sashimi, which will be made to order, you understand."

"Yes, ma'am." She took off as if she'd been fired from a rifle.

By the time guests began to arrive, everything was ready and in place, including three men who arrived late to work the sushi/sashimi table. There'd been no word from the missing cook the whole time.

"This had better be good," Hannah appeared at my elbow to hiss in my ear.

"Of course, Ms. Tilton," I nodded. At that point, she was lucky I didn't hand her to a sushi chef to cut into bite-sized pieces.

The following six hours were grueling, but Hannah received numerous compliments on the food and drinks. The seafood pasta was especially popular, and I was grateful we didn't run out until everyone had a chance to taste it.

Just as I was helping rinse pans before they were loaded into the catering van, a man and woman walked into the kitchen.

I knew who they were—except I didn't. Yes, they looked exactly like Laurel and James Rome, Jr. "I hear you made the seafood pasta," the man said, giving me a smile. "I'm James Rome," he offered his hand.

Lie, I said to myself as I took his hand and shook. Laurel, however, was exactly who she said she was.

Somewhere along the way, James Rome Jr. had been replaced by a replica. I had a feeling Laurel knew all about it, too. Not only was the mystery deepening, it was spreading like a virus.

Where was the real Jamie Rome? How had Laurel replaced him? Why didn't they report the Ravens as guests for their anniversary party?

I had too many questions and absolutely no answers.

~

Kordevik

"Look," Anita said, "I can't obsess someone who's already obsessed —up to her hairline, in fact. You take that much control, there's nothing left to take."

"You're joking?"

We were in my Jeep, heading homeward after leaving Hannah's party as soon as it was polite to do so. Anita waited until we were halfway to San Rafael to drop her bomb on me. I'd wondered why she hadn't attempted to place an obsession when I introduced her to Hannah. Now I was learning the truth.

"She looked at you like you were prime rib and she was starving," Anita snapped. "If I could do something about that, I sure would have."

"At least Lexsi showed her a thing or two about cooking and serving guests," I sighed. "I overheard the catering staff discussing their head cook, who didn't show."

"I knew that bitch wanted to use this as an excuse to fire Lexsi," Anita fumed. "Now she's only safe until the next time Hannah wants her gone."

"Yeah, and we're still engaged until Ultra-Bitch finds a way to fire me, because I want no part of her," I said.

"I hope Lexsi gets out of there before Hannah gives her more grief," Anita stated flatly.

"Yeah," I agreed.

~

Lexsi

The last crate of equipment and supplies was loaded into the catering van while I made the fake Jamie Rome yet another martini with Grey Goose and imported olives. He'd had three since he and Laurel ventured into the kitchen.

She sipped her second fruit and rum drink—she'd inhaled the first one. That's when *he* came.

Just from the way he moved—smooth and nearly silent—I understood he was vampire.

Not just any vampire, either, but a very old one. I'd seen enough old vampires at Gran's palace to recognize one easily.

"Granger, come sit with us," Laurel invited.

"Thank you, but I was merely wishing to bid you good-night," Granger lifted Laurel's hand to his lips.

I realized at that point that I'd stopped breathing. Was this the one who'd killed Vann? Vann had been a close friend of the Romes. My brain churned with the possibilities.

"Young woman," Granger turned his old-world charm in my direction, "Your food was exceptional. Perhaps we'll meet again." I watched, openmouthed, as he glided out of the kitchen.

"Another martini?" Not-Jamie pushed his glass toward me. I lifted it with a shaking hand and set about making another drink.

By the time I made it home, it was past midnight. Hannah didn't speak to me on my way out the door, either. No words of thanks would ever pass those bright-red lips. She'd intended to fire me earlier.

Faux-Jamie liked my martinis, though.

Would that have a bearing on my treatment by Hannah the Horrible? I shuddered at the thought. Why was I hoping that whomever or whatever had replaced James Rome, Jr. would have any sympathy for an unimportant assistant?

If I hadn't been instructed to work where I was, I'd be turning in my notice the next day.

The possibility of far-reaching criminal activity between the Romes, Granger, Hannah and Claudia Platt astounded me.

After all, the Romes knew Granger, a powerful vampire. Something about him definitely pinged in the *Bad Vampire* category. Did Granger know Claudia Platt, too? Hannah obviously knew Granger, and she was a friend and employee of the Romes.

Vann had been, too, I reminded myself. Had he stepped over a line, somehow, warranting his removal? Why?

I was tired and nothing was making sense to me.

It didn't help that I felt as if I were being watched all the way home.

~

"We need to talk," I informed Kory and Anita when I walked past the kitchen island where both sat.

"Tomorrow." I continued walking toward my bedroom, shut the door behind me and leaned against it with a troubled sigh.

~

Kordevik

Anita went to bed shortly after Lexsi did. I stayed up another hour, helping myself to the bourbon I found in Lexsi's seldom-used liquor cabinet. I wondered what Lexsi wanted to talk about with us. Did she realize that Anita couldn't do anything with Hannah? Had Hannah fired her anyway?

Everybody at the party raved about the food, so it couldn't be that. I sighed and poured more bourbon in my glass. How had our lives gotten so fucked up? We should be together on Kifirin, and I should be doing my damnedest to make Lexsi happy.

"What's the problem, man?" Mason took a seat across from mine.

"Just the usual *my life is presently fucked up,*" I replied before downing my current dose of alcohol.

"Been there," Mason agreed. "Several times."

"Any word from Klancy?" I asked.

"He called from the hospital. They're letting the girl go Monday morning."

"So he's been watching both?"

"Yeah."

"You know that girl's dead meat if she stays in town past sunset," I said.

"I know that, too. Klancy and I talked about it. He may have something in mind."

"I hope it's something good. And effective."

"That makes two of us. If alcohol had any effect on me, I'd be drinking with you, bro."

"To your health," I held up my next shot of bourbon in a toast.

Lexsi

Sunday morning, early, I got a call from Farin. Not only had she gone out with Tiburon on Friday, but Saturday, too. She was bubbling over with how well they got along.

"Rick wants to ask you out," she said, abruptly changing the subject.

"Farin, no," I moaned. "I mean, I like Rick and all, I'm just not ready for this."

"Why not?" she demanded. I'd just refused her brother; she, as his loyal sister, wanted to know why.

"Because I was engaged until eight months ago," I said. "It uh, didn't work out."

"Oh my gosh, why didn't you tell me?" she breathed.

"It's personal," I muttered.

"Did he dump you?" she wanted to enact righteous indignation on my behalf.

"No, I dumped him, because I really didn't know him as well as I should."

"Did he cheat on you?"

"Farin, slow down, all right? I don't like talking about it because it upsets me. Maybe later, okay?"

"Oh. All right. I'm sorry I was gushing about Tibby, when you're still getting over—well, you know."

"Tibby?"

"It's his nickname. I gave it to him. Isn't that awesome?"

I didn't want to point out that even though Farin was an accomplished weather scientist, she was going on like a schoolgirl with her first crush. At least that's what Gran would have said. I'd never had a schoolgirl crush. Yes, I'd met plenty of boys and young men, but I'd also been engaged since infancy. There's not much you can do with that hanging over your head.

I guess what upset me most was I'd not only never met the one I was promised to, I'd never had any choice in the matter. What sane person wouldn't run away from that? I wasn't sure why he hadn't run away as well. Didn't it bother him that his wife had been selected for him? None of it made any sense to me.

Of course, I didn't know that he hadn't run away, too. I hadn't had contact with anyone except Aunt Bree since I'd left. Maybe he didn't show up either. Perhaps the guests had gorged on wedding cake and champagne while commiserating about foolish youth.

I realized I'd let my mind wander too far as I contemplated business cards with "Fool," written beneath my name. "Do you think it's too early to invite Tibby to the house for dinner?" Farin asked.

I'd lost an entire chunk of conversation by allowing my thoughts to drift.

"Alone or in a group?" I asked. "I think it's early for an alone dinner, but if you invite a few friends," I suggested.

"That sounds good. What are you doing next Friday night?"

"Farin, I don't know," I answered honestly. "The way Hannah's going, I could be looking for another job by then."

"What should I cook?" Farin had already ignored my excuse.

"Don't go overboard," I said. "Something simple to start with. There's no sense in trying to make a fancy dinner when you're nervous about whether he'll like it or not."

"What do you think he'll like?"

"What did he order at dinner?" I asked.

"Pork chops the first night, Steak the second."

"I have a good recipe for pork loin, and you can make it in a slow cooker if you want. It's practically foolproof and great with potatoes and a green vegetable or salad."

"Can you e-mail it to me?"

"Sure. I'll get it to you by the end of the day."

"Look what the cat dragged in," Anita said when I shuffled into the kitchen.

"Hey, I've been on the phone with Farin for more than an hour," I retorted. "She wants to cook for Tibby."

"Tibby?" Anita lifted an eyebrow.

"Yes, they've gone straight to pet names," I said. "I think it's serious."

"Please tell me he isn't calling her Fairy," Anita said.

"No, it's Fair Lady, or so I hear."

"Almost as bad."

"Hold further conversation until I have coffee," I grumped, holding up a hand.

"Did we wake finally?" Kory stalked into the kitchen.

"Yes, we did. We need coffee. And silence from all minions until said coffee is consumed."

"Is there anything for breakfast?" Watson rambled in behind Kory, looking like he'd wrestled a sea monster instead of sleeping.

"Nice look," Anita smiled into her coffee cup.

"I cooked all night last night," I made my excuse to Watson while waiting for coffee to brew. I wasn't in the mood to make breakfast for anybody.

"I can make bacon and eggs," Kory offered.

"Great. I'll help," Watson said.

I kept my mouth shut and took a seat next to Anita while we watched them fumble their way through making breakfast. It wasn't horrible, as it turned out. I learned that Watson liked toast with his butter, while Kory preferred his slathered with strawberry jam.

"I met the Romes last night," I began.

"How were they?" Watson asked.

"Thirsty. I made five martinis for the guy who's posing as James Rome, Jr. He likes his made with Grey Goose and imported olives. Laurel had three rum and fruit drinks and didn't even wobble afterward."

Watson stared at me as if I'd turned into something he didn't recognize. "You're sure?" he said, his voice hitting a higher note.

"Yeah. I made them, so of course I'm sure."

"You know where they went afterward?"

"No idea—they were talking to Hannah when I left. Kory," I turned to him, "I met a vampire named Granger last night."

My statement was met with dead silence—from everybody. "What the bloody hell?" Kory breathed eventually.

"He was there and talking to the Romes. It made me wonder if they knew what he was. I also considered his role in Vann's death."

"Go back to the part where you said someone is posing as James Rome, Jr." Anita said.

"It's not him, I guarantee it. My truth meter gave a thumbs-down on that."

"What the fuck is going on?" Watson blinked at Kory. "Claudia insisted that I stock plenty of Grey Goose and imported olives for her visitors, last night."

"Might be a coincidence, but I doubt it," Kory shook his head. "What the hell do the Romes have to do with Granger and Claudia?"

"Donna and Abe Raven were at the Romes' anniversary shindig, only the Romes left the Ravens' names off the guest list after they were murdered," I said. "I checked with the society editor at the downtown office—the Raven's weren't listed and there were no photographs included. The photo of Vann posing with the Romes wasn't there, either."

"The Ravens were at that party—you can see Donna Raven's jacket in the photograph the Romes supplied for Vann's memorial tribute. He was definitely at that party," Anita confirmed.

"Here's another question—Vann knew the Ravens were at that party. Why wasn't he pointing that out in his newscast when he covered the crime?" I asked.

"You think he was told not to mention it?" Kory's eyes locked with mine. I could tell he knew something else, but wasn't willing to volunteer information.

"Vann may have been persuaded, like Hannah has been persuaded," Anita said. I understood then that Hannah was obsessed in some way.

"But why?" I asked. "It makes no sense."

"I have no idea what you're talking about, and I'm not sure I want to know," Watson held up both hands.

Lie. He knew something, but like Kory, wasn't willing to share.

"You may be better off not knowing," Kory told him. "You could live longer."

"At least we don't have to go to work today," I sighed and sipped my coffee.

❧

Kordevik

I skipped to my borrowed condo to get more clothes and make sure the place hadn't been compromised. Nothing was amiss as I gathered shirts and jeans from the closet, and nabbed an extra pair of boots before skipping back to Lexsi's place.

I discovered what had been left on my bed when I got there; two sets of black blades, all spelled against heat and fire, the larger set ten feet in length and sheathed in fireproof scabbards.

Li'Neruh Rath had delivered these in my absence. As the larger blades were the proper length and weight for my full Thifilathi, I imagined that sooner or later, I'd probably need them.

At least the walk-in closet was large enough for me to set them on the floor beneath the lower rods. I hung clothing over them, to hide the weapons as best I could. It worried me that whatever was brewing around us had begun to take a nastier turn.

Lexsi, if she found my blades, would know exactly what they were. Her father had two sets that looked much the same. These were mine —from my home on Kifirin. I'd checked the Grey House marks on the pommels to make sure.

It didn't surprise me that Li'neruh may have had a purpose in bringing me to Earth to serve my sentence. I felt it my duty to protect Lexsi, and if I could get to the root of the mysteries swirling about us, even better.

I considered, too, that I hadn't seen Granger at the party; he may have shown up after Anita and I left. For obvious reasons, I was glad I hadn't seen him and he hadn't seen me. Things could have gone very wrong afterward.

After all, I'd already burned down one of his houses. It wouldn't look good if I burned another where he'd been invited as a guest.

My thoughts turned to working out—it wouldn't hurt to drive to the gym and get rid of the restless energy that consumed me. Exercise would calm me down and help dismiss unnecessary worry.

I intended to drag Lexsi along, whether she wanted to go or not.

Lexsi

"I'm a member, you're my guest," Kory hauled a gym bag from the back of his Jeep. He'd insisted I come to the local branch of his gym to work out. I knew exercise would help with my worries, I just wasn't in the mood.

He refused my refusal, so here we were, in the parking lot outside King's Fitness Center.

Before, all my lessons and exercising had been mostly private, with only one or two instructors. This time, I'd be on display and I wasn't sure how I felt about that. If I joined a gym, I intended to go at a time when it wouldn't be too busy, or filled with weekend clients only looking to hook up.

"Come on, Prissy Pants," Kory teased. "Let's get your sweat on."

"That sounds so attractive," I mumbled and followed him toward the door. "Jerk."

"Double P."

"Single J."

"Is that a reflection on the one letter, or my marital status?"

"Maybe both."

"Fine. For that, we'll work out extra hard today."

"You're not the boss of me."

"Then you get to sit there while I work out extra hard."

"Sounds like fun," I muttered.

"Do I detect sarcasm?"

"You're drowning in it."

Kory thought to push me. He'd never met Uncle Sal, that was obvious. Sal never let me slack for any reason. Yes, I was somewhat out of shape and knew I'd be sore the next day, but I got through weights, running on a treadmill and throwing a few punches at a bag after a long period of stretching.

What bothered me about it, however, was the attention from other guests. Three men came by and attempted to make conversation. Kory, who was working out nearby, frowned at all of them. I think that may have served to warn others away. The jock at the reception desk offered to show me where the showers were after I was done with my workout.

I thought Kory was going to physically assault the man when he put an arm around my shoulder. The touch wasn't welcome and I dipped to get away from his embrace. "You're that girl on the news," he said, awkwardly dropping his hand. "Planning to make this your regular workout spot? I can sign you up on the way out."

"I usually work out at home," I said, attempting to fend him off. "He," I nodded toward Kory, "made me come with him today."

Kory chose that moment to walk toward me. Reception jock backed away. Kory had his shirt off and his abs put reception jock's to shame.

"We'll shower at home," Kory said, snatching his towel from a nearby bench. I struggled into my jacket on our way out the door; Kory stomped along as if he were itching for a fight.

The ride home was silent, except for engine and road noise. I couldn't have said if asked directly whether I appreciated Kory's jealousy. A part of me enjoyed his reaction; another part insisted that I take care of myself.

"I'm getting a headache," I announced, just before we turned up my street.

"Noted," Kory grimaced.

"Look, I didn't realize that would happen," Kory settled on the barstool next to mine. I was wrapped in the biggest, softest robe I had after showering and washing my hair. A hot cup of tea was in my hands, but I stared blankly into space without drinking.

"I really didn't expect it, either. I'm just not used to that. Is it awful that I wanted to knee him in the crotch?"

"No," he chuckled. "I'd have enjoyed that."

"Me, too." I smiled as I sipped my tea.

Kordevik

Mason always wakes the moment the sun drops below the horizon. He drinks bagged blood before joining the rest of us. Tonight, he had news when he walked into the kitchen.

"I just heard from Klancy," he sighed. "Mike and the woman have disappeared from the hospital."

Granger had fired another volley. I worried that two bodies would be found eventually. He had no use for humans if they betrayed him in any way, so their prognosis wasn't good.

CHAPTER 8

L*exsi*

Kory drove me to the hospital, where Farin and Rick were already waiting for information. Barricades were set up to keep the curious and uninvolved away from the hospital doors.

After a few minutes, Tiburon joined Farin as we sat at a nearby coffee shop, hoping for good news to come from sporadic news conferences given by the Hospital Administrator and local Chief of Police.

When I saw Chet and Jesse arrive without a reporter to set up in the space allotted for news crews, Kory and I walked outside to join them. I expected one of the weekend crew to report on the disappearances but so far, nobody had come.

"This is something Vann would have jumped on," Chet remarked as he fussed with the camera on its tripod.

"Didn't they tell you who was coming?" I asked.

"Hannah was supposed to meet us. As you can see, she's not here." Chet was disenchanted with the news diva already.

"Let me call Lee," I said, pulling my cell out and punching his number.

"Lexsi?" Lee said the moment he answered my call. "Are you at the scene? Good. I just heard from Hannah—she's stuck behind an accident on the Bay Bridge. Look, I know it'll be awkward for you later, but get in front of the camera to let our viewers know what's going on. The switchboard is lighting up at the station with complaints pouring in."

"All right," I said, working to keep the shudder from my voice. "I'll do what I can."

It was difficult doing the reports with very little prep time, but I got through them. Eventually, Farin, Tiburon and Rick joined Kory on the sidewalk nearby while I told viewers what I knew—or at least what I could report.

It wouldn't do, after all, to tell them that a vampire was likely behind the kidnappings and that things didn't look good for either victim. Twice, we cut to quick interviews with police, who still had nothing to report, and interspersed that with one-on-ones with employees from the hospital.

The police had already acknowledged that Vann was killed and Mike cut and beaten after reporting on the same incident—concerning an initial bar fight and ultimately ending in the bar exploding and then burning down.

I reported that there'd been no word from the Fire Marshall as to the cause of the explosion and subsequent fire, and likely it would take several more weeks before any findings could be released. Forensics experts were going over both hospital rooms, hoping to find evidence; then we learned that at least one other hostage had been taken, too.

A young man working with the housekeeping staff was missing, and he'd last been reported on the same floor as both victims' rooms.

Kordevik

Lexsi did an outstanding job, explaining the information she'd received from the police, then pulling in the Fire Marshall's office after Clawdia's was mentioned in the press conference by the Chief of

Police. She stayed in contact with the weekend crew at the station, who were busy setting up and interviewing hospital employees and other witnesses at the hospital around the time of the suspected kidnappings.

Hannah didn't show until nearly midnight, hissing like a coiled snake. She snatched the microphone from Lexsi during a lull and went to work, although she began by fabricating speculative bullshit.

"We're done, here," I grabbed Lexsi's hand and pulled her away. The others followed us across the street to the coffee shop, which remained open to serve news crews and others who'd gathered for progress reports.

"They're not going to find them," Tiburon muttered. Farin held onto his arm and began weeping. He comforted her in Spanish while Rick looked pale and defeated. He'd visited Mike that afternoon in the hospital, when everything seemed fine.

Things were no longer fine.

Lexsi looked weary. If I thought she wouldn't protest, I'd have lifted her and carried her to the Jeep. Instead, I traded her hand for an arm around her shoulders and held her up as best I could while we walked six blocks to my vehicle.

Mason wasn't there when we got back to the house; Anita had waited up to tell us he'd gone hunting for clues to the kidnappings. Watson had also gone out—to tend bar at the new place in Oakland. If I weren't so tired, I'd have gone to Oakland, too, looking for a fight.

Perhaps I was imagining things, but it didn't get past me that these kidnappings had happened the night after Granger, the Romes and Claudia had gotten together. "Come on, onion, it's time for bed," I led Lexsi toward her bedroom.

Anita lifted an eyebrow but didn't comment. Lexsi was pushed gently inside her suite; I shut the door with a sigh and went looking for a few shots of bourbon before I dropped face-first onto my bed across the hall.

Lexsi

Lee looked like he'd been through a shredder when I arrived in his office the following morning. "Am I fired?" I blurted. Judging from Hannah's dark looks the night before, it would come as no surprise.

"No. She was on the phone with the Romes this morning, telling them she was planning to let you go—they told her she couldn't fire you because you held the network together last night while she was stuck in traffic."

"I'll bet she's happy about that," I muttered, lowering my gaze and allowing my shoulders to sag in relief.

"She shut up about it," Lee said. "Look, you probably know already that I have another job to go to in a couple of weeks. This is between you and me," he lowered his voice. "If you find yourself in need of a job, you have my number. I'd hire you any day." He turned back to his computer, letting me know the unscheduled meeting was over.

"Thank you," I whispered before walking out the door.

Hannah didn't hand me a single insult all day, but she gave me nasty looks to make up for it. She also refused to follow up on the investigations on the dead seals found in the bay and the Ravens' murders.

Both those decisions came as no surprise to me—Lee was leaving and it was her call to make. Any answers that came could link both those things back to the Romes, if my hunches were correct. Instead, I did research all day long for Hannah, regarding the kidnappings and subsequent lack of clues and evidence.

One thing did stand out, however.

Not once did she ask me to contact Claudia Platt regarding the role her bar may have played in Vann's death and Mike's disappearance.

The police were still attempting to connect the dots on the young woman who'd also been taken. I was at a loss to explain that, too, but suspected that Watson knew something. Unofficial word was she'd been attacked not far from Clawdia's Bar and a Good Samaritan took her to the hospital. Watson tended bar at Clawdia's before it was destroyed, and was now employed as a bartender at the new place, which I didn't have a name for. All of this was connected in some way —it had to be.

I worried, too, at times, that Granger knew of my involvement in getting Mike and Rick out of Clawdia's before it exploded and burned. I couldn't tell when I met him at Hannah's party; he'd given nothing away during our brief encounter.

Why were the Romes protecting my job? That also concerned me a great deal. It couldn't be because I made good martinis; I got the idea that Laurel was running the show anyway, so this was likely her decision.

Too many things didn't make sense, but I did plan on one course of action; I intended to get the name of the new bar, its location and find who was registered as its owner. I'd bet my salary for a year that Claudia Platt's name was nowhere near that property deed.

I'd also bet that her fingerprints and that of a certain vampire were all over it. I didn't speculate about the Rome's involvement, although I suspected it, too.

What the hell were they doing, and why the hell were people dying or being kidnapped because of it?

~

"We're having dinner with Farin and Tibby on Friday," Anita announced as she walked into the kitchen. She'd gotten home seconds after I did. I sat at the kitchen island, having a glass of wine while contemplating what to cook for dinner.

"She got to you, didn't she?" I accused, wagging a finger at Anita.

"Farin's overflowing with exuberance," Anita said. "Have more of that?" she jerked her chin toward my wineglass.

"Yeah. Have a seat. I'll pour."

"It's only Monday," Anita observed as she dropped onto a barstool.

I pushed a glass of the red I was having toward her. She accepted it with a grateful nod.

"Yeah," I agreed. "The Romes told Hannah she couldn't fire me, so I'm still employed. If her looks could kill, though," I shrugged and lifted the wineglass to my lips.

"The Romes are involved?"

"For now. I suspect they're involved in all kinds of shit, they're just hiding it."

"What's your plan of action?" Anita lifted her glass in a toast before drinking.

"I intend to find where Claudia Platt opened her new bar, and whose name is on the deed for said bar. My bet is that it's a shell corporation or some other, inane entity, meant to mislead us."

"But we have to find it, first, before we can check the records for the listed owner."

"Yeah."

"What's for dinner?"

"I don't have much in the fridge. I really needed to make a run to the store yesterday, but you see how those plans went astray."

"Yep. See that, all right."

"You think I can get away with hopping to the store and back, without anybody asking questions?"

"I will defend your secret to the death," Anita drank more wine.

"Cool. Be back in a few." I grabbed my purse off the island and skipped to the local grocery store.

Kordevik

"We've got to stop meeting like this," I told Watson when he climbed into the Jeep.

"Sorry, man, but I still don't have the insurance money from my car after Clawdia's blew up. All that's under investigation, so they won't pay my claim until everything is cleared up."

"At least you're working the day shift," I said as I pulled into

Oakland traffic. So far, Watson had arranged for me to pick him up far away from the new bar, and he hadn't given me the new address.

I figured it was at Claudia's orders. I hoped he hadn't told her I was the one giving him rides home, and that she wasn't having him followed for any reason. I hadn't noticed anyone suspicious on our drives to San Rafael, but that didn't mean it couldn't happen.

Something about all this was making my Thifilathi's scales itch. It wasn't a comfortable feeling, either. I'd never been forced to solve mysteries, before; I'd only gone where I was sent to fight whatever I was ordered to fight.

Our current situation was definitely forcing me out of my comfort zone.

"Is Lexsi cooking?" Watson interrupted my thoughts.

"No idea." I connected to her cell phone through the hands-free, just to ask.

"I'm making seafood stew," she said. Her words were accompanied by the sounds of stirring and pots and pans being moved about.

"That doesn't sound good," Watson whined.

"We'll be there soon," I said and ended the call. "You're in for a treat," I turned to Watson. "If this seafood stew is what I'm expecting, you'll be over the moon about it."

Lexsi

Kory timed his arrival very well; the stew was just coming off the stove when he and Watson walked in. I hadn't had time to put fresh-baked bread together, so I'd bought the best I could at the store deli. The loaves were hot and ready to be buttered when we sat down to eat.

I thought Watson was going to howl with joy after his first bowl. He ended up eating three large bowls of seafood stew, with generous hunks of buttered bread. Kory laughed at him—they sat on the same side of the island, where Watson ate with the enthusiasm of a very hungry pup.

Anita didn't say anything, but she did push the plate of bread in Watson's direction. She hid a smile as she did it, too.

"Dude, are they working you that hard?" Mason wandered into the kitchen. Sunset had arrived and the vampire was awake. I found it comforting that we had a natural clock to announce that event in a polite and subtle fashion.

Mason had commented on Watson's appetite and the increasing pile of bread crumbs around his plate.

"Moving barrels out of an old winery," he lifted his bottle of beer to salute the vampire. "Heavy shit," he added. "Claudia wants the whole thing cleared out; some of that stuff has been there for ages."

"She moving?" Kory asked.

"Yeah. Said she wanted to get out of the Bay area for a while."

"No doubt," Anita said. "Otherwise, we might detect the stench of singed fur."

"She's my boss," Watson pointed his spoon at Anita.

"Yeah, I get that. My question is this—*why* is she your boss?"

"Not talking about that." Watson rose abruptly and strode to the dishwasher to place his bowl and spoon inside.

Don't upset him—we may need his help, I sent to Anita.

I know—I just can't figure him out, she replied. *He seems like a good guy, yet he's working for, well, that.*

I know. At least I'll be able to tell if he ever lies to us about any of that.

True.

"Excellent meal, onion," Kory said, breaking me away from my silent conversation with Anita.

"Why, thank you, Single J," I gave him a smile.

"Hey, now," he grinned. Honestly, when he smiled, I could definitely understand why Hannah wanted her red-polished hooks in his underwear.

"Sex is natural," Uncle Aurelius always said. "There's nothing to be ashamed of." I knew he was right, but still I'd never been tempted.

Until now, that is, and it was with someone that my family wouldn't approve of. Lifting my bowl from the island, I headed for the dishwasher. I could see and hear the conversation with my father now.

Dad, I think I want to have sex with a human.

I figured the fireworks would commence after that. In his mind, humans were not only weak, but short-lived, while I was of an immortal race.

Not a good pairing.

Besides, sex could complicate everything. Perhaps it was better to back away from Kory, because we had mysteries to solve. In a very plural sense.

Kory knocked on my bedroom door the following morning, at an unacceptable hour. "Get your stuff together, we'll go to the gym close to the station," he said. "I'll take you to breakfast afterward."

"Will there be more of those," I didn't know what to call them.

"The people there at this hour are only interested in getting their sweat on. They're not looking for a date."

"Awesome. Let me get my stuff."

He was right. Nobody bothered either of us and I was grateful. I got through my workout, realized I was still sore from Sunday's exercise and worked through it anyway. Uncle Sal would be disappointed if I hadn't.

Breakfast came next, and I had to admit I didn't mind sitting across the table from Kory, who knew exactly what he wanted to eat and ordered it with coffee. I had eggs and toast, with coffee. He got me to work in plenty of time, but had to drive Fiona Hall to the downtown offices right away.

Perhaps she knew the others talked about her and her long-term affair with an exec, but chose to ignore it. I merely hoped the exec's wife was fully informed and accepting of it; if she weren't and found out, trouble would surely come.

"They found the third kidnap victim in a field outside Vichy Springs," Lee said, handing me a thumb drive as I walked toward my cubicle. "See what you can make of that information. Hannah isn't here yet," he added. "Probably won't be for another two or three hours."

"On it," I nodded.

The early-morning crew had already reported on the sketchy information released by the police, and a reporter was in Vichy Springs, hoping for updates. Lee wanted information to feed to Hannah for the evening news.

Stuffing the thumb drive into my computer, I settled in with a cup of coffee to see what we had so far.

Kordevik

I'm worried, Watson texted.

About what?

About the body found east of Vichy Springs, came the reply. *No, it's not close to Claudia's new place, so don't start with the speculation*, he said. *I heard from another source that prints were found around the body. Not human prints.*

I'd already heard the story from Fiona—all the way to the downtown office building. How the third kidnap victim, who worked at the hospital, had been found in a field near Vichy Springs.

You thinking it could mean exposition? I texted back. I'd pulled into a hardware store parking lot to have this conversation—I didn't want a ticket or an arrest, because Watson was having a werewolf meltdown.

Yeah. Look, if I hear anything, I'll let you know. I thought the other, well, you know, was involved. This doesn't look good.

I hear that, I agreed. *Stay out of trouble. You're in enough as it is.*

Only because I know you, and I have to keep that to myself, he replied.

Right back atcha, I texted, surprised that autocorrect didn't intervene in my unconventional wording.

Sorry, man. Keep forgetting about that. I'd be in wolf heaven if it weren't for you.

You got that right.

Gotta go, dude. Break time's over.
OK.

~

Lexsi

The body looked as if it were attacked by wild animals. Police were consulting rangers and other experts, who also examined the tracks around the body.

Wolf prints.

Very large wolf prints.

I knew what that meant; they didn't.

With Claudia being Watson's boss, I suspected she was in this to the tips of her ears. At least I knew what she was, now. It was possible she was either a Packmaster, a Second or high in the pack she belonged to. She had too much authority to be otherwise.

Watson did her bidding, I knew that much. I worried that she'd eventually tell him to do something we would all regret.

It made me want to follow him to her new bar in Oakland, but there was probably a way around that. I turned to searching city and county records for any business in Oakland that had recently applied for a liquor license.

In the middle of that research, my cubicle phone rang. "You have a call on line two," the receptionist du jour informed me. "They asked to speak only to you."

"All right," I said. "Thanks."

"This is Lexsi Silver," I said after punching line two.

"That body doesn't belong to Brad Nolen," a voice growled. "They have preliminary ID through clothing and jewelry. That's not Brad." The line went dead before I could ask questions.

After stewing about that information for a moment, I called Lee on my cell phone to get the name of the journalist in Vichy Springs. I then placed a call to Dan Logan, the early-morning investigative reporter.

"Hi, Dan," I said when he answered. "You may not remember me, this is Lexsi Silver."

"I remember you," he suddenly had a smile in his voice.

"That's great," I said. "Look, I just got a tip that the body may not be the third kidnap victim, like everybody says. Are they doing forensics and running dental records?"

"Yeah, but the cops think this is a done deal—the body's pretty chewed up, but the clothes match the description."

"I'm concerned about that," I said.

"I'll look into it. Man, if this is true, we could have a real scoop on our hands."

"Exactly," I said. "Keep me informed, if you wouldn't mind."

"Sure will. Thanks for the call."

By three o'clock that afternoon, after some pushing and harassment of the Coroner's Office by Dan Logan, we knew the dental records didn't match. In fact, they weren't even close. News Seventy-Four was the first to have the information, too.

Hannah was almost gleeful as I handed the information to her. She began her evening broadcast with the information I'd given her, peppered it with more speculation as to what may have happened to the real Brad Nolen, and ended with the question as to why someone had gone to a great deal of trouble to make the unidentified victim appear to be Brad Nolen.

I left work after seven that night and skipped home because Kory called saying he had an errand to run. He'd told me to take a taxi or get another driver to take me.

I didn't intend to do either. I had a perfectly good way to get home; I just had to be careful enough that nobody noticed. That meant I walked out the employee entrance, waved at the guard on duty and then traveled several blocks toward the nearest bus stop before ducking into an alcove housing the locked door of an empty shop. After making sure nobody had noticed, I skipped to the house.

"Bout time," Anita said when I set my purse and jacket on the island.

"Hey, one of us was stranded at the station. I won't name names, but I'm pretty sure it wasn't you."

"I have lasagna in the oven," Anita put on her best, self-righteous tone.

"Then I forgive every transgression you ever committed," I sighed. "I love lasagna."

"Any word on who the poor soul actually was? The one found east of here?"

"Forensics has the body, and they're working to match dental records. The last word I had was that it definitely wasn't Brad Nolen. I hate that his family went through that—thinking he'd been found that way. They identified his clothes and shoes. Somebody went to a lot of trouble to do that."

"This whole thing is just crazy," Anita agreed. "Look, change into your comfy clothes and help me put a salad together. Lasagna should be ready about then."

"It already smells good," I said. "Be out in a few." Gathering my stuff, I took off toward my bedroom.

Kordevik

"Man, you look like you moved into a cave with spiders," I said when Watson climbed into my Jeep. He was covered in cobwebs and smudged with unidentified dark substances.

"I told you they hadn't used that cellar in a while," he grumped. I could tell he wasn't happy with his current line of work, too.

"Who's been tending bar?" I asked.

"Stella and Jake," he shrugged. "Half weres," he added. "When the cellar's cleared, I'll be back at work as usual."

"Where is it?"

"The bar?"

"No, the cellar."

"I promised Claudia that I wouldn't say."

"What about the bar, then?"

"Look, I don't want you going down there. Granger's already seen us together, remember? I don't want to jog his memory."

"I'm surprised he hasn't looked harder for either of us," I pointed out. "Mason, too."

"He had bigger fish to fry, with those three he snatched from the hospital."

"Yeah, but he has them already. Doesn't he? What's to keep him from tracking us, now?"

"What if he doesn't have them?"

"What the fuck are you talking about?" I jerked my head in Watson's direction.

"It's the way Claudia's been acting. Since I haven't seen Granger, I can only go by the way she is. She isn't happy about something, I know that much, and if it were due to something I'd done, she'd sure as hell let me know about it."

"Then how can we go about finding out if Granger doesn't have his hostages, or that he's not involved in that fiasco east of Vichy Springs?"

"No idea, and I'm not about to ask Claudia. Every day I go to work, I worry that the hammer will drop."

"Someday, you're gonna tell me what she has on you, man."

"Fat chance," he muttered and went silent. I'd just confirmed my suspicions. Claudia did have something on Watson, and I'd managed (in a backhanded way), to make him admit it.

My next quest was to discover what it was. That could take time. Lexsi's text came while I mulled over my options.

I waited until we were stopped at a stoplight to glance at my phone. "We're having lasagna—Anita made it," I said after reading the text. "It'll be waiting when we get there."

"Aw, man, I need a bath first," Watson whined.

"I can toss you off the bridge and into the bay," I offered.

"I like my water warmer than that," he shot back.

"How much longer?" I asked.

"Huh?"

"Until Claudia's cellar is emptied?"

"No idea. She sold the old barrels to another winery. At least I didn't have to truck them down the valley."

"If you hurry with your shower, we may be able to save lasagna for you," I teased.

"You better save some."

"You better hurry."

"Bet on it."

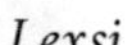

Lexsi

"No, completely coat the pork loin in the seasoned flour, then brown on all sides in the sauté pan. Once that's in the slow cooker, then sauté the mushrooms in more butter in the same pan," I told Farin on the phone. "Put the mushrooms in the cooker, then use the wine to deglaze the sauté pan. Add the cream and roux after that and stir until it thickens. That covers the pork loin in the slow cooker and four hours later, you have a wonderful meal."

"You make it sound so easy," Farin sighed.

"Come on, you can do this," I said. Kory and Watson stepped into the kitchen at that moment; Watson looked like he'd been shoved through a sewer pipe—to clean it.

Kory grinned at me; Watson grimaced at Anita's disapproving look before loping down the hall toward his bedroom.

I barely recalled my agreement to help Farin cook on Friday because Kory walked toward me, pulled me close and kissed my forehead.

"I uh, have to call you back," I told Farin and almost dropped the phone.

Daddy, I want to have sex with a human ran through my head as Kory let me go and went to the cabinet to get plates for the table.

Kordevik

"Need a word, man," Mason said after dinner. He'd been up for an hour, but didn't disturb us at the table while we ate.

"Where?" I asked.

"Somewhere private."

"Then come outside. We'll go down the hill a little way."

We walked for a block before I skipped him to a local hangout and ordered a beer for both of us.

"What do you have?" I asked.

"Word that the three kidnap victims aren't really victims. It was a proactive grab, from what I hear."

"By whom? And how would they know?"

"Klancy has connections," Mason lowered his eyes. "He notified somebody, but didn't expect anything to come of it. Something came of it. He only found out tonight—after sundown."

"Are these unknowns on our side?" I asked.

"He didn't say. All he'd say was that they were in a safe place—at least that's what he was told. Nobody can know this, you understand? Word could get back to Granger."

"I can keep a secret," I lifted my beer glass. "Keep me informed, if you wouldn't mind. I hope this isn't some kind of turf war with Granger. I don't like it when people are used as pawns."

"I don't think it's like that," Mason frowned. "At least I hope not."

"Too bad we can't tell their friends and family. Just to give them some relief."

"You can't; it could get Klancy killed," Mason pointed out. "He's a good guy. Don't want that to happen."

"I hear you. Look, if Klancy thinks he's in danger, tell him to contact me. I'll see what I can do."

"I'll let him know," Mason agreed. "Finish your beer; we ought to get back."

CHAPTER 9

Tuesday, in between running errands for Hannah, (which included a latte and dry cleaning) I searched public records for recent liquor license applications.

I found six, two of which were dated the day before. Still, I included them in the list to check out. Claudia wasn't a stranger to breaking the law; it wouldn't surprise me if she'd opened another place before doing the necessary paperwork.

I was standing in line at the coffee shop when Dan Logan called. "Hi, Dan," I said after seeing his name pop up as the caller.

"Hey, Lexsi," he said. "I just got something from my friend at the Coroner's Office. Turns out our dismembered corpse was a wanted man."

"Really?"

"Sure is. LA County's been looking for him for a while, but everybody figured he'd escaped to Mexico. Nobody heard from him in a while, I know that much. Wanted in a couple of murders, and suspected in a few others."

"No way," I said. "Who could have done that—traded a criminal for a kidnap victim?"

"Nobody knows. Police don't have a clue, but won't admit it. They're just clearing out their files on Gentry Mullins."

"Wow," I said. "Do you want to take the lead on this? Your contacts gave us the scoop."

"I've been informed that Hannah gets spoon-fed everything we find. I wanted to call you instead of her—for the obvious reasons."

"I'm so sorry they're doing this to you," I moaned. "It's just not fair."

"Neither is her attempt to get you fired over nothing," he responded. "Word gets around, you know."

"Yeah, I guess it does. Look, I'll get on this quick. Otherwise Princess Hannah won't get her lead-in for tonight."

"Thanks, Lexsi. I just didn't want to talk to Dragon Lady if I could avoid it."

"Not a problem. Thanks, Dan."

"Information on Gentry Mullins," I set Hannah's latte on her desk and handed her a tablet with all applicable data on the criminal.

"Why should I be interested in that?" Hannah lifted the latte and drank.

"Because that's whose remains were found east of Vichy Springs," I informed her. "Somebody dressed him up as Brad Nolen before he was torn apart by predators."

"Really?" I didn't like the glint in Hannah's eyes as she lifted the tablet and began to scroll through the information.

"Came straight from a source at the Coroner's Office," I said. "The police are doing a happy dance because they can close the files on Gentry, but they still don't know why all that happened or where Brad Nolen and the others are."

"Set up an interview with Brad Nolen's parents," Hannah said. "We need to milk that grief."

"Huh?" I stared at her in shock.

"What I said. Set it up, little bitch. Tomorrow, if possible."

"All right." I left her office before she could say something else that infuriated me. I will admit to imagining all the ways Hannah might die accidentally before Wednesday. None of them were accompanied by imagined tears.

Brad Nolen's parents wanted a forum to beg his kidnappers to release him. Hannah wanted a sob story to increase her ratings. I predicted a head-on collision of sorts.

In the interim, I received information on an entire busload of migrant farmworkers who'd gone missing near Tulare. Shortly afterward, a church van loaded with eight people heading across the Texas border into Mexico to do mission work, was also reported missing.

I thought Hannah ought to cover those incidents, too, and sent her information, just to be told that it wasn't as important as other things she planned to cover, one of which was doggy dress-up day in Sacramento.

I sent a quick text to Anita, instead, to let her know strange things were afoot. Before Anita could reply, Hannah ordered me into the editing room to review the doggy dress-up footage from a Sacramento affiliate, so I had to turn off my phone and look at pet costumes all afternoon.

It didn't keep me from wondering how busloads of people could vanish in two different states. Altogether, nearly forty people were unaccounted for, with no clues as to their whereabouts.

Kordevik

I heard about the missing buses on the radio while waiting in the designated parking lot for Watson. I dashed off a message to Lexsi, asking if she had information on it.

I do, she replied, *but Hannah refuses to cover it.*

WTF? I texted.

I'm confused, too. Nearly forty people are missing, the vehicles can't be found and nobody knows anything. Wait, something's coming in.

What?

They found the migrant worker bus in a ravine. Ten are missing, the rest are dead.

I swore, but didn't text that to Lexsi. *You still at your desk?* I asked.

Yes. Hannah's been on an irrelevant tear most of the afternoon.

No word on the bus in Texas?

Nothing yet.

Crazy. The other stations are getting the jump on us with this.

I know. Lee just shakes his head and hides in his office. I've hooked up with an affiliate in Texas and have something ready to go in case Hannah changes her mind.

That's good. Look, Watson just walked up. Gotta go, onion.

Watson was dirty, disheveled and disgruntled when he slid onto the passenger seat.

"Dude, you really ought to find another job," I said. "I need the carwash to spray the inside of my truck."

"Don't start, man," Watson growled. "Claudia already chewed our butts today because we weren't moving fast enough."

"Why's she in such a hurry?"

"No idea. We got the place cleared out, though. Hope she's happy."

"What's next, then? Back to tending bar?"

"Demoted to errand boy," he huffed and turned away to stare out the window. "She said I acted rashly when Granger's vamps came into the old place with the girl."

"And I acted rashly with you," I thumped the steering wheel with the heel of my hand. "She'd rather have you cleaning up the blood of a murder victim than calling out the ones causing the trouble?"

"Look, I don't understand this any better than you do," he snapped. "Let it go, man. You have a price on your head and I'm doing cleanup and errands."

"Are they actively hunting me? Granger's bunch?" I asked.

"So far, the witnesses are afraid to connect the dots for Granger," he turned to blink dark eyes at me. "They see you as somebody who can fight vamps. After your successful bit of rescue and arson, the truth is, they're more afraid of you than him. He doesn't like that, or so I hear."

"Then quit Claudia. You can find something else to do. Get out of town. She sees us together, that could be trouble."

"No, man. That won't happen."

"Which one won't happen?" I demanded. He turned away again.

"Neither," he mumbled. "Let it go."

"You're being morose again."

"Shut up."

Lexsi

I got home after Kory and Watson did and found them having sub sandwiches with Anita at the kitchen island.

"What's the word on the bus people?" Anita asked.

"Ten people still missing from the migrant worker bus, and the other passengers, according to police reports, died of asphyxiation. So far, nobody knows how that was accomplished. Hannah was forced to run the stuff I collected from the station in Texas."

"What about the other bus?" Kory asked before tapping the barstool next to his.

"No word, yet. Let me change, first," I sighed. "I just want out of these clothes and shoes. They smell like Princess Hannah."

"Then make it quick," Kory said. "I saved the roast beef for you."

"Really? That sounds so good," I said. "I'll hurry."

"Do you want to go with me to Farin's for dinner Friday night?" I almost stuttered while asking the question. I'd waited for a bit of privacy to ask; Kory and I were loading the dishwasher after we finished our sandwiches.

"You're asking me out?" He went still for a moment.

"Does that offend you? Look, forget it," I turned away. It had taken a great deal of courage to get the question past my lips. Instead of saying yes or no, he'd questioned my invitation.

"No. Nothing like that," he said after a moment. "I was just surprised, that's all. Yes. Of course. When do we leave?"

"You sound like you're ready to go, now." The smile I gave him trembled slightly.

"I am," he declared. "Look, I usually have to do the asking," he pulled me into a hug. "This is so—refreshing."

His arms felt welcoming. Safe. Still, a shiver of anticipation went through me.

Daddy, I want to have sex with a human.

Hannah's interview with Brad Nolen's family on Wednesday went just as I feared it would. She asked inappropriate questions, resulting in tears from his parents. I wanted to punch her for that—they had enough grief of their own without Hannah the Horrible adding to it.

Chet and Jesse frowned as they recorded the interview; Hannah hinted at times that the parents may have had something to do with their son's disappearance, which was so outrageous and disrespectful I wanted to punch her a second time.

I worried she'd sit in on the editing session, playing the tears and denials for all they were worth.

Difik.

Another thing that showed up alongside the news of the missing bus from Texas was that a Texas death row prison inmate was scheduled to die in two days.

No surprise—several states still had the death penalty. That news was mostly ignored in favor of the missing busload of volunteer missionaries, which hadn't been found. Authorities and volunteers were still searching for them and their vehicle.

All of the missing were young men from a state college, who belonged to a religious organization. They spent their summers helping those in need by building or repairing homes in small towns hit by storms and such. The organization was a national charity group and one highly thought of, regardless of your religious convictions or opinions.

The man on death row, on the other hand, had been convicted of killing at least ten women—in horrific ways. I'd done research just to check. He was a vicious man, known for his perpetual scowl and frequent profanity-laced outbursts. He'd exhausted all his appeals—even with a wealthy family paying the best attorneys they could find to get him off death row.

Definitely not a candidate for man of the year. Still, I put a short piece together to send to Hannah, in case she wanted to use it as filler. Visions of her doing a one on one with that character and with no guards present were quickly squashed—this man would tear her apart with his hands.

Good-bye, Loftin Qualls, you won't be missed, I said to myself and sent the e-mail to Hannah.

≈

Hannah's piece on the Nolen family was received with mixed reviews at best; nobody liked the browbeating of Brad's parents and they voiced their complaints all day Thursday.

Hannah forced me to respond to those complaints. I didn't attempt to defend her, and the words *sorry* and *apologize* were emailed many, many times. I doubted the negative response would sway Hannah in her next interview with distraught relatives. It ought to, but it wouldn't.

It made me wonder if this were part of the obsession Anita spoke about, or whether that part was all Hannah. Either way, her heart was ice and steel with nothing to thaw it, including the tears of frantic loved ones.

The surprise came just before I was scheduled to go home; one of the young men from the Texas van had wandered into a building in downtown Dallas, disheveled, dirty and confused.

He was currently at a hospital, but there was no further word on his condition or whether he knew where the others in his group were. I went to Hannah and gave her the information I had, plus a phone number for our contact at a Dallas affiliate.

"This is everything?" Hannah waved the thumb drive at me.

"So far. I've asked for updates when they come in; someone at the Dallas station will send whatever they get," I said.

"Then I expect you to take the calls," she snapped. "Get anything new to me before eleven."

"Of course."

That meant taking my work phone and laptop home, but it could be done. Other assistants did it all the time. I also coordinated with the overnight and early-morning crew, calling Dan Logan first and sending the collected information links to his email address.

"I'll let you know what Hannah has for the late broadcast," I told him.

"I can coordinate with Jim and the night crew," Dan said. "You think Lee will let me fly to Dallas?"

"You ought to ask. Hannah wasn't interested in making the trip."

"Sounds like a plan," he said. "I'll let you know what Lee says."

"Thanks, Dan. This case is just too weird," I added. "Something bothers me about all of it."

"Yeah, it makes no sense," he agreed.

"Bringing work home?" Anita asked when I made my way into the kitchen, loaded down with my laptop case, purse and jacket.

"Yeah. They found one of the men from that church van in Texas— in Dallas, of all places. I was worried they'd find bodies across the border or something. They were in Brownsville, the last anybody heard from them."

"That's more than five hundred miles away," Anita frowned. "Have they questioned him about the others?"

"The last I heard, he was confused and disoriented, in addition to being filthy. That means we have nothing new on the others."

"And nothing new on the ten migrant workers still missing?"

"Not a word. You know what I find fascinating?" I asked.

"What's that?"

"That all the missing are men in their twenties and in good health. There were three kids and several women in their twenties on the migrant worker bus, along with several older men. None of them survived."

"All of them citizens of Mexico?"

"That's in the police records," I nodded. "All here legally, so there's no reason for them to run, especially since some of them left friends and relatives behind on that bus."

"I think I was followed on my way home from work," Anita announced. "I'm worried that whoever is behind the attacks in the restaurant parking lot is getting interested again."

"They know you're here?" I whispered.

"I think I lost them at the foot of the hill," she shrugged. "I didn't see them after the last stoplight before turning up our street."

"When did you check on your place last?" I asked.

"Two days ago. You think I ought to check again?"

"Yeah. I don't trust them or whoever sent them."

"I think the Romes have gotten a whiff of what I'm after," she said after a few moments. "They're not firing me because they want to get me out of the way, and keeping me employed is the best way to keep me in their sights."

"You're not making me feel any better about this," I moaned. "You told me to quit. Why aren't you taking your own advice?"

"Because I like to see my enemy coming," she said. "I can take care of myself most of the time."

"Yeah, but they have Granger on their side," I warned.

"Hmmph."

"Come on, let's go to your place, then we can stop at the deli and pick up soup and sandwiches. I'm too pooped to cook tonight."

"I hear that. Come on, we'll visit the rooftop across the street first, in case they're waiting for us to walk inside the building."

"Sounds great," I grumbled. Stuffing my work phone in a pocket, I nodded for Anita to take my arm and fold space.

Kordevik

At least Watson was cleaner Thursday evening when he climbed into my Jeep. "Ordered and loaded booze all day long," he said, leaning his head against the headrest and closing his eyes.

"You don't sound happy," I said. "You look better, though."

"The half wolf bartenders shoved their human tails in my face all afternoon," Watson sighed. "Both of 'em not worth a butt sniff," he added.

"TMI," I said. "Honestly, butt sniffing is over the top."

"Only for non-werewolves," he responded, weariness in his voice. "I'm losing part of my income by not collecting tips at the bar."

"Then go work for somebody else, man."

"Can't. Can't explain it, either. Sorry. Mason said he followed some of Granger's vamps last night," Watson volunteered—probably to get me off the subject of his finding other work.

Mason took Watson to work every morning before sunrise. I picked him up before sundown. So far, it had worked fairly well. "What were Granger's vamps doing?" I asked. "How did he manage to tail them and not get caught?"

"From overhead, or so he says," Watson opened his eyes. "They were sniffing around the gym not far from your condo."

"Fuckers," I muttered.

"I wouldn't go back there if I were you," Watson closed his eyes again. "Compulsion to report you wouldn't turn out pretty."

"So they all know what I look like, then? When I'm human?"

"I guess they do," Watson gruffed. "It was only a matter of time, man. Granger's seen you like this," he jerked his chin in my direction. "Others have seen—whatever it is."

"What happened to witnesses being more afraid of me?" I demanded.

"If your life's on the line when they ask questions," he didn't finish.

"Right. You know if they take me down, you'll have to find another ride home. Hell, you'll probably need another place to stay, too."

"Huh?" He sat up straight and turned his now-wide gaze on me.

"You think Lexsi will let you stay if you get me killed and place her in danger at the same time? Mason won't like it either, because he'll be next."

"Are you trying to make me feel worse than I do already? If so, mission accomplished," Watson snapped.

We didn't talk the rest of the way home. When we got there, Lexsi and Anita were gone.

～

Lexsi

We should have been more careful. Since the building still stood and nothing seemed amiss, Anita and I assumed it hadn't been touched, her part of it included.

How wrong we were.

After a few moments on the roof of a building across the street, when nothing happened out of the ordinary, Anita folded us into her apartment. There, everything was fine—nothing out of place, just as she'd left it.

I watched as Anita ambled toward the front door to get the mail dropped through the slot. It was junk mail—I knew that. She received her regular correspondence at a post office box.

I barely had time to glance upward; a transom window topped the doorframe. I almost saw the red glint too late. I can't begin to describe the fear and fury that overwhelmed me; Anita's enemies wanted her dead.

"No," I shouted at her as she bent to lift the cards and envelopes from the floor.

It would be more than difficult for me to describe what happened next, because in my memory, it's merely a blur.

I can only say that I came back to myself on the roof of the building across the street, Anita held tightly in my arms and covered from the fire and explosion by my Thifilatha's wings.

Kordevik

"What the fuck happened?" I shouted as Lexsi, wearing Anita's raincoat and nothing else, pulled a stunned Anita toward her bedroom.

"Kory, no," she moaned. "Anita almost got killed. Not now, okay?"

"What?" Watson, who'd been drinking shots of Crown at the kitchen island, almost leapt from his barstool.

"Somebody booby trapped her apartment," Lexsi said. "She needs to lie down, she's shaking."

It didn't get past me that Lexsi was shaking, too.

"I'll help," Watson slid to Anita's side. Instead of putting an arm around her, he lifted her in his arms and almost ran toward her bedroom.

"Lexsi? Baby? Are you all right?" I asked.

"Everything is terrible," she whispered. "Really, really terrible." Blue eyes closed as she slumped in my arms.

Lexsi

Anita escaped burns and extreme harm, but even my Thifilatha couldn't protect her completely from the blast waves. She had multiple bruises on her back and right thigh.

I had a Thifilatha.

Only my mother and my great aunt had ever shown that ability. I had six older sisters. It had never manifested in any of them.

I didn't know whether to feel proud or terrified.

I was terrified anyway; the moment my Thifilatha manifested, I'd destroyed my clothing and my work phone.

That meant calling the station, telling them the lie that I'd lost it and asking for a replacement. Hannah would be furious if I failed to send her updated information as promised.

Kory almost refused to drive me back to the station after I fainted. At least Watson had appointed himself as Anita's nurse and fussed over her while she attempted to push him away.

Kory wanted to shout at me for going to Anita's apartment. He didn't shout. His words were slow and measured as he explained something I already knew—that Anita and I were lucky to be alive.

We didn't tell him how we escaped the explosion, only that I saw the red light and grabbed Anita away from the door. He still thought we'd been outside the apartment and somehow, my clothing hadn't survived, along with my work phone. Hence, the emergency drive to the station for a replacement.

At least I hadn't received any frantic emails from anyone on the laptop, which had been safe at home.

After a while, Kory settled for a deep frown and stopped lecturing. All I could do was hang my head and look guilty, because I was. I'd suggested we check on Anita's apartment, and we'd set off the subsequent explosion.

Kory never said it, but he was terrified. Perhaps he really did care for me and wasn't just looking for sex, like most human men. I'd gotten a scolding as a result. I wanted to tell him I was sorry and that I hadn't expected a planted bomb, but that would only open the lecture floodgate again.

I was scared enough and felt guilty enough already. At that moment, I wanted to be a storybook hero—one who took all the terrifying things in stride and handled near-death experiences with cool confidence.

Instead, I hugged myself while sitting on Kory's passenger seat as he silently fumed beside me.

"We've turned the other one off already," the night producer handed me a replacement phone. "Try not to lose this one, okay?"

"I promise," I nodded. "I'm so sorry I lost my phone."

"Don't worry about it—Vann lost phones all the time," the man waved his hand. "With everything that's happening, I think we're all somewhat scattered."

"Thank you," I breathed and held back from giving him a hug.

I checked messages the second I left the building. Hannah hadn't left me anything and I was grateful for that. About halfway home, however, we picked up a tail.

Kory saw it first and pointed it out. I shivered as I watched the vehicle's headlights in the passenger side mirror. I also saw Kory's face settle into a grim mask. We took unnecessary turns. The vehicle always stayed behind.

"Wouldn't vampires or werewolves leave their headlights off?" I whispered as Kory steered his Jeep through another false turn.

"You'd think so, but they may be attempting to throw us off," he replied. "Or it could be humans," he added.

I made myself smaller in my seat—I wasn't human. How did I tell him that? After turning Thifilatha, I was even farther from human than I'd been four hours earlier.

"We may need to stop at a bar or restaurant," Kory said after a while. "We can't keep driving all night."

"You think they'll come in after us?"

"If they do, they'd better be ready for the consequences," he muttered.

"Yeah." I wanted to shiver again, and wondered if my Thifilatha would respond if I wanted it to. The last time had been purely by accident.

"Have you had anything to eat, tonight?" he asked.

"No, there wasn't time and I'm really not hungry," I began.

"Then we'll stop at the all-night diner near the highway," he said and made a turn to go in that direction. "If people are around us, maybe it'll keep them from causing trouble."

Ten minutes later, we pulled into the small parking lot of a twenty-four-hour restaurant. My feet crunched on gravel scattered across a dimly-lit, unswept stretch of concrete.

At that moment, the restaurant's front door, with a flashing *Open* sign in the adjacent window, felt like a safe haven.

I hoped it continued to feel that way.

Kory opened the door for me, just as our tail pulled into the parking lot. I barely got a glimpse of a dark SUV before Kory shoved me through the restaurant's door. I blinked; the fluorescent lights overhead nearly blinded me as we walked to the tiny hostess stand to request a table.

We were led to a table against a window, where we sat while the hostess handed us menus and asked if we wanted coffee or something else to drink.

"We're with them," two men walked up just as the waitress turned to go.

I gaped—these didn't look dangerous, but what did I know? One of the men, of medium height with light-brown hair and copper eyes, grinned and took a seat across from me. His companion, a taller man with dark hair and darker eyes, sat across from Kory.

"I'm Davis Stone, Jr., from the Salt Lake City Pack," he introduced himself and produced a badge. "This is Thomas Williams the Third, from the Sacramento Pack. We need to speak with you concerning official business."

CHAPTER 10

*L*exsi

These two werewolves, employees of the Joint NSA/Homeland Security Department, knew Kory and I worked for the Romes. They knew a lot of other things, too, one of which was that Kory, for some reason, was wanted by the supernatural underground. I had no idea why, but I was determined to ask him about it later.

"We found the remains of your work cell phone at Ms. Grant's apartment after the residence was destroyed," Davis turned to me. "We know you didn't plant the bomb," he added. "You and Anita Grant are lucky to be alive."

"Then why are you here?" Kory demanded.

"Because we're investigating Granger—and several other unsavory characters," Thomas declared. "Davis is my boss, and he asked me to help get those two away from the hospital. Unfortunately, Brad Logan witnessed the rescue, so he was also taken. They're all safe," he added.

"Thank goodness," I covered my face with both hands, which were now trembling.

"I need to order something for her," Kory announced. I realized he was talking about me and dropped my hands. "She hasn't eaten," he explained.

My stomach gurgled a response, which caused my face to warm.

"What we want," Davis said after the waitress took our order, "is to figure out what, exactly, is going on and who is involved. Frankly, this whole thing stinks, but we don't understand why. We think the Romes are involved, too, but again, no reason has appeared. What are they into? We have no idea."

Davis and Thomas knew as little as I did about what was going on. They knew about the bar explosion; their thoughts were that the same person or persons were responsible for planting the bomb at Anita's apartment.

I was afraid to tell them some of what I knew. Afraid they wouldn't believe me, mostly. For now, I'd keep those things to myself.

Plus, I'd lose my job if the Romes discovered I'd spoken with authorities. Keeping said job would enable me to stay on top of their involvement in whatever it was, plus keep me informed of new events, no matter how remotely connected they could be.

"What do you want from us?" Kory asked, his words dry.

"Information," Davis shrugged. "Whatever you can give us. It may help to unravel this mystery, before we find there's a *too late* attached to the whole thing."

"That will only paint a larger target on my back," Kory snorted.

"We may be able to offer some protection," Thomas' smile was tight. His words were sincere, only there was a note of incredulity attached. I had no idea why.

I could tell Kory doubted his words, because he snorted a second time.

"You're aware of what Granger is?" I asked. Clearly, their department understood what werewolves were, since they'd introduced themselves as members of separate Packs.

"We know all about vampires and shapeshifters," Davis said. "We have several working in the Department, as you've already guessed. They know their secrets are safe with us—some have been employed by the Department for decades."

"I started five years ago," Thomas grinned. "I love my job."

"What can you tell us about the body found east of Vichy Springs?" Kory asked.

"Not much," Thomas evaded the question.

His statement was both truth and lie—he knew things but they were to be kept secret. I decided to let that go for now. My food arrived, along with more coffee for Davis and Thomas and a burger for Kory.

I ate while our visitors outlined their plans. They asked for news regarding specific activities inside the San Francisco portion of Rome Enterprises. They also wanted information on certain things, such as employees acting or saying anything out of character, or of people disappearing without a logical explanation.

I worried that they knew about Sirenali and that they might be more interested in Anita if they knew that's what she was.

Anita wasn't a part of what was wrong; she was attempting to resolve at least some of it. They never asked about her, however, and what I was doing at her apartment.

That surprised me. *I* would have asked those questions.

"Look, we'll be in touch," Davis rose and stretched. Thomas nodded at Kory and me when he also stood, handing each of us a business card. "Just remember, sometimes the smallest thing can mean something, especially in a situation like this. Call the number on that card if you have information. We'll take care of the check on the way out."

I watched as both turned and strode toward the cashier's stand, walking with the easy grace of confident werewolves. "If they have Brad Nolen in a safe place," I said, my lips feeling numb and the words foreign on my tongue, "then who dressed Gentry Mullins in Brad Nolen's clothes? My next question is this; why did they dress Gentry Mullins in Brad Nolen's clothes?"

Kory didn't answer me at first; instead, he pulled a ten from his wallet and tossed it on the table as a tip. "Come on, onion, let's go home," he murmured. With his hand beneath my elbow, he helped me stand. I was grateful—I found my legs were shaking when I rose to my feet.

Kory didn't speak again until we were halfway home. "I think somebody—a werewolf somebody—or perhaps more than one, was sniffing after the kidnap victims," he said. "My assumption is that when these not so law-abiding werewolves caught the scent from Brad's clothing, they went after him. Turned out to be too bad for Gentry Mullins, known criminal."

"Do you think Gentry Mullins may have been involved in what's going on?" I asked. "And somebody wanted him out of the way, for whatever reason?"

"Good question. I'll have to think about that. We really don't have enough information to even speculate at this point. I wish those two werewolves had told us what they knew about it."

"Yeah. I got the idea they were holding that stuff back from us."

"Baby, they're just looking for ways to get inside information. Never forget that. These people—sometimes they don't care about collateral damage, as long as they get what they want. Don't put yourself in danger just to answer a few of their questions, all right?"

"Yeah." I pulled my jacket tighter about me and stared out the window. I didn't intend to tell Kory that I wanted the same questions answered, and I wasn't going to let the Romes kill Anita because she'd become something of a nuisance to them.

I was more than grateful that Kory had his eyes on the road instead of me when a tiny curl of smoke escaped my nostrils. Somewhere inside me, the impossible had manifested and my Thifilatha wanted nothing more than to teach the Romes a lesson.

"Early-morning gym tomorrow," Kory announced as he pulled into the driveway.

"Yeah," I agreed. "Dinner at Farin's tomorrow night."

"Yeah."

~

I learned shortly after I arrived at work that Farin's oven wasn't working, which precipitated her visit to my cubicle, where she asked to move the dinner to my place so we could make bread and roasted vegetables to go with the pork loin.

"Sure," I agreed. "Just bring your slow cooker to the house and we'll finish everything in my kitchen."

"I love you," Farin faked a kiss at me before trotting away to do the morning weather report.

"I love you, too," I called out after her.

Hannah got the idea midmorning to interview someone at the Coroner's Office about Gentry Mullins' remains. Frankly, I didn't give a damn about Gentry Mullins—he murdered people and managed to elude police for years. I imagined that his victims who managed to survive were breathing relieved sighs at his unusual passing.

At least we skirted Dan's source and went with the Deputy Coroner, who wanted his fifteen minutes of televised importance. We set up in an office, which had windows with a view of an autopsy room. Thankfully, it was empty.

"I can't comment about anything found on the body," Deputy Coroner Jeremy Rollins explained. "Those items are being examined by the Forensics Department and we can't release any information."

"Surely you can tell me something," Hannah purred. If she hadn't been on camera, she'd probably have trailed a manicured finger down the Deputy Coroner's face and wordlessly offered herself in exchange for information.

That thought made me go still for a moment. What if she'd been directed to do just that by the Romes? Anita said she was obsessed to her hairline, so anything was possible. Blowing out a breath as silently as I could, I added one more thing to my long list of items to investigate.

The problem was, my list was too long already, and I really didn't have a good excuse to tail Hannah after work hours.

I did, however, know someone who could and be discreet about it.

Tonight, after Mason woke, I intended to ask him what he thought about following Hannah, just to see if she'd make good on the silent invitation she'd issued to the Deputy Coroner. If she did, I expected her to ask for information he would refuse to give through legitimate channels.

I doubted her individual interest in any of that.

I didn't doubt Granger, Claudia and the Rome's interest, though. Vampires could be stealthy and had extremely good hearing. Perhaps Mason would agree to help me out; he lived in my house rent free, after all.

While Hannah continued to talk to Jeremy Rollins and Chet and Jessie packed their gear, I let my mind wander to the anonymous call I'd gotten about Gentry Mullins being the victim found outside Vichy Springs.

I really, really wanted to know who'd called. The voice didn't sound like Thomas or Davis, but they had equipment to disguise their voices if they wanted. Either way, I hadn't heard that voice again, but was sure I could identify it if I did.

Why had he called me? Shouldn't he have called Hannah or someone else more important at another station?

I considered that there were some mysteries I might never solve, and that troubled me. I also considered that I could have more of my mother's talents than just cooking; she'd been a valuable agent for the Alliance Security Detail when she was younger. She'd taken down drug lords, mass murderers, slave rings and who knew what else?

So many of those things she wasn't allowed to talk about, that's how secret they were. It made me think of my half-brother, Bel Erland. He and I used to speculate on some of Mom's escapades, but we'd never really learned the truth of them.

Still, it was fun to imagine Mom leveling her wrath against those who deserved it. I hoped I could be as effective as she was if the need arose.

Poor Kory—if he knew what I really was and what I could become, he wouldn't waste any time running in the opposite direction.

Humans didn't fall in love with people who could become fifteen feet tall and burn anything they desired with just a touch.

The positive side of that, of course, was that we could also shield anything or anyone we chose from fire; it had no effect on a Thifilathi or Thifilatha. My race had been designed to walk through molten lava without feeling its effects.

No human would want that. To them, I'd be a monster. A silver, bat-winged-and-scaled monster. Mom's Thifilatha was gold; Great-Aunt Glinda's was white.

I wondered how my Thifilatha found its way to silver.

Regardless, it matched my last name. Perhaps somewhere in the cosmos, the Mighty were smiling at the coincidence. Or, perhaps they'd planned the whole thing. With them, one could never be sure.

I considered, too, that so far, only my smaller Thifilatha had manifested. I imagined it would be roughly equivalent to my mother's, which was close to seven feet and I believed my full Thifilatha would also be the same, at fifteen feet.

Either would scare Kory witless. Still, I intended to protect him with everything I had if Thomas and Davis were right about the criminal portion of the supernatural community placing a bounty on his head.

At least Anita appreciated what I'd become. If I hadn't, we'd both be dead.

"I'll get that," I lifted Chet's tripod and followed him to the van. Hannah spent another five minutes talking to Jeremy while we loaded everything and then waited patiently for her in the parking garage.

Kory hadn't driven us today; he had other assignments at the downtown headquarters. George, whose skin was as dark as his smile was bright, drove us instead. I liked him very much—I'd already seen photographs of his two sons and his wife. I'd promised to make cinnamon rolls for him to take home the following Friday, so he could treat his boys.

If Anita wanted evidence that the Romes practiced discrimination, she only had to look in George's direction. He had a degree in journalism, yet the closest he could come to being a journalist with

Rome Enterprises was driving Hannah and others like her on outside assignments.

Uncle Tybus' words came to me, then.

You won't be able to change everything for the better, young one, he'd said. *Change what you can as well as you can.*

Lee would be leaving in another week. I intended to call Anita and then have an unscheduled meeting with Lee before he left for his new job.

Kordevik

"My ex is pregnant," Watson announced as he climbed into my Jeep Friday afternoon.

"Not with yours, I hope," I said.

"I wish it was mine," he muttered.

"Hey, I thought you and Anita," I began.

"I like her, man, but she's not a werewolf."

"Ah. I see where this is going. You weren't high enough on the totem pole to be a candidate for your female."

"Yeah." Watson slumped in his seat.

"You know, I probably understand that better than you think," I said, checking traffic before pulling away from the curb.

"What do you know about that?" Watson demanded. He didn't believe me—that was evident.

"I know about being left at the altar, because my woman didn't want anything to do with me," I said.

Watson turned his head in my direction and lifted an eyebrow in sudden interest. "It was an arranged marriage," I went on. "She hadn't even met me and decided to leave me standing there."

"Dude, that sucks," Watson said.

"Yeah."

"Well, at least you have Lexsi, now. I see how you look at her."

"Dude, my intended *was* Lexsi. She just doesn't know it. She thinks

I'm human. You breathe a word of this and I'll burn every bit of fur off your balls, man."

"You mean you're courting her *now?*"

"Yeah. Look, this is how it's done with my kind. Someone's chosen for you and you show up at a wedding. She decided to run away instead. I have to convince her to love me back before I tell her anything."

"Well, all I gotta say is you hit the jackpot, man. That woman is smokin' hot."

"I know that already, so keep those wandering eyeballs to yourself."

"Dude, I'm not encroaching on your territory. If I need somebody, I'll hook up with Anita."

"Hey, Anita deserves better than somebody looking for the casual hookup, all right?"

"You don't get to tell me what to do," Watson went into morose status in a blink. "I like Anita. It's her choice, too, you know."

"Fine. Just—don't mistreat her or lead her on. Anita almost died the other night, so she's vulnerable."

"I'll be honest with her." He hunched into his jacket and turned away from me. Because he was turned away from me, I allowed a curl of smoke to escape my nostrils. Every man ought to realize that every woman was equal and precious. Watson didn't appreciate someone playing with his emotions by giving the woman he loved to another. Anita, by extension, didn't deserve to have her emotions toyed with, either.

Perhaps if he'd lived more than a thousand years, as I had, he'd see that for himself. On Kifirin, High Demon females were extremely rare. To be promised one in marriage soon after her birth was nothing short of a miracle.

I was nobody important; I still found it extraordinary that I'd been selected as Lexsi's mate.

Until she ran away from me, that is. At times, I figured this was punishment for a misdeed somewhere in my past. I suppose the extraordinary thing in this chain of events was that Lexsi and I ended up on the same planet, and in the same city.

Destined to meet, an inner voice informed me. "We're having pork loin for dinner," I told Watson. "I hope you're hungry."

~

Lexsi

I threw a cake together while helping Farin and Anita do vegetables and a salad. Tiburon was scheduled to arrive any moment when Kory and Watson came through the door. Both needed to change before sitting down to eat; Kory grinned when I asked if he intended to wear what he had on.

"Not for dinner with you, onion," he said and took off toward his bedroom. Watson took the hint and did likewise. If he hadn't, Anita might have hauled him toward his closet herself.

Tiburon arrived on time; Farin got a kiss and the bottle of wine he'd brought with him. The smile on his face told me he was in love with News Seventy-Four's daytime meteorologist.

"This is a really good red," I acknowledged when Farin handed the bottle to me.

"I'll open it," Kory offered. I handed it to him and went looking for wineglasses. Rick arrived while Kory was pouring wine. He'd brought flowers.

Farin said he liked me. If I could have turned a brighter shade of red, I surely would have. Kory frowned when Rick leaned in to peck me on the cheek. "Uh, I'll find water," I burbled. "For, uh, the flowers. Yeah."

I turned away as quickly as I could without appearing rude. I thought I'd explained things well enough to Farin. Whatever she'd told Rick, it hadn't been the right thing, or enough of it. I'd have to tell him myself, as uncomfortable as that felt.

I wanted to splash cold water on my face instead of filling a crystal vase with it. The flowers, the vast majority of them roses, didn't smell as sweet as those outside my window on Avendor. For a moment, a wave of homesickness hit me.

"You all right?" Anita's voice was soft as she came to stand beside me.

"I told Farin I wasn't interested," I mumbled. "What am I going to do?"

"Tell Kory later," she said. "Rick ought to know better."

"What if he doesn't?" I moaned.

"Then you'll have to tell him how things are yourself."

"I feel sick," I whispered.

"Come on, you have to perk up and eat," she scolded. "People are wondering what's going on with you."

"Great." I wobbled toward the table with a fake smile on my face and a knot of vipers roiling in my stomach. I ended up sitting between Kory and Rick and barely choked down a minimum amount of food.

How could I have known that things would get worse? Rick started talking about Mike and how much he missed him. He choked up when he speculated that Mike could be dead and he might never know it.

That's when Kory's hand gripped mine under the table—a silent warning that we couldn't tell what we knew. We'd been warned by Davis and Thomas that spilling that secret could jeopardize their investigation.

Rick's emotional admission only made it more difficult for me to say what needed to be said. *What am I going to do?* I moaned in mindspeech to Anita.

I didn't think about the direction this could go, she admitted. *I don't know what to tell you.*

I can't be a substitute for Mike—that would be a lie, I returned.

I know. I don't do obsessions on close friends, she added. *Unless it's for their safety.*

Understood—that's the right thing to do.

You look green, she pointed out.

I feel really sick, I admitted. *If I throw up on Rick, it will ruin Farin's dinner.*

"Baby, is everything all right?" Kory asked. Rick's head swiveled in our direction faster than I thought possible.

"I don't feel good," I mumbled and scooted my chair back. A part of me felt embarrassed, another part felt relief that it was Kory and not Rick with me in the hall bathroom while I lost everything I'd eaten for dinner.

~

"Tell me," Kory said softly.

I lay flat on my back on the edge of my bed while Kory rubbed my belly with a gentle hand. I had an arm across my eyes, shutting out the dim light in my bedroom.

"I thought I told Farin well enough that I wasn't interested in Rick," I whispered. "I guess that was a spectacular failure on my part. I don't want to hurt his feelings, since he's so upset over the Mike situation," I added.

"Onion, I think he understands things now," Kory murmured.

"I'm sorry—I just didn't know what to do and it made me feel so sick," I apologized. His chuckle surprised me.

"Onion, I was worried there for a few," he admitted. "I'm not offended by vomit, I promise. I've seen plenty of worse things in my lifetime."

"That doesn't make me feel much better. What if I'd barfed on you?"

"I'm wash and wear," he replied. "Not a problem."

"I've ruined Farin's first home-cooked meal with Tiburon."

"You haven't ruined anything. They're still eating, drinking and talking. Even Rick."

A light tap sounded on the door. I thought it was Anita. "Come in and join the fun," I called out.

Mason walked through the door. "Everything all right?" he asked.

"I'm better, now that I upchucked," I admitted.

"I sort of got that scent," Mason said.

"Can I ask you for a favor?" I pulled my arm away and struggled to sit up in bed. Kory helped by placing extra pillows behind my back.

"Of course," Mason agreed.

"I think Hannah plans to sleep with the Deputy Coroner, just to get information he's not allowed to share. Is there some way you can tail her after hours?"

Kory's expression was one of surprise, while Mason lifted an eyebrow in response to my question.

"What sort of information?" Mason was suddenly all business.

"Well, she was asking about what, if anything, was found on Gentry Mullins' body—besides Brad Nolen's clothes. The Deputy Director said he couldn't release any information. Hannah started batting her eyes, then. If Chet, Jessie and I hadn't been there, she might have climbed onto an autopsy table with him, to get what she wanted."

"You think she came up with that on her own?" Kory asked.

"No. I don't think that would have occurred to her. I think she's asking for someone else."

"I talked to Klancy shortly after sunset," Mason said. "He doesn't like the way things look, and says he's hearing some rumblings, but there's no proof."

"Was he specific?" Kory asked.

"Not particularly," Mason shrugged. "I was thinking about going hunting with him tonight. I'll see if he's interested in tailing Hannah with me."

"You'll do it?" I asked.

"Yeah. This whole thing is more than strange. Something's going on; we just have to find out what it is."

"Mason," Kory said, "I want you to listen in if Hannah gets the information she wants."

"Already on it, bro," Mason grinned. "Former police officer, remember? And, when I tell Klancy, he'll be curious, too."

"Can I meet him, sometime? Klancy?" I asked.

"Sure," Mason nodded. "I'll get going—we'll check the likely places for Hannah's tryst with a Deputy Coroner." Mason left my bedroom so swiftly he was almost a blur.

"Mason is reliable," Kory sighed. "If there's a way to get the information, he'll find it."

"Do you trust Watson?" I asked.

"Yeah," Kory said.

"I just worry that Claudia will connect the dots, and it will either not go well for him, or not go well for us."

"I think she has something on him," Kory admitted. "He won't say what it is, but he's trapped in that job. She treats him like shit, too, when he works his tail off for her. He won't willingly tell her anything, onion. Count on it."

"I understand," I said. "I'm just worried, that's all."

"I know. We'll sort it out, okay?"

I closed my eyes when his fingers brushed a stray lock of hair behind an ear. It would be a lie if I said I didn't want more of his hands—on my face, my body—on intimate places none had ever touched before.

Another knock came.

"I hate to interrupt," Anita said when she poked her head inside the door. "But Rick's condo was just destroyed."

exsi

By the time we arrived at Rick's condo building, we couldn't park anywhere near it. It wasn't just Rick's condo—the entire structure was damaged in the blast.

Residents were huddled outside on nearby sidewalks as firefighters attempted to extinguish the blaze engulfing the rest of the building. Other news crews were already on-site, with Seventy-Four noticeably absent.

"We can send a live video feed to the station with my cell phone," I said, handing the phone in question to Anita. "Just hold it steady and make sure you get my voice and the building behind us."

That's how News Seventy-Four ended up with the story—with a makeshift newsfeed from a cell phone. We even interviewed Tiburon, whose condo was also destroyed in the building. He informed us that this wasn't his only home, but still, things precious to him had been lost.

Rick, his arms around Farin, looked completely lost while Tibby spoke with me and Anita recorded the interview. I had an idea why Rick's apartment was targeted; the enemy thought he knew where Mike was.

A thread of worry for Farin ghosted through my mind, too, while Kory fielded calls from the night producer at the station and relayed directions to me during brief interruptions.

After all, if the enemy hit Rick's place, they could get Farin's, too, so they could solidify their presence and level further threats. By the time a crew arrived from the station, I was happy to hand it over to them.

Kory, Rick and Tiburon approached a police officer who stood guard at the perimeter. He said the building would likely be a total loss, and as yet, not everyone was accounted for.

We'd already relayed that information to the station, so there was nothing new. Why did they want Mike so badly? What about the young woman who was taken—did they want her, too?

"Kory, do you think we should check on Farin's apartment?" I asked as we made our way back to his Jeep and Tibby's Cadillac. It had taken both vehicles to transport all of us.

"Not without a police escort," he growled softly. "You know what happened to Anita's place. They may be waiting for someone to show up there, now."

"But," I sputtered.

"Let me call some friends, okay?"

I knew exactly who he wanted to call—werewolf agents Stone and Williams. If anybody could check Farin's place for explosives, they surely could.

"Make the call," I said, allowing my shoulders to slump. When I'd run away from an undesired wedding, I never thought I'd end up neck deep in something like this.

"We'll be there in a few," Kory waved the others on. Tiburon nodded and led Rick, Farin and Anita toward his car while Kory and I stopped outside a closed sandwich shop to make the call.

"Davis Stone, here," he answered on the first ring.

"This is Kory Wilson," Kory identified himself. "I need a favor."

"Does it have anything to do with the condo bombings down by the wharf?"

"In a way. We figure Rick Armstrong's condo was the main target, so we're worried that Farin, his sister, may be targeted too. Is there some way we can get one of your agents to check out her place before she goes home?"

"Yes, and it may be a good idea if she stays elsewhere while we watch her place for a while," he answered immediately. "If there's a remote chance she could be on their hit list, then we'll explore all our options. I'm guessing they think Rick knows where Mike is, and he'll be getting a call or a letter, if he hasn't already."

"That's what I think, too," Kory admitted.

"Where is he going to stay, tonight?" Davis asked.

"Probably with us," Kory admitted.

"Give me the address and we'll come talk to him."

"That sounds great." Kory rattled off my address. I hoped they'd be discreet when they showed up—I didn't want the enemy to find us because they were watching Davis and Thomas, too.

"It may be late before we get there," Davis admitted. "We'll check Ms. Armstrong's house, first, and let you know what we find."

"Thank you," Kory breathed a sigh.

"I appreciate the call," Davis said. "This may provide good leads in the case."

"I hope so. I'm a little tired of it, to be honest," Kory admitted.

"Kory?" I said after he'd driven us halfway home.

"What, baby?" he said, without taking his eyes off the road. A heavy fog had settled in and it was difficult to see the road ahead.

"Why did they take that woman when they got Mike away from the hospital?" I asked. "They never said Mia Cummings saw anything; only that Brad Nolen did."

"Yeah. About that," Kory's voice was flat. I knew immediately that he'd withheld information. "Look, this is the reason they have a price on my head," he said. "One night, I was in Clawdia's, having a drink at the bar and talking to Watson when several vamps came in. They had Mia and Mason with them. Mason looked half-dead and for a vamp, that's pretty bad. They intended to have a public execution for both; Watson had other ideas. He pulled a rifle from beneath the bar and the fight started. All I could do was get him and Mason to my place after the fight; Klancy took Mia to the hospital for treatment."

"So Klancy weighed in on this?" I asked.

"Yes." That was a partial truth. I let it slide. He still hadn't told me the whole story, but someday, maybe he would. For now, I was content with what he'd said, that he'd gotten Watson and Mason away from the vamps, so of course they wanted him dead. Mason, too.

Watson—I had no idea why he wasn't dead already. He still worked for Claudia, and if he and Kory were ever linked—I squashed that thought.

"Do you suppose those vamps worked for Granger?" I asked instead.

"There's no doubt of that," he replied.

"Perfect."

"Is that sarcasm?"

"Yeah."

"My dad always said sarcasm was a good way to express anger," Kory said. "It's preferable to destroying people or property."

"He sounds like a smart man."

"He is."

~

Kordevik

When Lexsi asked if she could meet my father sometime, I had to bite my tongue to keep from saying that it had been a given, if she'd only shown up at our wedding.

"Maybe sometime," I answered her question. "He doesn't live in California."

"Oh."

She didn't pursue the subject and I was glad; I worried that I'd have to lie and make up a place for my father to live on Earth. "I hope Mason has news for us," she changed the subject.

"Yeah."

"Kory?"

"What, baby?"

"Please be careful. Those people—vampires or whatever they are who want you dead? Well, I don't want you dead."

"I don't want me dead either, but it's nice to hear you say that," I told her. "Look, don't worry, they haven't caught up with me yet."

"But they bombed Rick's place tonight, and a lot of other people are homeless because of that. What if that's what they're planning for —all of us, too?" Her voice shook when she said the words, and that troubled me. Yes, she'd already been placed in danger when Anita's place was destroyed.

"They haven't got us yet, and I don't intend to let that happen," I replied. "Don't borrow trouble by letting your worries get the best of you."

"You sound like my grandmother," she whispered.

"Then your grandmother is really smart," I said. After all, her grandmother was Queen of Le-Ath Veronis. You didn't hold that throne by not being smarter than just about everybody.

"She is." Lexsi hugged herself. "Sometimes, I wish Gran were here. She'd know what to do."

"I think we can handle this," I said. "We're better than they think," I added. "Granger and his bunch, I mean."

"I sure hope so. I'm not just worried about you and me. I'm worried about Anita, Farin and the others, too."

"I know. I promise to do everything I can to keep all of them safe."

"Yeah. Me, too."

Her words were loaded with meaning, as if there were something she wasn't telling me. Something she was reluctant to tell me. I let it go for now—our relationship was still somewhat fragile, and pushing her to tell me could serve to separate us. I wasn't willing to risk it.

I wanted to hold her in my arms and kiss her. I also knew what the first kiss would do. Lexsi wasn't ready for that.

Hell, *I* wasn't ready for that.

Mentally, I cursed the burden set upon High Demons—the one

that said a High Demon male's first kiss would render his female High Demon mate unconscious, so he could place his claiming marks.

At least the act of placing claiming marks no longer made the female ill for weeks; Li'Neruh Rath had effected that change. My saliva would heal the bite marks my smaller Thifilathi placed, and that was a welcome change.

If I kissed Lexsi, then sank my long canines into the back of her neck as was warranted, she was bound to notice when she woke.

It would also mean we were mated, in a very real sense.

She'd already run from me once, for the same reason.

"Here we are," I pulled into the driveway after several moments of silence.

"Yeah." Lexsi didn't sound happy.

~

Lexsi

Davis and Thomas arrived two hours after Kory and I did, at nearly three in the morning. I'd almost fallen asleep on Kory's shoulder when the doorbell rang.

"Wake up, onion, we have company," Kory breathed against my hair. It was justice, perhaps, that both our werewolf visitors looked as weary as I felt.

"Farin Armstrong's apartment was wired to explode when anyone approached the door, just like her brother's condo," Thomas informed us. "If they're here, we'd like to speak with them. We've deactivated the bomb, but left the wiring in place; we don't want unexpected visitors to get blown to bits. We hope the enemy will still think the bomb's live."

Kory turned to me. "I'll get Rick up, if you'll wake Farin," he said.

I drew in a breath; Farin was in bed with Tiburon, and I really didn't want to disturb them. Squaring my shoulders, I gave Kory a tired nod and headed for the hallway. Tiburon answered the door when I knocked.

"We have two agents from the Joint NSA and Homeland Security

Department here," I said. "Farin's apartment was wired, too. The agents want to talk to her and Rick."

"We'll be right out," Tiburon said and closed the door.

"They're on the way," I told Davis when I reached the kitchen. "Want coffee or something stronger?"

"How about both?" Thomas asked. "It's been a long night."

"Yeah. I get that," I agreed and started brewing coffee.

Rick, dressed in a pair of Kory's sweatpants, shuffled into the kitchen first, with Kory right behind him. Davis and Thomas stood, produced badges and introduced themselves.

"We expect you to get some sort of notification from the ones who destroyed your condo building," Davis began. "They'll want to know where Mike Ellis is, because they think you have that information."

"Huh?" Rick's face expressed his confusion.

"They don't have Mike," Thomas explained. "We do."

"What's this?" Tibby walked in, holding Farin's arm.

"Mike, Mia and Brad are all safe; we have them in a safe place," Davis said. "That's why when you start getting messages threatening you or someone you care about unless you tell them where Mike is, call us immediately. Your life may be in grave danger."

"Like it isn't already?" Rick snapped.

"It is, but you're a public figure, as is your sister. It will be more than difficult if you disappear suddenly. People are already beginning to panic over seemingly random bombings. Your apartment, Ms. Armstrong, was wired to explode if you went back there," Thomas turned dark eyes in her direction. "I suggest staying here with Ms. Silver if possible, or, failing that, we can find a place for you. I warn you, however, we'll have to place discreet guards so you and your brother can be kept as safe as possible when you travel to and from work."

"But," Farin's lower lip trembled.

"Chica, don't worry. Granger is nasty business and these here— they can protect you during the daytime. I assume you have something just as good to protect her during the evenings?" Tibby turned a hard stare on both agents.

"We have several agents who can hold their own against Granger."

"She knows they're vampires; we've had that discussion," Tibby pointed out. "Farin, both these men are werewolves." He jerked his head toward Davis and Thomas.

"And you're a shapeshifter," Davis huffed. "Have you told her that, yet?"

"I was getting to that," Tibby announced.

"What the hell?" Rick began.

"Whoa," Kory held up a hand. "Look, let's not out everybody in the room, okay?"

"Who's outing whom?" Mason walked in with someone else.

"Mason?" Thomas blinked at the vampire before extending his hand to shake. "Man, I wondered what happened to you."

"Shot and left for dead," Mason shook hands with Thomas. "I haven't seen you since school, dude."

"I was worried I wouldn't see you," Thomas observed. "I guess you know my secret, now."

"Yeah, but I can't say it's unwelcome at this point. Lexsi, Klancy and I got the information you wanted," he turned toward me. "But I'll be damned if it makes any sense."

"A necklace?" Davis shook his head. "That doesn't make sense. What kind of necklace?"

"She said it was a metal coin of some type," Mason said. He and Klancy sat at the kitchen island while the rest of us had something to drink, and explained what they'd learned from listening in on Hannah's sexual tryst with the Deputy Coroner.

I got the idea that Mason was slightly disgusted by some of what he'd heard. Klancy, an older vampire, sat in silence while Mason described their evening activities.

"Did Jeremy Rollins verify that Gentry was wearing the necklace?" Davis asked.

"This is where it gets really strange," Mason said. "Rollins said there was no necklace. He said Gentry was only wearing a metal wristband."

"She was leading him on," Kory huffed. "She asked about something he wasn't wearing, in an attempt to get the real information. I'd bet she wanted to know about the wristband all along; she just didn't want him agreeing with her about a fictional necklace so he could get what he wanted from her."

"Sneaky," Rick said.

"We'll have to ask about the wristband," Davis said. "Look, we need to go. You all have our number now—call if you see or hear anything unusual, or if you feel your life is threatened. We'll have discreet guards in place for Rick and Farin, beginning tomorrow morning."

"Thank you," Tibby nodded. "I, too, will keep her as safe as I can."

"At least I know Mike is all right," Rick said.

"Bear in mind—you can't tell anyone about this visit, or it could jeopardize even more lives," Davis said. "This is classified information, you understand."

"I won't do anything to place Mike in more danger," Rick snorted. "I'm just glad he's alive."

"What am I supposed to do about my clothes and things?" Farin asked.

"I suggest borrowing something until you can buy extras—you can't go back to your place. In addition to the explosives planted on-site, it may be watched. After all, they can attempt to blackmail your brother through you."

"You will stay away from that place," Tibby said. "I will not have your life threatened again. If you need clothing, I will pay for it."

"Mason, will you and Klancy see us out?" Davis asked as he rose from his seat.

"Sure," Mason nodded.

The rest of us watched as they walked toward the front door. At least fifteen minutes passed before Klancy and Mason returned.

"I just got offered a job with their department," Mason breathed. "Klancy, too."

"You gonna take it?" Kory asked.

"Hell yes," Mason said.

"I, too," Klancy spoke. "It will give my life purpose."

I didn't say it aloud, but I was already a Klancy fan. He reminded me very much of Uncle Aurelius, who'd also been vampire. I was glad he was on our side, too.

"Mason and I will keep watch the rest of the night," Klancy said. "You may sleep in peace, knowing we are on guard."

I didn't sleep in peace, as Klancy suggested. Instead, my dreams were filled with vague terrors, deaths and a search for something I couldn't find. When I woke on Saturday morning, I felt more tired than I had the night before.

When I wandered into the kitchen, I found Anita and Watson having coffee at the island. I had no idea where Watson went the night before, only that he'd been missing when we returned from the site of the explosion.

"Don't ask him where he's been, I've already done that," Anita stood to get more coffee.

"Did he tell you?" I asked while I waited for my turn at the brewer.

"Nope."

"No breakfast for you," I informed Watson and went to get eggs from the fridge.

"I went to see my sister," he mumbled. I almost dropped the egg carton, I was so stunned.

"Well, well, now we know how to get secrets from Mister Furry Butt," Anita crowed.

"I have to wait until her husband is out of town," Watson hung his head.

"You two don't get along—the husband and you?"

"Man, if I could, I'd kill the bastard," Watson growled.

"What bastard are you killing?" Kory walked in, his hair damp from a recent shower.

"His brother-in-law," Anita said.

"Dude?" Kory leaned down to look into Watson's face.

"All right, I'll admit it—Claudia forced my sister to marry the worst werewolf ever," he said. "Enough, okay?"

"That's gotta suck," Anita said.

"It does suck."

"Is your sister all right?" I asked.

"She hates him, but there's nothing she can do," Watson admitted. "There's nothing either of us can do."

"Werewolf politics," I said without thinking.

"What would you know about it?" Watson demanded.

"Just an educated guess," I fumbled.

"Hmmph," Watson said. "Only another werewolf will understand this mess."

"Well, how about some eggs and ham, then?" I asked.

"I'll take that," he agreed and dropped the subject.

"We still don't know what Claudia has on him," Kory said later, when he and I sat on the back patio having more coffee after breakfast. The early fog had cleared enough that we could see the waters of San Rafael Bay far below.

"Information is slowly seeping out of Watson," I said. "Maybe he'll trust us enough eventually to tell us."

"I hope so. Whatever it is, I'd like to find a way to get him away from her. She can pull him down with the rest of her minions, if he's not careful."

"You think she'll get pulled down? We don't even know what she's doing, except purposely getting her bar destroyed."

"Davis and Thomas think she's involved with Granger, who's behind these bombings. They're trying to get Mike back, too, you understand."

"Don't you think this is carrying the revenge thing a bit far?" I asked.

"I don't think it's revenge that's driving them," Kory responded. "I think Mike was a dead man, just like Vann was, before they managed to get away. My guess is they saw or heard something they shouldn't have."

"Then I hope Davis and Thomas are asking those questions," I said.

"I'm sure they are. The thing is, Mike was hurt pretty bad. He may not have remembered anything. That doesn't mean he won't," Kory held up a hand. "I think Granger wants his hands on Mike, to finish the job before he remembers."

"Wow. I never thought of that," I breathed. "This just keeps getting worse, doesn't it?"

"Looks that way. I'm surprised they haven't found this house yet. We're all together, here—wouldn't take much to get rid of all of us at once."

"Are you trying to scare me more than I am already?" I squeaked.

"No, baby. I shouldn't have said that." He stood and covered the distance between his chair and mine. "Stand up," he said.

"But," I said.

"No, I'll take a seat, you sit on my lap. I'll hold you."

"But," I said again.

He folded my hand in his and pulled me to my feet. I was in his lap in less than five seconds, his arms wrapped tightly around me as his warm breath fanned my temple.

"That's better," he breathed before kissing my temple. "We should have enough to fight back if Granger attacks," he reassured me.

Again, I wondered if my Thifilatha would come if needed. Snuggling into Kory's warmth, I closed my eyes and prayed to the Mighty that it would.

~

Kordevik

Vampires I could handle—for the most part. My vulnerability would be in those around me. Farin was a target because Rick was Mike's best friend. What would Granger do if he learned how important Lexsi was to me?

I worried that he already had that information, and was merely waiting for an opportunity to take her. King Jaydevik told me that she'd never manifested a Thifilatha. All the worse for me, because it rendered her nearly human. Yes, she had fighting skills, but those skills only worked against humans. Vampires and werewolves were a different story.

I tightened my arms around her and wished we were on Kifirin, sharing this embrace. Nothing would threaten her there; High Demon females were treasured by the race.

That's sexist thinking, Li'Neruh Rath's mental voice interrupted my thoughts. *Lexsi made her choices, as have you.*

I wasn't about to argue with the god who ruled Kifirin. Even if I disagreed with him, which I did.

Wise, his laughter rang in my head.

~

Lexsi

Kory drove Anita and me to the grocery store while Tiburon took Farin and Rick to a local department store to buy clothing. Watson borrowed the TinyCar and disappeared again.

"Let him be—he has his own demons to battle," Kory sighed and pointed me toward his Jeep.

It was a human phrase, which had a double meaning to me. The High Demons had an old saying, too; *I have demons to battle* was an excuse to get away on their own for a while, either to spend time with friends or to be alone. To humans, it often meant that something troubled them; something they were ill equipped to handle.

Watson certainly appeared ill equipped to handle his troubles, some of which we didn't know.

You can't help if you don't know what the trouble is, Gran always told me. A part of me hoped we'd learn what Watson's troubles were—all of them—before they destroyed him. Or before Claudia destroyed him. He never spoke about her to me; I'd catch his lies if he did.

I wondered how he and Kory had become friends—how else

would Kory have been allowed in a supernatural bar without being thrown out? Klancy must have held off the vampires while Kory got Mason and Watson away, but that didn't explain Mia Cumming's escape.

Kory said Klancy got Mia to the hospital. How had Klancy done all those things by himself? Did someone else step in to help?

Blowing out a breath and shoving those thoughts from my mind, I pulled out my cell phone to check the grocery list I'd put together. The pantry was nearly bare since so many were staying at the house, now. Groceries were going to cost a ton of money.

Rick and Farin were washing new underwear and other necessities when we got home. The Jeep was filled with groceries; Tiburon helped Kory unload while Anita and I put things away.

Since Friday night, I hadn't once thought of work. I counted that as a blessing. With Tibby and Anita's help, we put chicken enchiladas together. I'll admit the boxer was a great help in the kitchen. He explained that his grandmother taught him to cook—he was quite fond of his abuela.

"She lives in San Diego," he explained. "Mama moved to Vegas with my stepfather."

"I think I'd like to meet your abuela," I smiled.

"She would be happy to know that. If she visits, I'll introduce you."

"He asked me to come to Vegas with him, for his next fight," Farin arrived in the kitchen, carrying a basket of clean laundry.

"I'm not sure I could sit there and watch someone try to hit a friend," I said, giving Farin a smile.

"Tibby will handle it," she shrugged.

"Awesome. Dinner's almost ready. Round up the troops."

Work crossed my mind again after dinner. Kory asked Watson to help clear away dishes and clean the kitchen; Watson had shown up in time to eat, as if he could scent the food from wherever he'd gone.

Rick stepped in to help and I was grateful. He'd been mostly silent since he'd learned that Mike was alive.

That's when I went to my bedroom to check my laptop for any news that had come through over the weekend. I'd gotten information from the sister station in Texas; the survivor who'd appeared in Dallas was now missing again. His parents were making impassioned pleas for him to come home. Journalists speculated that whatever trauma he'd suffered while he was kidnapped had caused him to disappear again.

The other thing I received was an addendum to the execution scheduled for Friday evening; the prisoner was now dead, but a video had been included with that information. Journalists were sometimes invited to witness executions; it was obvious someone from the station had gone.

The video images came with sound, depicting the prisoner as he was led into the room where the lethal injection would be administered. He looked straight at the window as he wept and insisted on his innocence.

"I didn't do it," he repeated.

Truth.

"I'm not Loftin Qualls," he shouted.

Truth.

Ohmygodohmygodohmygod.

CHAPTER 12

*L*exsi

"What's this about?" Anita asked as I pulled her inside my bedroom and shut the door.

"He's dead," I whispered.

"Who's dead?"

"Loftin Qualls. Well, somebody who looked like Loftin Qualls."

"What the hell are you talking about?" Anita demanded. "Are you all right?" Her eyes narrowed as she attempted to feel my forehead.

"I'm fine," I said, although I let her feel my forehead anyway. "Loftin Qualls, you know who he was?"

"That rapist-murderer millionaire?" she asked.

"Yeah. That's the one. I think somebody else died in his place."

"That's not plausible," Anita said. "He's been on death row. How could they sneak somebody in to trade places with him?"

"Money?" I suggested. "His parents have loads of it."

"Here's my next question—where would he go if he did get out? Somebody would surely notice."

"Not if he looked like somebody else," I hissed.

"What are you basing this on?" she asked.

"I can show you the video somebody at the sister station in Texas sent to me."

"Let me see it."

We watched the video together; I told Anita that the prisoner depicted was telling the truth. She turned to me then, her eyes widening in shock. "You're sure about this?"

"Yeah. As sure as I've ever been," I nodded. "I don't know what to do about this."

"Tell those guys who were here the other night," Anita said.

"Oh. Yeah. Right. Uh, how do I tell them that I know truth from a lie?"

"There's that," Anita blew out a breath. "Look, they still need to know. Did anybody fingerprint that guy, or check DNA?"

"I don't know," I moaned. "What I do know is that somewhere, the real Loftin Qualls is on the loose and probably looking for more victims."

"Yeah. I didn't consider that."

"They're going to think I'm nuts," I sighed.

"Who?"

"Davis Stone and Thomas Williams. The werewolf agents," I replied.

"Then hold off for a while and think up a good way to explain it," Anita retorted. "But know this—he could kill between now and then."

"I know that."

"Look, I'll back you up as well as I can, but you have to convince them."

"I'll try. I have no idea what Kory will say."

"Lexsi, look at me," Anita said. I turned my gaze on her. "A murderer may be loose and already killing," she said. "That execution was two days ago."

"I know."

"Have you checked to see if there are any murders that could be attributed to this asshole? I heard he always got creative when he killed."

"Don't remind me." I felt sick for the second time in two days.

"Then make the call."

"All right. They'll kill me, then Kory will kill me," I mumbled and pulled out my cell phone.

~

"Kory," I approached him. I'd found him having a drink with Watson at the kitchen island.

"What is it, onion?" he asked.

"I called Davis and Thomas."

"What for?" He was on his feet in a second, his drink forgotten on the island.

"I need to talk to you in private before they get here," I said.

"All right." I reached for his hand, discovering that mine was shaking. What if he didn't believe me?

What if nobody but Anita believed me?

In truth, I was beginning to doubt myself. Nobody at the prison suspected anything—after all, they'd ignored the prisoner's claims and executed him anyway.

"Tell me," Kory said after I shut the door to the laundry room. At least it was empty at the moment.

"A prisoner was executed at a Texas Penitentiary," I began. With my voice trembling, I explained what I'd seen and heard. "He wasn't lying, Kory. You have to believe me."

~

Kordevik

Gulis were extremely rare, but I couldn't deny that it ran in her family. Her mother, from what I'd heard, was a guli—a truthspeaker of the High Demon race. They always recognized truth from a lie.

"I believe you, onion," I pulled both her hands into mine and squeezed them gently. "We just have to find a way to convince our agent friends to believe you, too."

"Oh, thank goodness." She pulled her hands from mine and

wrapped both arms around my waist. That's where we were—in the laundry room, wrapped in an embrace when Anita knocked on the door to inform us that Davis and Thomas had arrived.

Convincing two werewolves proved to be a tougher job.

"The body's been cremated," Davis informed us. "There's nothing left to check," he added.

Lexsi was stricken by the news and huddled against me.

"His parents took custody of the body almost immediately and sent it to a facility for cremation," Thomas confirmed Davis' words and shut off his cell phone.

"Then I suppose you'll have to keep your eyes and ears open when the new murder spree commences," Anita's words were dry.

"If he's alive and his parents are involved, they ought to send him out of the country for treatment," Davis rose from his chair. "We'll send discreet requests through channels, in case any unusual murders crop up."

"We'll look into it as well as we can, but you have to understand that what's going on here takes precedence," Thomas said.

I thought Lexsi would collapse with the news. They may as well have told her they didn't believe what she'd said. The results were much the same. I had to congratulate anyone involved in this mess for destroying the body as quickly as they could.

For all anyone else knew, the real Loftin Qualls was dead.

"Thank you for your time," Anita said, her words as cold as the snow on Baetrah's winter summit.

"Keep us informed," I said.

Davis half waved as he and Thomas headed for the door.

"Come on, baby, I'll walk you to your room," I whispered against Lexsi's hair.

Lexsi

My sleep was troubled and sparse that night; I was grateful when Kory knocked on my door and reminded me of our trip to the gym before going to work. Mason and Klancy were still awake—dawn was still two hours away when we left the house.

My mind still churned about the how of replacing a psychotic killer with another person, who would be executed in his place. If this were another world, I could conjure up a way, perhaps, but Earth in the here and now had no such resources.

"Stop worrying about it," Kory patted my hand. "Buckle up and let me know if you see anybody following us."

"Okay."

I didn't look forward to dealing with Hannah at work on any day. Today was far worse than other days.

A potentially innocent man had been executed, while the real criminal had gotten away, somehow. My first boss was dead, and had been replaced by another from the legendary Hades. Rick, Anita and Tiburon's homes were nothing but ash. Farin couldn't go home and Kory had a price on his head, placed by vicious vampires. Watson worked for someone I perceived as evil, who was also in bed with previously mentioned vampires, as were the owners of the company I worked for. What else could possibly go wrong?

"Sweat it out of your system," Kory advised as he drove through an intersection. "I've always found exercise to be a good way to clear my head and put things in perspective."

"Thank you, Obi-Wan," I said.

"Just trying to help. I'd like to see a smile on your face again," he added.

"Yeah, well, there's not much to smile about right now. I have to deal with Hannah the Horrible today."

"Hannah's not so terrible," Kory teased. "Deep down. And covered by a big pile of rocks."

The laugh escaped before I could hold it back.

Before Hannah got in, I'd already checked with the station in Texas. I wanted to find out if anyone had interviewed Loftin Qualls' parents. I'd know whether they were telling the truth, too.

The family requested that the media respect their privacy at this time, while they grieve for their son, came the reply.

Of course they'd asked for privacy. I imagined that somewhere, they were spiriting said son away to a safe place, so he could plot his escape and murder again. Frustrated, I lifted my now-empty coffee cup and headed for the break room.

"Any word on the missing again kidnap victim?" Lee was in the breakroom, pouring a cup of coffee for himself.

"Nothing." I'd checked on him, too, before I began my quest for more information on Loftin Qualls' parents. "They're looking for him—his family, the police, even the FBI is looking. I have the newsfeed from the Texas affiliate; forwarded it to Hannah first thing for her to take a look."

"I got compliments this morning from on high at the national news level," Lee said. "On your phone camera coverage of the condo explosion downtown. I was told it reminded them of old-school journalism, with a very modern twist."

I mulled that over for a moment. "What was the holdup on sending a weekend crew down there?" I asked.

"Well, the way I heard it, both drivers on duty thought they could go out drinking without telling anyone. That left us scrambling to find somebody to drive the van into the city. It took a while, as you well know."

"Does that happen often?" I frowned at Lee. "That the weekend drivers just go off on their own instead of doing their jobs?"

"First time ever," Lee shrugged. "Both got fired for it."

"Wow. That sounds so—irresponsible."

"Good thing you were there," Lee said. "You saved our bacon. Again."

"It was an accident," I said. "Farin's dating Tiburon, and her brother's condo was in the same building. We went to see if there was anything we could save. That's why I was there to begin with. At least we got the news out—Rick and Tibby's condos are a total loss."

"Rick Armstrong, the weather guy?"

"Yeah. Farin's brother."

"We tried to hire him, but the other station offered a raise to keep him there. Damn fine meteorologist."

"So is Farin," I said.

"I know. The Romes wanted a man as chief meteorologist. Remember, you didn't hear that from me," he added and walked out of the breakroom.

That information was something I could pass along to Anita, for her files. I needed to talk to her anyway, about George. The wheels were turning as I walked back to my cubicle.

I wanted to argue with Hannah about the assignment, but didn't. She'd just call me little bitch again and I was more than tired of that insult. She wanted me to go to a downtown hotel and interview the chef, who'd created a new dish that everyone was raving about.

"You know something about cooking, little bitch. I don't." She wiggled her manicured fingers, letting me know her hands never touched food except to eat it. "Oh, and if you see Kory, tell him I expect him to drive me to the downtown offices at noon—I'm having lunch with the CEO."

"Of course." I fumed as I left her office—she was still attempting to get her claws into Kory's back. Preferably during sex.

"What's wrong?" Farin stopped me as I marched toward my cubicle to call Kory and George.

"My gag reflex is at def-con five," I grumped. "Can't you smell it from here?"

"Smell what?"

"The knee-deep vomit in Hannah's office," I whispered.

"Oh," Farin covered her mouth to suppress a giggle.

"I gotta go," I said and waved as I continued down the hall. "Luigi Del Vigo is waiting to be interviewed."

"Good luck. I hear he's a tyrant in the kitchen," Farin called out.

"Yeah."

Luigi was just as much a spiteful tyrant as everyone said he was—behind his back. They all claimed he was a culinary genius to his face.

The dish everyone was making such a fuss over was snapper in a special cream-chili-paprika sauce. The sauce recipe was a closely-guarded secret, and he evaded any questions regarding its ingredients.

"Here, taste," he offered a plate of snapper with a dollop of the sauce, which had come straight from the kitchen.

I lifted an eyebrow at my first bite—yes it was very good, but his secret ingredient was guava paste. It paired well with the pepper-jack cheese used in the recipe. The sweet balanced the spicy, making the sauce a desirable accompaniment to the fish.

I wasn't about to leak his secret—he could keep it. I was determined to improve on his recipe, though, and make the dish at home—with shrimp and pasta, instead of snapper.

I finished the interview with Luigi, who was more interested in selling himself than his food, helped Chet and Jessie pack up and called for George to meet us in front of the hotel.

Kordevik

"Have you set a date for your wedding?" Hannah held up a mirror and primped in the back seat of the limo while I drove her toward the main office downtown.

"Not yet," I said, attempting to keep my voice civil. "Anita and I are discussing it."

"I think you can do better." She snapped her compact shut and smiled into the rear-view mirror.

"I've done well enough," I said, trying unsuccessfully not to grind my teeth.

"She's a nobody," Hannah added, as if she hadn't heard my reply. "Besides, you can always get a little on the side. Nobody will know."

"I'm not interested in that," I said. "Sorry." I wasn't sorry. Frankly, I wanted to stop the car, jerk Hannah out of the back seat and wring her neck. Maybe a Deputy Coroner liked what she had to offer, but I wanted no part of Hannah (the Horrible) Tilton.

I hoped the CEO would give her all she wanted, just so she'd leave me alone. I pulled up to the curb and got out to open her door. She held onto my hand too long as I helped her from the back seat; I had to pull it away from hers as gently as I could while mumbling nonsense about parking tickets.

"I'll text when I need a ride back," she blew me a kiss. The doorman didn't miss the exchange when he opened the door for her.

Cursing under my breath, I slid onto the driver's seat and buckled in. Gossip would likely travel at the speed of sound, letting Anita know before the day was out that her supposed fiancé was diddling Hannah Tilton.

While pulling away from the curb, I considered turning in my notice, which would be a direct violation of my parole on Earth. That, in turn, would sentence me to an extra five years in this special version of hell.

Lexsi

Anita picked me up after work, her mouth set in a grim line.

"What happened?" I asked.

"Hannah."

"What did she do?" I asked.

"She made a spectacle of herself when Kory dropped her off at the Rome building," she said. "Now everybody thinks my fake fiancé is having sex with her."

"So they're all talking about you behind your back, then?"

"Yes. It didn't bother me at first, until they started calling me blind and stupid."

"Then call it off. Kory will have to think up another excuse to keep Hannah away."

"I want to give Hannah a piece of my mind instead. That's not possible, since she's already obsessed by somebody else."

"Maybe we ought to hunt the one who obsessed her, then," I said.

"Maybe we ought to rip his head off his neck, after forcing him to remove the obsession," Anita grumbled.

"My guess is, he's in league with the Romes up to his hairline, in addition to being best buds with Granger and Claudia," I observed. "Did you get the info on George?"

"It's in my purse. Thanks for the tip on the Romes practicing sex discrimination, along with all the other versions."

"It's the least I could do," I shrugged. "Since you're engaged to my boyfriend and all."

"What's for dinner? I'm starved," Anita said.

"Well, something different if you'll stop by the grocery store first."

"I'm all over that," she replied and pulled out of the station's parking lot.

~

"This is like Luigi's sauce, only better," Farin sighed after tasting the shrimp linguini I'd fixed for dinner.

"You've had his?" I asked.

"Yeah, Tibby took me. That was good; this is so much better. How did you get him to give you the recipe?"

"He didn't. I tasted his sauce today during an interview. I knew pretty much what was in it after that, so I thought I'd make some improvements. Turned out well enough," I said.

"It's better than awesome," Watson held out his plate for more. Kory hid a grin and speared a shrimp with his fork. I could tell he liked the food, too.

Rick's eyes were on me while I ate; I didn't say anything, although it made me uncomfortable. At that moment, I wanted Kory to have mindspeech, so he'd know. He looked up at me just then.

"Any word on that missing kidnap victim?" he asked.

"Just a random report. Somebody who was half drunk while crossing the border back into the States swears he saw the guy in a car with two others, but nobody is giving the report credence."

"Why would he be crossing the border anyway?" Farin asked. "Seems to me, he'd avoid the area after being kidnapped the first time."

"That's what most people, including the border guards and local police are saying. Border guards say they never saw anything, and they were checking cars."

"So there's really nothing new," Rick said, lifting his glass of wine to drink.

"No, there's really nothing new. Lee gave you a compliment today," I said.

"Me?" Rick set his wineglass down and blinked at me.

"He said you were an amazing meteorologist. Said we tried to hire you, once."

"I remember. It was last year, when Trey Downing retired. I turned it down."

"He turned it down because of me," Farin sighed and stared at her plate. "Rick wanted me to be promoted. You see how that turned out."

"Just because the Romes are jackasses doesn't mean you didn't deserve the promotion," Anita pointed out. "Because you did."

"I agree," I said. "I told Lee what I thought about the whole thing. I mean, Gerald is okay, but he's no Farin Armstrong."

"Yeah—his clothes are a dead giveaway," Watson quipped.

Kory snickered before slapping a grinning Watson on the back.

Farin rolled her eyes while Rick tried not to laugh. "See—this is the difference between men and women," Anita began. "We were discussing Farin's superior abilities, while you three only consider the way she dresses."

"That's not true," Watson disagreed. "We were considering the way Gerald dresses. Have you seen those godawful golf pants he wears every Fourth of July?"

"With knee-socks—don't forget those," Rick chuckled.

"Have you seen him at national conventions?" Farin asked. "I saw him last year—he wore shorts, black socks and sandals to a meeting. When pictures of that got out, Lee told him he could only wear suits at public functions from now on."

Everyone at the table laughed.

We were clearing dishes away when I got the call from Lee. "Can you come in? Hannah's off tonight and this is important."

"What's important?"

"A women's shelter in Austin was attacked. Six are confirmed dead," Lee replied.

"How?" I asked. "How were the women killed?"

"The six confirmed deaths all died in their beds. They're checking now for signs of rape before they were—ah—dismembered."

"I'll be there as quick as I can," I said and ended the call.

"What's this?" Kory took the phone from my hand and tilted my chin up with a finger.

"I think the real Loftin Qualls just left his calling card at an Austin women's shelter."

We were clearing dishes away when I got the call from Lee. "The FBI is now involved," I reported an hour later. "As yet, no witnesses have come forward and information regarding the identity of this killer is unavailable. A massive manhunt is underway and several K-9 units have been called in to join the search."

Lee, who'd been called in just as I had, gave me a nod when the segment ended. "We'll let the others have it now," he said. "I'm concerned that whoever did this is long gone."

"I worry about that, too," I said. I had more information than Lee might ever have, and it frightened me. Not only had Loftin Qualls managed to get out of jail, leaving someone else to die in his place, he'd gotten past security at a shelter to kill six women who'd gone to bed early.

Everyone else at the shelter had to be moved after they were questioned. How had those women died without anyone seeing or hearing something?

"Still no word on that missing kidnap victim?" I asked.

"I checked around eight tonight—still nothing," Lee shook his head. "Look, go home. You have an early morning tomorrow. I don't expect Hannah until around noon."

I suspected that she was spending the night with the recently divorced CEO, but I didn't say it. Lee probably suspected the same thing. Anita would suffer through all the gossip Hannah started, while Hannah would skate through another affair because everybody was afraid to talk about her infidelities.

Afraid Hannah would get them fired, I reminded myself.

Maybe she was in bed with James Rome, Jr., who wasn't really James Rome Jr.

The hair on the back of my neck prickled.

How had I not put this together before? Somewhere, the real James Rome, Jr. was likely held prisoner or trapped somehow, because he looked like someone else. At least I hoped he was. Like Loftin Qualls' replacement, he could also be quite dead.

How were they doing this?

Why were they doing this?

Had Laurel found a way to get rid of her husband, and replace him with someone she liked better? I didn't use the word love, because I doubted Laurel actually knew how to do that. When I'd met her, she may as well have worn a T-shirt that said *Power Hungry and Self-Serving*.

Loftin Qualls had money; his family had even more money. Had Laurel approached them with an offer, in exchange for an obscene amount of cash or favors of some sort?

I went in search of Kory so we could go home, while my brain sifted through possibility after possibility.

~

"Here." Kory set a glass of bourbon in front of me. "It's the best I could find in the liquor cabinet. Watson's been drinking more than I thought."

I hated bourbon. I intended to drink it anyway, or I wouldn't sleep. While some images of the women's shelter were shown on the news during my broadcast, none of them were the horrific ones—of the hallway splattered with blood after the killer went from room to room.

Boot prints could be seen, even from the distance the photographs had been taken. My guess was that the shoe size wouldn't match Loftin Qualls'; it would match someone else's.

"Don't dwell on it tonight; you'll waste the booze," Kory set another glass of bourbon on the island and took the barstool next to mine.

"Easy for you to say." I lifted my glass and swallowed as much as I could, before setting the drink down and struggling not to gag.

"Take it easy. I don't mind holding your hair while you barf, but the experience has to be unpleasant for you," Kory teased.

"Can we not discuss barfing?" I mumbled and buried my face in my arms.

"Hey, now," he pulled my hair aside and massaged my neck. I wanted to moan with pleasure, his hand felt so good against my skin.

"You're really tense, onion," Kory breathed against my hair.

He was right. I felt as if I were about to burst with the information I held inside me—information that still came no closer to a resolution of any kind.

If Laurel Rome were behind all this, why did she need the Qualls' money? She had plenty of her own.

Why was she—and the man pretending to be her husband—in league with Granger and Claudia? What parts did they all play in this? Did Hannah know anything? Was the Sirenali who'd obsessed Hannah involved in this, too?

"This is so fucked up," I muttered. Kory's hand went still on my neck.

"What's fucked up? Never mind, I know the answer." He went back to massaging my neck, before switching to both hands and moving to my shoulders. Before long, he pulled me to my feet and herded me toward my bedroom. If he'd asked then, I'd have let him spend the night in my bed.

He didn't. Instead, he pushed me through the door and shut it softly behind me. I felt abandoned as his footsteps faded down the hall.

~

Kordevik

A much younger High Demon wouldn't—*couldn't*—have controlled his Thifilathi.

I barely did it. With her neck exposed and my hands on it, the animal part of me almost manifested. Lexsi would have been scarred for life if I'd allowed it to happen, physically and emotionally.

Placing claiming marks while the recipient was awake was horribly painful. Besides, Lexsi believed me to be human. When she recovered, she'd likely never want to see me again if I'd let my Thifilathi loose.

Fuck.

What was I going to do? She was probably wondering why I hadn't kissed her yet.

Double fuck.

Not only were we drowning in a mystery we couldn't solve, our relationship might disintegrate because I couldn't behave like a normal human suitor.

Yes, I wanted to march back to her room, get in bed with her and do what any normal male would do—make love to the woman of his dreams. Perhaps six months ago, I'd have been so pissed I'd have placed my claiming marks and let things fall out as they would.

That was before I knew her.

Before I loved her.

Fuck.

CHAPTER 13

Lexsi

"Hannah looks like she's been rode hard and put up wet," Farin snickered as I poured coffee in the breakroom. It was nearly noon and I was having a fourth cup to make up for a mostly sleepless night.

"She's here?"

"I saw her walking toward her office just now."

"Your equine reference has not been lost upon me," I held up my free hand.

Farin giggled. She was in a good mood—as she should be. Tibby had shown up after dinner the night before and slept in Farin's room.

I couldn't help comparing her experience with mine, which left me frustrated, unfulfilled and sleeping alone.

Yes, it would be my first time, but I wanted it with Kory and nobody else. At least Farin wasn't obsessing over the people who'd planted a bomb at her apartment. Davis and Thomas were doing a good job on that front.

"What's the latest on those murders?" Farin asked as Gerald Castleman, the station's chief meteorologist and her boss, walked in.

"The FBI and local police haven't given us any new information," I

183

replied. "All we have is what we had last night. I've even contacted someone I know at a Texas station—they're in the same boat, with very little to report."

"Storms in the Austin area tonight," Gerald said while pouring coffee. "Rain may wash away evidence."

"I'm worried that there wasn't much evidence last night—or today," I said. "Nice to see you in early, Gerald," I saluted him with my coffee cup. Farin grinned behind Gerald's back as I walked out the door.

Kordevik

"No, we're having lunch, during which we will break it off," Anita hissed as she took my arm. I'd gone to her office to pick her up for our impromptu lunch date; she'd called me midmorning to inform me that we were going out.

"So, it makes you look better and me worse at the same time?" I whispered. Yes, I did my best to hold back my anger. After fighting my Thifilathi the night before, this really wasn't a good time for Anita to get me riled up again.

"Hey, I was helping you out," she snapped. "But after Hannah's stunt, this has to end. I didn't sign up to be the subject of nasty gossip. You're on your own, now, with that witch."

"Where do you want to have lunch?" I spoke in a normal voice.

"Oh, pizza sounds good."

"Pizza it is."

"Here," Anita handed the engagement ring back to me. We sat in a small pizza place six blocks from the Rome Building, waiting for our order. "I can't tell you how awkward it felt wearing that, when all you can do is watch Lexsi," she added.

"Thanks for helping me—or at least trying to help me." My words were sincere as I pocketed the ring with a nod. "I'll try to get the money back from the jewelry store."

"Yeah. I'd suggest offering it to Lexsi, but she deserves her own ring, not one worn for a while by someone else."

"You think she'd take anything from me?" I snorted.

"She might," Anita shrugged.

"There are things that have to happen first," I said. "One of those things is getting a certain vampire and werewolf off my back."

"There's that," she agreed. "I'm surprised you haven't seen more of them, to be honest."

"I think they're scared witless and hoping some other fool will look at the reward offered and try to take me off guard."

"Why would they be scared witless?" she asked, sucking on her straw. I watched strawberry lemonade move through the plastic tube for a moment before I realized what I'd done.

"Hmmph. I don't have to answer that," I said.

"I think you ought to tell Lexsi there's more to you than meets the eye. Just like there's more to her."

"You think that will solve anything?" I tossed out a hand. "You don't even have half the story and you're trying to give me advice."

"I know enough," Anita snapped at me. "I sure as hell hope you're bulletproof in every way, too, because you're probably going to need it."

"I can take care of myself." Rising from my chair, I slammed it beneath the small table and stalked out of the restaurant.

A bullet tore a hole in the sleeve of my favorite jacket before I could skip away.

Lexsi

"He wasn't in the Jeep when it exploded," Anita attempted to calm me down. She'd shown up at the station five minutes after I got the report of a car bomb near a pizza restaurant. Cell phone images sent by people near the site identified Kory's Jeep perfectly, right down to the tag, which survived the bomb.

"Then where is he?" I shouted.

"Shhh," Anita jerked her head toward the hallway. Heads were poking out of doorways to see what was going on.

"I'm here," Kory stalked in, looking as if he were prepared to wrestle a bear.

"What happened?" Anita fingered the hole in Kory's jacket. He jerked his arm away.

"Somebody tried to shoot me, that's what," he muttered angrily. "Then they blew up my Jeep."

"Oh, no," I whispered. "They tried to kill you twice?"

"As you can see, they were unsuccessful both times," Kory said. His words were calm and measured. I watched his eyes, though—a fire burned in their depths. He was so angry he could probably kill with his bare hands.

"Have you uh, talked to the police?" I asked. Kory in this mood frightened me. Things had taken a dangerous turn and I wasn't sure how to react.

"I called our new friends," he growled. "They're on the way to pick me up."

"Are they taking you home?" I asked.

"No. I'm taking a few days off. They said they have a safe place for me to stay."

"But," I began.

"Let it be, onion," he said and turned to walk away.

Kordevik

I intended to hunt the bastards down who tried to kill me, but I needed help from Davis and Thomas. They were already hunting Granger; I wanted their leads. They'd already promised to keep eyes on Lexsi; I didn't want to place her in further danger because I was staying at her place.

That's why I'd asked if they had a place for me to stay. They'd already checked my condo—it was wired, too. Someone was watching it discreetly, just as they were Farin's.

I stood under the awning at the station's entrance, waiting for the two werewolf agents to arrive. They'd already described their vehicle, so I wouldn't be convinced to climb into the wrong one.

"Want a ride?" Davis' passenger-side window rolled down, revealing his face.

"Yeah." I lifted the gym bag of clothing I'd gathered from my bedroom at Lexsi's and strode toward the vehicle.

The back seat of the SUV was roomy, comfortable and had a new-car scent to it. Stowing my bag on the floor on the opposite side, I shut the door and nodded at Thomas in the rearview mirror.

He pulled away from the curb.

Yes, I felt horrible, walking away from Lexsi like that. I'd done it for a multitude of reasons. Not least of those was that our relationship had progressed faster than I'd expected. It was past time for a first kiss, which I couldn't deliver until she understood the consequences.

In the eyes of our race, it meant we were married. The wedding she'd skipped out on had been a mere formality—for those other races in attendance. Once my Thifilathi claimed her, she'd be marked—and mine—for life.

Strange, how getting to know her in the real sense shifted my views on the subject. I wanted—needed—her consent before I placed my claiming marks.

She didn't need to know that I intended to fry vampires and werewolves; whoever was responsible for the attempts on my life, as well as Anita's, Rick's, Farin's and Mason's.

Lexsi, no doubt, was included in that list somewhere, merely by association.

"Mason says you have unusual talents, although he wouldn't elaborate," Davis turned in his seat to look at me. "He says you're extremely dangerous, actually."

"I intend to be extremely dangerous all over the ones who tried to kill me." An outward breath of smoke accompanied that statement. Davis' eyes widened in surprise.

~

Lexsi

Not only had Kory disappeared with the werewolf agents, Hannah, somehow, had managed to get Fiona Hall fired. Yes, she was a drain on the company, and everybody knew she was having an affair with an executive in the downtown office, but Hannah had done it in the most spiteful way possible.

It was why she'd forced Kory to drive her downtown the day before; to convince the CEO (by sleeping with him), to have Fiona officially transferred to the LA station while the executive involved only received a warning on his personnel record. Fiona was fired via e-mail by the LA station's General Manager before she could pack a bag.

Fiona had zero prospects of finding another job as a result; Hannah had effectively destroyed the woman. Fiona wept while clearing out her desk; Hannah asked (loudly) whether someone could shut off the noise.

Grateful that nobody saw the plume of smoke that escaped my nostrils, I sent information to Hannah for her six o'clock broadcast. Fiona's fate would have been mine, too, if Hannah had her way.

I didn't think her obsession had anything to do with the jealousy and nastiness, either—in my opinion, that was all her and nobody else.

"The word is displacement," Farin handed me the battered dictionary from her cubicle.

"Paper?" I held it up.

"Are you pointing out the obvious, or attempting to shame me for destroying trees? I've had that dictionary since I was in grade school. Mom bought it for me."

"All right," I lowered the book and set it on my desk. "Why are you asking me to look up displacement?"

"It'll be the defense mechanism one," she said and turned to walk away.

I went still. Hannah still wanted to fire me, and she'd probably attempted to fire Kory because he'd disappeared on her. Someone had to tell her that Kory was taking a leave of absence after his breakup with Anita; it was the excuse he'd given, anyway.

Hannah wanted him to be her exclusive driver from now on. He'd put a stop to that, albeit inadvertently. Her joy at getting Fiona fired was drowned by her subsequent anger at Kory.

Why did the Romes want such a spiteful bitch working for them? It made no sense—nobody in the industry liked her or considered her talented, let alone a normal human being. I only had to listen to gossip to know what everybody thought of her.

No matter how bad it gets, things can always be worse, Gran says. That's why I didn't send mindspeech, begging Aunt Bree to allow me to crawl away from the cesspit that contained Hannah Tilton and the Romes.

I knew I was more upset than usual with my job, because Kory had abandoned me. He'd become my sounding board and my solace—more so than Anita, even, and she was willing to go to war for me.

Kory abandoned me.

Yes, I knew most romances among humans didn't work out.

It was still a blow. Panic threatened—I shoved it down.

To keep from crying in my cubicle, I continued my search for the ten missing men from the California bus. At least one from the Texas bus had shown up. None from the California bus had been found, even with dogs and planes searching the area.

I made calls to the sheriff's office, local law enforcement and anyone else I could think of to contact, just to see if anything new was available.

I kept at it, too, until word came that an employee at the Coroner's Office had disappeared, along with some of the evidence collected from Gentry Mullins' body.

I'd bet my salary the missing items included a metal wristband.

~

Kordevik

"We asked for that evidence, dammit," Davis half-shouted into his phone. "Your office dicked us around about it, too. Now you're telling me it's gone—along with an employee? Look, I don't care that it looks like a kidnapping. Find both. Now."

Several seconds went by while Davis listened and fumed. "Look, I know you screwed around with Hannah Tilton, so she could pull that information from you. Did you tell anybody else?"

More seconds ticked by. "You'd better be right, and you better be there when some of my agents arrive. Clear your calendar, because you'll be answering questions all night. We'll also be questioning Ms. Tilton, so the truth would be your best plan of action. Yes, I do want to see all the photographs."

I wanted to see the photographs, too, and wondered if Davis would allow it. After all, I could have some insights that he wouldn't, since he'd been confined to Earth all his life.

~

I saw the photographs. Like Davis and Thomas, there was nothing to be made of the plain, silver wristband. It fitted over the wrist like a cuff, with the traditional opening at the back.

"Without the actual piece, these are meaningless," I handed the photos back to Davis.

"I know." He breathed a sigh and shook his head. We were in the evidence section of the coroner's office, where Thomas' wolf was sniffing about, attempting to detect the scent of the kidnapper. So many other scents were likely present, so the effort was futile.

"Useless," Thomas was back to human and grabbing his clothing from a nearby chair. "I'd have to go through every employee and separate their scents, when I have nothing from the kidnapper to compare with the others."

"What about security cameras?" I asked.

"Detectives have already looked at those," Davis sighed. "Images get fuzzy right after the kidnap victim walked into evidence, and when it clears, he and the wristband are missing."

"I don't think you'll understand this," I began, "but one of the first things wizards and warlocks learn is how to interfere with electronics."

"Wizards and warlocks?" Thomas stopped in the middle of pulling on his pants.

"Trust me—they exist," I said. "Just not naturally on this world. So, unless there's been some serious evolving, if this is a warlock's work, then he isn't local."

"You're serious about this, aren't you?" Davis studied me for a moment.

"As serious as the proverbial heart attack," I shrugged.

"So, you've met some of these people?"

"Yes, just not here. On this planet."

"What the hell are you saying, man?" Thomas zipped his fly and frowned at me.

"That there are more things in heaven and Earth, man," I replied. "These would be not from Earth, though."

"If that's what it is," Davis pointed out.

"It would explain a lot," I countered.

"We need to talk to our boss, then," Davis said. "We'll drop you off at the house in Petaluma, then check in with her."

"I'm going to Petaluma?"

"It's a safe house. You'll be fine."

"Not worried about that," I said. "I wanted to be closer to San Rafael."

"It's only twenty miles or so," Thomas said. "Close enough."

"Hmmph." The thought of being even twenty miles away from Lexsi disturbed me. I wanted to be closer than that. Just far enough away to draw Granger and his flunkies in my direction and keep them away from her.

"It'll have to do; it's the closest one, unless you want to get a place in the city."

"No, thanks," I said. "Petaluma will be fine."

"We'll get a vehicle for you, too, just in case," Davis offered.

"You mean you'll let me out? Voluntarily?"

"I assume you can protect yourself," Davis' words conveyed sarcasm. "I also assume you're attempting to protect Ms. Silver and the others at the San Rafael house."

"You assume correctly," I allowed a curl of smoke to escape my nostrils.

"That's new," Thomas observed.

"There's more where that came from, I assure you."

"I don't suppose you know anything about why Granger's Nob Hill mansion burned down, do you?" Davis asked.

"I have nothing to say on the subject," I replied. "Can we go to Petaluma, now? I have some thinking to do."

Lexsi

I told Anita I'd get myself home after she sent mindspeech offering to pick me up. At least Hannah spent most of the afternoon in her office with the door shut after getting a frigid reception from everybody at the station.

I'd sent her research on all the topics requested, and included some she hadn't requested. She planned to do a follow-up on the recent spate of bombings, but didn't have new information and wasn't really interested in uncovering any.

I no longer cared; Kory's departure had left me in limbo; keeping my mind occupied with work had served to distract me for a while, but when it came time to go home, I was at a loss. I felt as if I'd been left adrift on the ocean in a small boat with no oars.

That's why I skipped straight to my bedroom at home, curled up on the bed and hugged a pillow to me. I'd been abandoned, and it hurt.

A lot.

That's when it hit me. I'd never gone to check out the bars I'd researched in Oakland. That would certainly distract me. Scrambling off the bed, I grabbed my cell phone and scrolled through my notes to find addresses.

After checking area maps on the laptop, I skipped to the first bar on the list.

~

"Well, look at you." The man swayed as he talked, a drink held loosely in his hand. He smelled awful. It only took me ten seconds to realize that this bar was humans only; the music was far too loud for vampire or werewolf ears.

"Look at you," I responded to the man. "Excuse me, I have to visit the ladies room." I turned to walk away. He grabbed my arm. I tossed him against another patron sitting at the bar.

The noise from the fight that ensued ended the moment I skipped away.

Bar two was a kink bar. I got out of there fast.

Bar three was upscale and attached to a restaurant.

Bar four—well, that was the one. It was called Tooth and Nail instead of Clawdia's, but still alluded to the supernatural crowd by its name. On the paperwork, it was called something different and belonged to a corporation, listed as DSG Enterprises.

I was determined to research the corporation the moment I got home.

"What the hell are you doing here?" A vampire detached himself from his leaning position at the end of the bar and approached me.

"Just looking for a drink," I replied as coolly as I could. He was so large, I imagined that a wooly mammoth occupied one branch of his family tree. The excessive hair, of course, was what gave him away, though.

"You need to run along, missy," he snarled. "This bar ain't for you."

"Then I'll run along," I snapped.

He reached for my arm. I jerked away.

"Hey, we're looking for her," a vamp with three followers rose from a nearby table.

Time to go.

"Keep looking," I snapped, punched woolly mammoth in the face and skipped away.

"What the hell did you think you were doing?" Anita demanded the moment I arrived in the kitchen. "You should never walk into one of those places by yourself."

"What places?" Farin wandered in, Tibby right behind her.

"Supe bars," Anita said.

"Which one?" Tibby asked.

"A new one in Oakland. They call it Tooth and Nail."

"Punny," Tibby nodded. "Haven't been to that one."

I'd forgotten that he'd been outed as a shapeshifter. I just didn't know what he shifted to. Since being nosy about those things was considered quite rude, I didn't ask.

"Four vamps there recognized me," I said. "I was forced to make a quick exit."

"That's the worst thing you could have done," Anita scolded. "They'll be better prepared to grab you next time."

"There won't be a next time; that's Claudia Platt's new bar, count on it," I defended myself. "I'm going to do research on it tonight, to see what I can find."

"What are you looking for?" Farin asked.

"I intend to find out if Claudia has hidden partners in the business," I replied.

"What's going on?" Watson shuffled into the kitchen, looking as if he were starving.

"Found Claudia's new bar," I informed him. "So you didn't have to tell me." I turned and stalked toward my bedroom. Watson could fend for himself if he were hungry. I wasn't in any mood to cook.

Kordevik

"Klancy's watching Lexsi's place; Davis asked me to move in with you—in case you needed backup." Mason dropped a duffle on the kitchen floor and offered a grin.

"What I need is to find Claudia's new bar," I said. "I intend to let Granger know I'm looking for him."

Mason went still for a moment—a stillness only vampires can achieve. His unblinking gaze was as fathomless as a silent, cold lake as he considered my intentions. "What the fuck, man?" he said after a while.

I realized I'd frozen in place while he studied me. "What I said," I turned away. "If you don't want to come with me, and I warn you, you won't be traveling in any conventional sense, then make yourself at home. I'll be back later."

"You may want to know what your destination is," Mason pointed out.

"That's what I intend to find," I said.

"I know where it is."

"What the fuck?" I turned on him swiftly.

"Sometimes," Mason said, "It's a good idea to use compulsion, if for nothing else but to keep friends safe. I asked Watson where the place was, then told him to forget I asked. For his safety, you understand. You also understand that if he ever tells Claudia where we are," he didn't finish.

"Yeah. I get that. Claudia better bring a fucking army if she intends to take me down." Mason watched the puff of smoke I'd breathed dissipate before speaking again.

"I'm not sure this is the best course of action," Mason observed.

"Then what do you suggest? Granger tried to kill me twice today. That didn't go so well. If he finds out I have friends," it was my turn not to finish a sentence.

"You think he'll go after them to get to you?"

"You're vampire, you've had dealings with that murdering psychopath already. You tell me what he might do."

"You have a point." Mason agreed.

"Does Granger know you're a King Vampire?" I asked while Mason studied the problem in silence.

He went still again. "What the fuck do you know about King Vampires?" His voice was as cold as the snow on a granite peak.

"I know that Granger likely placed compulsion. I also know it didn't do a damn thing to you. You're young as a vampire, dude. Any normal vampire would have stood there when ordered and let Granger's goons slice him to death. Instead, you fought them off and managed to kill at least one of them. King Vampires are notorious for their fighting skills. Queens, too, or so I hear."

"You know too damn much," Mason crossed arms over his chest and turned away from me.

"Your secret's safe with me," I held up a hand. "Look, give me the address of the bar and I'll leave you alone."

He turned back, then. "What about you? Are you susceptible to compulsion?"

"Nobody from my race is," I said. "It's the way we were made in the beginning. Truth is, my kind were created to keep the dark worlds in line, including the vampire and werewolf planets. We sort of fucked that up after a while, but the compulsion thing still has no effect on us."

"What about Anita?"

I snorted more smoke in a humorless laugh. "Anita, well, imagine the strongest vampire compulsion you can, and take it to the tenth power. It's called obsession. Don't mess with her, man."

"What about Lexsi?"

"Lexsi won't be susceptible to either, but she's vulnerable in other ways. Females of my kind, well, they generally don't turn. She only has some decent fighting skills she learned growing up. If anybody touches her," I growled.

"Look, I get it," he held up a hand. "I'll go with you tonight. The bar is called Tooth and Nail." He rattled off the address in Oakland. "I warn you, Granger's vamps are probably there, waiting for us to arrive. We may have a fight on our hands the second we walk through the door."

"Not a problem," I flexed my hands and formed fists. A fight was exactly what I wanted.

~

Lexsi

I searched through county records, looking for more information on DSG Enterprises. I'd hit a dead end with what was filed on the liquor license, so I started digging for information on Clawdia's Bar.

There, Claudia Platt was listed as sole proprietor. She'd had no website or any other social media presence that I could find; not surprising, considering what she was. Word of mouth in a closed community was likely her best advertisement. Somehow, they'd all gotten the word on the change of address in Oakland, too. That's when it hit me.

Klancy.

Klancy might know how word was spread on all things supernatural. Shoving my desk chair back, I marched out of my bedroom and went in search of the vampire.

"Lexsi," he offered a nod. I'd found him on the patio, standing on the edge of it while listening for anything unusual and sniffing the air for strange scents.

If anybody came close to the house, Klancy would know.

"How do you know," I began. "Well, how does the supernatural community hear when there's a change—like the address for Clawdia's Bar and things like that?"

A low chuckle rumbled in his chest. Until now, I hadn't heard him laugh. "E-mail," he replied. "From a no-reply source. Nobody knows who sends them, they just appear."

"You mean there's a supernatural webmaster out there, who sends out notifications?"

"Yes. If your name disappears from the list, you are in very deep trouble with the community in this area. Mason's name disappeared from the list. Kory was never on it, although he should have been."

"What do you mean he should have been?"

Kory was human.

"Perhaps I err in saying this. You, perhaps, should have also been on the list."

"You can tell by scent," I said as understanding blossomed.

"Yes." He smiled when he nodded.

"I should have known—my grandmother can do the same thing," I muttered.

"While I have not encountered your race before, it is not human, young one. Neither is Kory's."

"He could have told me," I blew out a breath. "I suppose it doesn't matter now, since he left me behind."

"He has no desire to place you in danger," Klancy turned away to study the lights surrounding the bay far below. "You think he has abandoned you? I feel he is protecting you—by separating himself from you and the others in this house."

"And here I am, whining about it. Thanks, Klancy." I turned to go back inside.

"You are welcome."

~

Kordevik

"You sure you want to do this?" Mason squared his shoulders as we studied Tooth and Nail from across the street. At least all the neon worked in the sign placed over the door.

The place was windowless, like Clawdia's, with a heavy, wood and metal door leading into the bar. Two vampires walked in while we contemplated our mission. "I'm ready if you are," I said, clenching my fists.

"Let's do this," Mason nodded.

The moment we walked in, conversation stopped. I was used to seeing Watson behind the bar. Two people stood behind this one—a man and a woman, who appeared to be related.

Perhaps these were the half-werewolves Watson disliked. Nobody approached us as we made our way to the bar. Halfway there, I began the shift to my smaller Thifilathi. My clothing burned away while my skin turned to black scales. Gasps could be heard when my height increased and curved horns formed above my ears. I blew clouds of smoke, which caused those nearby to cringe. Two scooted chairs back to give me space.

"Where's Granger?" I growled as I fisted the male bartender's shirt in one hand and lifted him off his feet.

"Put him down." The female pulled a shotgun from beneath the bar and pointed it at me. Smoke drifted from my nostrils as I turned my head in her direction.

"Put the gun down," compulsion dripped from Mason's voice. As directed, she lowered the gun and set it back on the shelf.

"Where's Granger?" Mason demanded before I could repeat my words.

"I don't know," the half-were whispered. "Nobody's seen him for days."

CHAPTER 14

*L*exsi

Watson borrowed the TinyCar to get to work. I didn't care; I had my own form of transportation and it was much faster than driving. It also allowed me to go to the gym beforehand, without a ride from Kory.

Klancy's revelation the night before troubled me, too. Was Kory a shifter? If so, what kind? Shifters came in all shapes and sizes—the size and mass of the person often had little to do with the animal they became.

Normal-sized humans became rabbits, squirrels and other small creatures. I considered that while running on the treadmill. What if Kory was a small shifter? Was he too embarrassed to tell me what he was?

Either way, he wasn't here to discuss it with me. Perhaps he didn't want his secret out at all. I still hadn't heard from him—what if Klancy was wrong and Kory was done with our relationship?

I realized I'd only make myself sadder if I continued to worry about it, so I showered, slapped on makeup, skipped to my favorite alcove near the bus stop and walked the rest of the way to the station.

It was Thursday, and I'd promised George cinnamon rolls on

Friday. That meant I'd be cooking when I went home for the evening. I had George's résumé on my computer, too, thanks to Anita.

Time for a meeting with Lee, before he left the following day.

"You have a minute?" I asked after knocking on Lee's door.

"Sure." He offered a half-smile. "What's on your mind?"

"This." I handed him a flash drive with George's information. "George is working as a driver for Rome Enterprises, when he has stellar records from a New York college and ran his own news program there."

"Our George?" Lee took the flash drive while staring at me.

"Yeah. Seems somebody only thought he was good enough to be a chauffeur for the company."

"I'll take a look," he promised. "You're not thinking about jumping ship, too?"

"Maybe someday. Possibly soon," I said. "I have a few things to do here, first."

"They're replacing me with Hannah's old boss from LA," Lee dropped his eyes and stared at his desk for a moment. "Those two," he shook his head. "Lexsi, don't let them bully you. You know what to do if that happens." He looked up at me, concern in his eyes.

"I do, and I appreciate it. More than you know. By the way, I'm bringing cinnamon rolls and maybe a few other things tomorrow," I said. "I hope you like them." I turned and walked out of Lee's office, to find Farin waiting outside the door.

"Can we have lunch today?" she asked.

"Sure." I studied the frown on her face. "What's wrong?" I added.

"Rick. He's acting weird."

"In what way?"

"I'll tell you over lunch."

"Okay. Twelve-thirty all right?"

"Yeah."

The reason Farin and I didn't ride together to work was that she had to be there at four for the early broadcast, while I didn't have to show up until two hours later. Working out at the gym was becoming a habit, and I didn't want to give it up. Keeping in shape could save my life, should someone attack me again.

"Have you ever taken self-defense classes?" I asked as Farin turned to walk away.

"No, why?" She turned back to me, with a puzzled frown.

"I think it's a good idea," I shrugged. "Ask Tibby if you can work out at his gym." I turned away this time. Hannah would be at work in an hour or so, and I had research to do.

~

There was still nothing new on the women's shelter murders in Texas; I spoke with someone at the affiliate in Texas. They were following up on the case but had nothing new, either. They worried the FBI was keeping any new information under wraps.

I worried about that, too, but from a different perspective.

The Texas station wanted to do follow up reports; I wanted to know whether anyone was linking Loftin Qualls to the deaths, or were considering them copycat crimes. So far, nobody had said his name, although the deaths could easily be attributed to him, were he alive and on the loose.

Meanwhile, I did further research on the states still allowing the death penalty; Oklahoma had an execution scheduled in the next month. Perhaps it would pay off if I did research on that prisoner, too.

Nothing new had been reported on any of the missing people from the California migrant workers' bus, and there was no further word on those college students missing from the Texas bus.

My fingers itched to punch Davis' number on my cell phone, but I held back. I had questions for him; that much was true. I also wanted to find out how Kory was doing. I knew better than to ask where he was; it was likely a safe house and that information was confidential.

Stay safe, I sent Kory in mindspeech, knowing he'd never hear my words.

~

Kordevik

I almost dropped the weights I lifted; Lexsi's mindspeech shocked me so much. I considered making a reply before deciding against it. She'd know immediately that I wasn't human, let alone most any other creature native to the planet.

She probably didn't know that Granger hadn't made an appearance in days. Even the vamps in the bar knew nothing—Mason and I checked.

I found it humorous that none of them wanted to make a frontal assault on me, too, especially when my smaller Thifilathi did the questioning. Perhaps the news of so many of their burned or destroyed brethren held them back.

I really didn't give a shit. I wanted my hands on Granger and the sooner the better, in my opinion. I didn't like watching my back while humanoid and frankly, Granger had it coming.

If I discovered Claudia had thrown in her lot on Granger's vendetta against me, then she could expect a visit from yours truly next.

Mason had gone to meet with Davis and Thomas after we'd gone home the night before; he didn't say what he'd discussed with them and I was asleep when he got back anyway. I'd taken Tiburon up on his offer to use the gym where he worked out. Except for the manager and two boxers going after it in the ring nearby, I had the place to myself.

Perhaps I should tell Tiburon to invite Lexsi and Farin to work out here. They had everything necessary and few people there to use it. I considered, too, that the full moon was approaching. That meant all the weres and shifters would be going crazy.

Lexsi might need extra protection during that time; anything that shifted always felt bolder and angrier during that part of the month. I spoke of my kind, too; we became territorial during the moon-shift. I always skipped into the high hills surrounding the Bay area, where fog often drowned out the noise when I released a roar or two.

"Hey, bro." I discovered Tiburon grinning down at me while I bench-pressed eight-hundred pounds.

"I didn't see you come in," I said.

"Most people don't," his grin grew wider. "I just have to avoid the rat traps they put out."

~

"You're a rat? For real?" I asked. Tibby and I sat in a diner down the street from his gym; I'd gone a few rounds with him when he asked, then agreed to have lunch with him.

"For real, man. My grandmother—she's the Rat Shifter Packmaster in San Diego."

"You're worried about telling Farin, aren't you?"

"Yeah." Tiburon sounded depressed. "She probably thinks I'm a tiger or something. How do you tell your girl you're a rat?" Dark eyes reflected his concern; he was in love with Farin, there was no question about it. He was also terrified she'd reject him if he told her what he was.

"Damn, dude, you got some chops for a rat shifter," I declared. I was bigger, faster and stronger than any human or shifter, yet he'd gotten in a few punches. Snark Demonio deserved his nickname and reputation.

"I hope Farin sees the same thing, instead of thinking I'm vermin."

"If she loves you, she'll never think anything of the sort."

"I don't know how to tell her," he added.

"Be honest and show her," I suggested. "Just make sure she doesn't scream at the sight of, well, the normal version. Make her understand that beneath the furry exterior, you're still you."

"Are you still you—beneath the scales?" his eyes met mine.

"One hundred percent. I'm just extra dangerous, that's all."

"How much can you bench press when you're like that?"

"You've only seen the smaller version," I pointed out.

"There's a bigger version?"

"Yeah. If you see that one anytime, somebody's gonna die."

"Is there a reason for me to be scared of you?" Tiburon asked.

"None," I shrugged. "Unless you decide to go into business with Granger."

"*Pedazo de mierda*, that one," Tiburon hissed.

"Agreed," I said. He'd called Granger a piece of shit. I was okay with that description, although I had others that would fit just as well. "You know I'm looking for him, don't you?"

"I understand this, after he sends bounty hunters after you."

"Anybody who shoots at me and blows up my car better be ready for the consequences," I said.

"If you need help that I can give," Tiburon shrugged.

"I'll remember that. If you need help convincing Farin, let me know. I'll do what I can."

"Thank you. I will remember that."

I wondered what to do with myself after skipping back to the safe house in Petaluma. I hated daytime television, wasn't hungry after my lunch with Tiburon and was already bored after ten minutes wandering around the house.

Mason was asleep in a darkened room; too bad, I'd have asked him what he'd heard from Davis and Thomas the night before. That's when my cell phone rang. It was Watson. I thought about not answering—after all, he could probably give me good information as to Claudia and Granger's whereabouts, he just hadn't done it.

"What?" I said, instead of hello.

"Dude, I need to see you. Like now."

"About what?"

"Somebody ran a light and hit Lexsi's car, man. You need to come."

"Is she hurt?" I was striding toward the door while I spoke.

"She wasn't in it. I was—I borrowed it. Dude, you need to get here fast. I'm about to lose it."

"Where the hell are you?" I demanded.

"At the corner of Comper and Parley." He named an intersection not far from the Tooth and Nail.

"I'll be there in a minute," I snapped and ended the call. Was he acting as bait so more of Granger and Claudia's hit men could take aim at me?

I decided to play it safe and skip to the top of a nearby building. That way, I could determine whether an accident really happened, or if it were a trap.

The scene when I arrived was exactly as Watson described—I just imagined it wrong. The SUV that hit Lexsi's TinyCar looked like an accordion, while the TinyCar didn't show a scratch.

Firefighters called to the scene were attempting to cut the other driver and his passenger out of the SUV while Watson paced on the sidewalk, his arms crossed tightly over his chest. He was about to lose it, and I could see why.

The SUV was larger, heavier and should have obliterated the TinyCar. If the laws of physics had applied, the smaller, lighter vehicle should have been sent sailing. It wasn't. It stopped right where it was hit, in the middle of the intersection.

Several witnesses were gathered on the sidewalk, too; I imagined more than one of them had called 9-1-1, because an ambulance was on the way. I could hear the siren coming closer the longer I examined the scene from my high perch.

"Fuck," I growled before I skipped into an empty alley and walked out of it. Watson smelled me before he saw me; his head jerked in my direction. He looked like a man who'd nearly died, only to find his salvation walking toward him.

"What the hell happened?" I mumbled as I stopped beside him.

"I don't know. I saw things, man. Things that don't make any sense."

"Things?"

"Well, people. One person. Woman."

"Who?"

"I don't know, man. Never saw her before."

"When?"

"After the car was hit."

"A witness?"

"No, man. Look, I don't know how to explain this."

"Are those two all right? The ones who hit you?"

"I don't think so. I smell death."

"But they ran the light," I pointed out. "They're in the wrong."

"They're werewolf," Watson hissed. "I think they've been following the car. I don't know whether they thought Lexsi was in it, or knew I was."

If they hadn't been dead already, I might have turned and killed them, in front of street cameras and a multitude of witnesses. "Answer questions for the police, then I'll get us out of here, TinyCar included." I didn't attempt to hold back the breaths of smoke that clouded the space between Watson and me.

"Please don't turn," Watson whispered. "I want to, too, and we don't need anybody seeing that."

"Hmmph." I blew more smoke. I wasn't going to explain to Watson on the street that I'd turned the night before and walked into the Tooth and Nail with Mason. Those werewolves should be following me, not Lexsi or Watson.

Thoughts of calling Lexsi to let her know about the car went through my mind, but I ignored them. Watson would have to tell her —after he told me about his unusual experience.

He probably had been knocked unconscious during the hit and imagined the woman. Still, I intended to listen carefully to what he said.

The TinyCar shouldn't have survived, after all, and Watson should have been the one cut out of it, instead of those two in the SUV. Nothing about this wreck made any sense.

It took more than an hour for Watson to tell his side of the story— that he'd been driving along when the SUV ran the light and slammed into him. Witness accounts backed up his statement, so the officers took his information and asked if he wanted a ride to the hospital.

He turned them down while both of us watched dead werewolves in human form being loaded into the back of the ambulance. They were on their way to the morgue and were completely covered by sheets.

So far, not a single person had walked out of Tooth and Nail and I wondered at that, too.

Still, I felt eyes on us; if Claudia or anybody inside the bar knew it was Lexsi's vehicle, they now knew Watson was connected to her in some way because he was driving it.

Unless Watson had been their intended target.

I very much doubted that, although he'd made a target of himself, merely by driving her car.

"You're not taking this car back to Lexsi's," I said as Watson and I walked toward the TinyCar. I hoped it would start; it had been hit really hard and could still be damaged.

It started right up after I folded my frame into the front seat. I was surprised my head didn't scrape the top; it turned out to be roomier than I thought.

Putting the car in gear, I maneuvered around broken glass and the SUV's front bumper, which had crumpled and fallen off. A wrecker was backing up to pull the vehicle onto a trailer; it had sustained too much damage to be towed anywhere.

"Did you know either of those werewolves?" I asked after we'd driven several blocks.

"No, man. Neither were from the local Pack. Where are we going?" He thought to ask.

"To see a couple of friends," I pulled out my cell. Yes, I broke the law by talking on the phone while driving. I told Davis when he answered my call that I wanted Lexsi's car gone over, in case there was a location device planted.

He gave me the address of a local garage and hung up.

Lexsi

Lunch with Farin was late; I ended up doing research for Hannah that she could have done herself. If it had been up to her, she'd have forced me to go without lunch. Lee sent me out the door before

Hannah could call my name again; already it was two o'clock and I was really hungry by that time.

"So, what's wrong with Rick?" I asked.

Farin and I sat in a sandwich shop that was usually filled to capacity at lunchtime. Since it was after two, the crowd had thinned out.

"He forgot Mom's cell phone number. I had to tell him it was on his phone."

"Why would he forget that?" I asked. "Has he hit his head or something? Is he still really stressed over the condo bombing and Mike's disappearance?"

"I didn't think so, but maybe he kept it all inside until this happened." Farin tossed out a hand in frustration. "We're supposed to have dinner with our parents this weekend. If he's still acting like this, they'll worry."

"You think somebody contacted him about Mike?" I asked. "Like Davis and Thomas said they might?"

"I don't know," Farin moaned. "Nobody tried to contact me."

"He's their first target," I said. "If they can get to him, then they don't need anybody else. Mike must have some special information for them to go as far as they have."

"I wish we could talk to Mike," Farin sighed. "Rick would probably feel a lot better."

"It could place all of us in more danger," I reminded her. "We have enough worries as it is."

"He keeps talking about Mike anyway," Farin said. "Maybe if you talked to Rick, he'd listen to you."

"I don't know whether that would help at all," I said. I recalled that I hadn't actually seen Rick in two days, although I knew he was still staying at the house. "Anyway, I have to make cinnamon rolls and cookies tonight after I get home. I promised George and Lee some treats for tomorrow."

"I'll help," she offered.

"Good. You can bake cookies while I'm making dough for cinnamon rolls."

~

Anita, I sent, Rick may have an obsession, or something else may be wrong with him.

I can check when I get home, she replied. *What's he doing?*

Farin says he's acting weird. He forgot their mother's phone number, when it was on his phone the whole time. Things like that. She says he keeps talking about Mike. That he wants to talk to Mike.

That's classic obsession, she said. *He's been ordered to squash his love for his family, in addition to other things, most likely. Part of that, of course, is telling the enemy exactly where we are. It's an old trick to get someone to betray family.*

What can we do about it? Anything?

He needs to be removed from anyone he might harm. My guess is that he came in contact with one of my kind, in a completely innocent setting. I doubt a waiter or a fan on the street would have raised suspicions of the agents tailing him.

Yeah. But what are we going to do? Somebody probably knows where the house is.

I suggest you call your friends as soon as you can. We may need a safe house, just like Kory.

I can't make cinnamon rolls at a safe house.

Your choice. Either way, we need to get Rick away from Farin—and the rest of us, too.

Lee says the jerk producer from the LA station who used to be Hannah's boss is coming to take his place on Monday.

I heard that, too. Look, gotta go. I'll see you at home tonight, and we'll decide what to do then.

All right.

~

Kordevik

Kory, I wish you could hear me, Lexsi mindspoke me, her mental voice anguished. *I think Rick has been obsessed. So does Anita. I don't know what to do. I don't want to leave the house, but the people hunting us may already know where it is.*

Watson and I stood inside the waiting area at an FBI facility, answering questions for Davis and Thomas while two people from their agency went over Lexsi's car.

"Look, I didn't recognize the woman at all. She may have been an apparition, for all I know," Watson declared.

"What did she look like? What did she tell you?" Davis asked, his voice calm. He knew, just as I did, that the approaching full moon left a werewolf agitated enough. Something like this jacked those feelings to a dangerous level.

"She had long, dark hair. I swear, she glowed, too—there was a light around her. She said the car and the house were protected. I have no idea what that means."

"Perhaps it was your brain, making an excuse for the car withstanding any damage," Thomas suggested.

I gritted my teeth at Lexsi's message and almost didn't stop myself from answering her. "I sure as hell hope you're right about the house and the car," I hissed as I stood. "Lexsi says Rick has been compromised in some way. If he stays in that house with her, and if anything happens to her," I didn't finish.

"What's this?" Davis was on his feet and pointing me toward the door.

That meant I was compelled to explain mindspeech, and that Lexsi had no idea I could hear hers. Either way, something had to be done about Rick.

"Hang on," Davis said. I watched him pull his cell phone from a pocket and select a contact number. "Hey, boss," he said when someone answered. "We have a problem. Kory says Rick Armstrong has been obsessed and may be dangerous. Any suggestions?"

Since my ears weren't sharp enough to hear the person on the other end, I waited in silence while Davis listened. "We can arrange that," Davis finally said. "It'll solve our problem for now, anyway." He listened again. "Yeah, they'll be looking for him, just like they're looking for Mike. Too bad we still can't get anything from Mike. It could crack this whole case."

Davis turned his back to me for the last bit of conversation. "Yeah, I'll make sure that gets done, too. It may force their hand on a few things. Thanks, boss." He ended the call before turning back to me.

"We have work to do," he said and strode toward the waiting room door.

~

I wasn't asked to participate, but Davis and Thomas arranged for three agents, in full disguises, to abduct Rick Armstrong from News Eighty-Two's parking lot after he got off work at midnight.

The other thing they'd arranged happened the following day; an exclusive from News Eighty-Two (besides Rick's abduction). The station had received video of field reporter Hannah Tilton meeting Deputy Coroner Jeremy Rollins at a downtown hotel.

~

Lexsi

Rick never made it home the night before. Farin was distraught until I got the call from Davis, saying they had Rick and that he'd be kept safe until the case was solved. Somehow, they'd heard something concerning his safety and moved in before the enemy could attack.

I felt better about the whole thing immediately; Davis said he was increasing security around the house so I shouldn't worry.

I also learned that Watson wrecked the TinyCar; Davis explained that it was in the shop, so they were providing a replacement vehicle for me and another for Watson.

That's why Farin stayed home after her brother's supposed abduction and the rest of us gathered in the breakroom for cinnamon rolls and cookies as a sendoff for Lee. I'd made sure to give George a separate box when I arrived, so he could take it home to his family.

In the middle of Lee's farewell speech to the staff, an intern ran in, babbling something about breaking news at Eighty-Two. A monitor was switched on and we all gaped as images of Hannah's tryst with Jeremy Rollins at a downtown hotel were shown, while the day anchor spoke about secrets divulged, an employee kidnapped and missing evidence at the jail connected to the Coroner's Office.

Hannah hadn't arrived yet; I wondered if she knew. None of us could take our eyes off the screen as the images of Hannah kissing Jeremy outside a hotel room door was shown repeatedly.

"Deputy Coroner Rollins has been suspended with pay until this investigation is concluded. Our calls to Hannah Tilton have not been returned."

"And Seventy-Four gets a black eye on my last day at work," Lee sighed and turned off the monitor. "Food is delicious, Lexsi. May I see you in my office?"

I followed Lee out of the breakroom, wondering what he wanted. I found out the moment he shut the door.

"Come with me," he said. "You don't want to stay here while everybody else drowns in this scandal."

"I want to," I replied. "I just can't do it yet."

"Lexsi, anybody who looks at your resume in the future is going to ask about the Hannah Tilton thing. You're her assistant. They'll assume you knew something. News stations don't want to be associated with anything like this. Quit now and I promise you'll have a job at Eighty-Two. Stay here, even for a month, and the taint may prevent the execs from allowing me to hire you."

"You think the Romes will fire Hannah?" I snorted. "I don't think you understand. There's something going on, here, and I intend to find out what it is."

"What do you have?" Lee took a seat at his desk and studied me.

"Nothing I can substantiate at the moment. As I said, I intend to uncover this."

"Here," he pulled a card from his pocket and handed it to me. "If you need an outlet to report your findings."

He already had business cards for his new job at Eighty-Two. "I'll let you know," I took the card and turned to leave.

"Silver," Lee said quietly.

My hand stopped turning the doorknob. "What?" I didn't turn to look at him.

"You're the best rookie I've seen during my thirty years in the business."

"Thank you," I said and opened the door.

I couldn't tell Lee that all my research skills and thirst for getting to the bottom of an apparent mystery could be traced back to Master Morwin, my Amterean Dwarf tutor. He'd taught me to think for myself and made me want to delve deeper into my assignments.

I left him behind when I went to the private college on Wyyld II. Admission there was reserved for the children of Kings, Queens, diplomats, presidents and anyone else highly placed in Alliance government. I'd graduated with highest honors, thanks to Master Morwin's teachings.

My continued thirst for the why and how of things had stood me in good stead as a rookie journalist. I hoped those skills continued to serve me as I attempted to solve the deepening mystery around me.

Hannah never came to work; someone else did her segments on the six and eleven o'clock news.

It was Friday night, I hadn't heard a thing from Kory, Rick was obsessed and gone, Watson wrecked the TinyCar, I still had no information on Granger and Claudia or how they were connected to the Romes, and why they were connected.

There had to be some sort of grand scheme, here, but I had no idea where the loose thread might be in order to unravel it all.

"Want some wine?" Anita plopped onto the barstool next to mine at the kitchen island.

"Yeah. What should we have?"

"Pinot Noir?"

"Sure."

"How about a sandwich? We have ham and roast beef," Anita cajoled.

"Fine."

"Hey." Watson shuffled into the kitchen and dropped two sets of car keys at my elbow. "Our loaners," he said.

"Thanks. How'd you get both home?"

"Werewolf agent," he said. "Sorry about your car."

"I heard it wasn't your fault."

"It wasn't. I survived. The other two didn't."

"What other two?" He had my immediate interest.

"Actually, the TinyCar is fine, Davis is having somebody go through it to check for bugs. They think those two in the SUV that hit me were out to get me or you."

"You're being talkative all of a sudden," Anita said. "Want wine or something stronger?"

"Bourbon," Watson said and took the seat next to Anita's.

"I already know you want a sandwich," she offered him a grin.

"Yeah."

While Anita pulled packages of deli meats, mayo and other things from the fridge, Watson turned toward me. "I saw somebody today," he said. "Right after the wreck. Dark hair, strange blue eyes, looked like she was glowing. She said the car and the house are protected. I know for a fact the TinyCar didn't have a scratch on it, and it should have been totaled. Me with it," he added with a frown.

Anita set a glass of bourbon in front of him.

"You saw Aunt Bree," I said. "This is her house and that's her car. I'm not surprised they're protected."

"That's not all she said," he wriggled uncomfortably on his barstool.

"What else did she say?"

"She told me to pull my head out of my ass and stand with my friends. Then she told me to tell you," he jerked his head in my direction, "that you have more of your grandmother in you than you know. She said something funny, then. She said you can find secrets in the mist. The last thing she said was, *take them down.*"

"Who is your Aunt Bree?" Anita asked.

"My grandmother's sister. I can't say exactly what she is, because I don't know. What I do know is this—when Aunt Bree talks, everyone pays attention."

"I'll drink to that," Watson raised his glass. I clinked my wineglass against his and drank.

CHAPTER 15

Lexsi

Yes, I was tipsy when I wandered toward my bedroom. Watson had already herded Anita toward his, while Tibby had shown up earlier and coaxed Farin into the kitchen to have a sandwich and a glass of wine with us.

They were still in the kitchen talking when I decided to go to bed.

I saw them the moment I opened the bedroom door. My blades, gleaming in the filtered light from the hallway, lay on my bed. An envelope lay atop the blades.

Closing the door, I flipped on the light and blinked in the sudden brightness.

Lexsi, the note began. *You must solve this mystery, with help from your friends. Terrible things are stirring, and they must be stopped before too much damage is done. Find the secrets while hidden in mist. As for the Romes, take them down.*

Bree

P.S. Be gentle with Kory when you discover his secret. He loves you.

B.

Moving the blades aside—they were spelled by Grey House and quite expensive—I reread the note.

217

She'd told Watson that I had more of my grandmother in me than I knew. My grandmother, the Queen of Le-Ath Veronis and a vampire, could easily turn to mist. Why didn't my father have that talent as well? He was half High Demon and half vampire. My mother was a quarter High Demon, but had received all the gifts a High Demon could possess, in addition to many other talents.

Had the misting talent skipped a generation? Why was I being told this now, instead of in my past?

And why had I not turned Thifilatha before? A small voice asked.

Because I hadn't needed it before.

There was one way to find out if this were true. I walked into the bathroom and turned on the light. After fumbling through my first few attempts, I eventually got the hang of it. My grandmother, a Queen Vampire, could become mist easily. It was a part of her heritage and the ability not only gave her invisibility, she could send her mist through any solid surface.

Bullets and other projectiles would go right through her mist without harming her. Many lives, including her own, had been saved by that one, incredible talent. I also possessed that talent, now, and hoped it would become just as formidable a weapon for me as it was for my gran.

Saturday morning, I cleared the desk in Aunt Bree's study. Then, I skipped to a local art store and bought a large corkboard, pins, paper and other supplies. I drank a cup of coffee while I wrote events on colored paper and pinned them to the corkboard, along with relevant photographs I printed from my laptop.

I included the bus kidnappings in California and Texas, the women's' shelter murders, Loftin Qualls' supposed execution and subsequent cremation, Hannah's party and the guests she'd invited, Clawdia's destruction, and everything else that had occurred that I had no explanation for.

"What's up?" Watson stood in the doorway, his eyes wide with curiosity.

"I'm trying to put all this together," I mumbled, pinning another paper to the corkboard. "None of it makes sense."

"You trust me to see this?" he asked, stepping inside the study and examining the corkboard.

"Aunt Bree came to you. She wouldn't appear before just anybody."

"Why do you say that?"

"Aunt Bree and her sister—my grandmother—are sort of powerful," I sighed. "If I were you, I wouldn't cross either of them."

"No plans to," he held up a hand. "She made me see the light, so to speak."

"Funny. Look, I know you got replaced at the bar—Tooth and Nail—I saw those two people in there Wednesday night before I punched the vampire bouncer in the face and got the hell out of there."

"You punched Willis?"

"Woolly mammoth Willis?"

"That's the one."

"Yeah. I punched him. He and three other vamps wanted to take me down."

"You're braver than I thought," Watson grinned.

"Dumber than you thought, more likely," I said.

"Word is that nobody has seen Granger lately, but I overheard something at the bar while unloading cases of booze yesterday morning," Watson said. "I didn't think it made any sense, but nothing else makes much sense either," He tapped the corkboard with a finger.

"What did you hear?"

"That Granger was with the devil."

"Huh? They said exactly that?"

"I extrapolated. It was noisy in the back, and all I could hear was *Granger is with devil.*"

"You think they meant a real devil?"

"I thought they meant *the* devil," Watson blew out a breath. "Like I said, it makes no sense."

"I wish I could talk to Mike. Granger and his bunch wants him back because he knows something. He either saw or heard something he wasn't supposed to, because they planned to kill him and Vann."

"I concur."

Kordevik

I heard from Watson after lunch. He was off this weekend; he'd claimed injuries from the accident and Claudia allowed him two days to recover. He was resting at Lexsi's place and eating enough for at least two people.

After all, he was on Granger's list, now; the more I thought about it, the more certain I was of that fact. Lexsi, too, because she was associated with me. If the house were protected in some way, Watson needed that protection just as much as Lexsi did.

In addition to Granger, I suspected Claudia was involved in arranging the accident to begin with, since two werewolves were following the TinyCar. Watson suspected the same thing, and I worried about his continued employment with Claudia. If he went back to work, he could end up dead.

Watson also told Davis and me that a werewolf he knew died Friday night—with no apparent cause given. Because the victim was werewolf, Claudia would likely have a private funeral and whoever it was would have merely disappeared, according to human records.

Watson suspected foul play, but had no way to investigate the death, which happened at the winery that Claudia purchased as her new home.

I still didn't know where that was.

You know Claudia will be watching you from now on, I texted Watson back.

What else is new? Came the reply.

What will happen if you don't go back? I asked.

I'll never get my girl if I don't.

How does your girl feel about all this, or is she just stringing you along?

I don't know the answer to that anymore. I'm worried about my sister, too.

I could almost hear the desperation in Watson's voice as I read the text. He was more than confused and I felt sympathy and kinship in his plight. I worried that the moment Lexsi learned who I really was, she'd run away again and I'd never have another chance with her.

My relationship with Lexsi teetered on a thin edge, and I blamed Granger and Claudia Platt for that. The Romes, too, since they were connected in some way.

Dude, turn on the news, Watson texted. *Hannah just got arrested for murdering that Coroner guy.*

～

Lexsi

I got word from Lee's assistant at the station, since Lee no longer worked there. Lee's replacement wouldn't arrive until Monday, and I was grateful not to hear the news from him.

Hannah was in jail for Jeremy Rollins' murder. That information was currently running on every station, including the national news programs. If this didn't cause Rome Enterprises stock to plummet further than it already had, then I would be much surprised.

I watched in stunned silence as images were shown of Hannah being led into a police station while reporters from every news outlet except ours bombarded her with questions. As expected, she kept her mouth shut.

At that moment, I wanted Kory with me. Somehow, I needed to get to Hannah and ask one simple question. A fear grew inside me—I doubted Hannah would do this sort of thing on her own and I also doubted that the Romes would let her take the fall for a crime they may have had a hand in.

"This is definitely fucked up," Anita gestured at the television screen Watson and I watched in the kitchen. Watson pulled her onto the barstool next to his and wrapped his arms about her shoulders.

"I need to see her," I announced. "I have to ask her a question."

"Look, this is no time to taint yourself further by getting anywhere near that bitch," Anita huffed.

"I may need your help to get to her," I said, ignoring Anita's warning.

"Why in the name of all the stars would I do that?"

"Because I'm afraid that isn't Hannah."

"What the fucking hell?" Watson stared at me in disbelief.

"Look, even if that isn't Hannah, what can we do about it?" Anita argued. "The authorities have her and they've made positive ID. I'm assuming that means fingerprints, Lexsi. We may be walking into a trap if we attempt to get in and ask questions."

"But that may be an innocent person sitting in jail," I countered. "Her only crime may be looking like Hannah. How, I have no idea, but something is up."

"See my previous trap reference," Anita's fists were on her hips, and if she were in her alternate form, I imagined her scales would be bristling, too.

"Fine. What do you want me to do, then?"

"Give it a day or two," Anita said. "Let's see how this shakes out. Surely you can wait until Monday."

"All right—maybe Hannah's old boss will be interested in visiting her. If I'm lucky, he'll ask for someone to come with him."

"I doubt that will happen, but sure. Whatever will keep you away from that jail is fine by me."

"You're really concerned about this, aren't you?" I asked. I couldn't recall Anita ever arguing this passionately about anything before. Her deep, green eyes studied me for a moment before she jerked her head in a nod.

"All right. We'll let this go for now, but I'm still saying that probably isn't Hannah. I'm worried the real, murdering Hannah is off somewhere, enjoying wine and pool boys at the Romes' expense."

"Pool boys? Damn, it sucks to be working middle class," Anita sighed. I smiled as the tension left her body.

"Hey, what about Watson?" I asked.

"Sex only—he made that clear in the beginning," she said. "And I'm okay with that."

"Then I hope it's damn good," I frowned at her.

"It's more than adequate," she grinned.

"Then I guess it's a good thing he's eating a sandwich on the back patio and isn't here to listen to you describe him as adequate."

"Hey, I said more than adequate," she pointed a finger at me. "Actually, it's downright hot, but I didn't want you to be jealous."

"Of what?"

"The fact that you're not getting sex."

"Oh, we had to play the sex card, huh?" My arms were now crossed over my chest. Did she know I was inexperienced in that department? Here I was, never having had sex with any male and feeling jealous, just as she'd said. Sure, I'd been promised to someone since I was an infant, therefore I'd pushed others away.

Perhaps I shouldn't have done that. If I'd taken what they offered, I wouldn't feel like such an ignorant klutz if I got the opportunity to have sex with Kory.

Since I'd learned he wasn't human, it raised my hopes that he'd understand when he discovered what I really was.

Kory, I want to sleep with you, I sent, glad for once that he would never hear a word of what I'd just admitted to him.

Kordevik

I choked on my drink, I was so shocked. No doubt she'd be embarrassed when she learned I could hear her mindspeech.

It didn't stop my cock from stiffening, either, at the blatant invitation. Another drink and a cool shower might be in order, to combat the effect Lexsi's mindspeech had on my body.

~

Lexsi

"Hannah just pled guilty at her arraignment." Barry, Lee's former assistant, informed me on the phone.

That's when I knew it wasn't Hannah who'd been arrested. She'd never capitulate, even in the face of overwhelming evidence.

"They're moving her to the county jail in San Bruno tomorrow," Barry added. "No word on what sort of time she'll do. We'll have a weekend reporter there—every other station will be there, too, so we have to have a presence."

"Do you want me to be there?" I asked.

"No. Separate yourself from this, Silver," he said. "You don't need anyone approaching you with questions."

"Yeah, I see your point," I agreed.

"If anybody manages to track you down, the standard response is *no comment*," he reminded me.

"Got it. Thanks for the update."

"I'll let you know if anything else crops up."

"Thanks, Barry. See you Monday," I said and ended the call.

~

Hannah's move to the San Bruno facility was scheduled Sunday afternoon. Both of Hannah's male assistants, who seldom showed up at the station, had refused to comment. If requests had come to the station, asking for a comment from me, they'd apparently been deflected already.

Local and national media were speculating wildly about the whole thing, and bashing News Seventy-Four for refusing to comment. In my estimation, it was a no-win situation. They did report that Lee had officially suspended Hannah before he left, and the murder took place shortly afterward.

Lee refused to comment, like everyone else. I had no idea what word, if any, had come from the Romes, and I wondered at the fact that they were content to allow their company to lose half its value in a single weekend.

After all, I suspected that they'd engineered the entire debacle, just to get the authorities away from Hannah and her willingness to do whatever it took to get information she wasn't allowed to have.

My guess was that whoever had the stolen wristband was either named Rome or employed by or associated with someone named Rome.

Aunt Bree hadn't said to take Granger or Claudia down. She'd told me to take the Romes down. I assumed they were at the bottom of this mess, with potential outside help.

Perhaps the devil that Watson mentioned.

In all my studies and research, I'd never heard of a race that called themselves such. There were demons, of course—High, Greater and Lesser. Every kind of shapeshifter you could imagine, creatures not dreamed of in any Earthling's imagination, too, but no actual devils.

Watson said he'd thought they meant *the* devil, but I doubted Granger would align himself with someone who reportedly handled fire on a regular basis.

Fire and vampires didn't mix well.

Fire and werewolves didn't mix well, either.

Frustration mounted as I stared at my corkboard in the study. Sure, I had another weapon in my arsenal, but what good did it do to become mist when I couldn't decide where to go first?

Gran would know—she and my mother were good at this sort of thing. Instead, the mystery lay in my inexperienced hands, and I was mucking it up.

Kory, I sent, *Watson heard somebody say the devil was with Granger. Like it was a real person. What does this mean?*

I didn't keep the anguished frustration from my mental voice. He wouldn't hear anything anyway, and it helped to say the words, even if they were silent.

My cell phone rang ten seconds later.

"Want to go out tonight?" Kory asked. "I think we can arrange to be almost invisible, and get some work done at the same time."

"Yes," I said, my voice breathless. "What time?"

"Meet me at Tibby's gym. You have that address?"

"Yeah, he left it here in case we wanted to go," I said.

"Good. Be there around eight. Go inside—I'll find you."

"Okay." Excitement began to rise—*I was going to see Kory.*

"Baby, I love you. I hope you know that," he said and hung up.

I'd have floated on clouds the rest of the day, except for one thing.

Fiona Hall, who still had her press credentials, showed up for Hannah's transfer. While other reporters shouted questions at Hannah, Fiona pulled a gun from her bag and began shooting. Hannah died before Fiona did—in the crossfire, as guards and police fired their weapons to defend themselves.

I felt shaky as I made my way inside Tibby's gym. Hannah and Fiona's deaths disturbed me greatly—after all, I doubted that Hannah was actually dead. A doppelganger had likely died in her place.

Fiona—even with Hannah ruining her life, didn't seem the type to shoot anyone. Was this the Romes' way of tidying loose ends, and serving the world tasty, titillating news as a main course?

I'd begun to look at everything with suspicion, as a result.

"I'm here," Kory spoke as I walked through the door.

He and Mason had come. Both wore hooded sweatshirts and jeans. Anyone would have had to get very close to recognize either.

My hopes were crushed that Kory and I would get time alone. Shoving those thoughts aside, I went to him and wrapped my arms around his waist.

"It's okay," Kory rumbled against my hair as his arms folded about me. I hadn't realized how chilled I was until he warmed me.

"What are we going to do?" I pulled away and lifted my eyes to his.

"We're going to do a bit of sleuthing," he gave a wry smile. "I still can't get Claudia's new home address out of Watson, so we're going to visit a few vineyards that have sold recently."

"I guess you heard about Hannah and Fiona," I sighed and dropped my gaze.

"Yeah. Doesn't make much sense. Come on, onion. Time's wasting."

Kory placed an arm around my shoulders and we followed Mason out the door and into the parking lot. Mason was scenting the air and listening carefully as we made our way to a late model SUV.

"This is our loaner," Kory explained as he climbed into the passenger seat after putting me in the back. "Mason got information from Davis and Thomas on the vineyard sales, so we're going to check things out."

"Good. I'm glad to be doing something useful," I said. "Sitting at home, trying to figure this mess out is driving me crazy."

"We're going to the area around Sonoma," Mason said. "Four vineyards sold there in the past year. Since we don't know exactly when Claudia made the purchase, we're checking all leads."

"Thanks for inviting me," I said. Mason pulled out of the gym's parking lot and headed for the highway.

"I thought you could use some distraction, after the day's events," Kory leaned around his seat to grin at me.

Damn, you're handsome, I sent. It was something I'd never say to him in person—at least not while Mason was with us. Kory blinked at me before turning back in his seat.

Deaf as a post. I sighed and settled in. Sonoma was nearly fifty miles away from San Francisco. We had a long drive ahead of us.

The first two places were small, boutique wineries completely unsuitable for habitation by a werewolf. The missing wine cellar described by Watson was also a definitive sign. The third winery, however, was the farthest out and looked as if it had possibilities.

"Klancy and I can come back to investigate, if Davis agrees," Mason said, driving past so he could find a place to turn around. Even from the road, we could see the huge doors leading into the man-made wine cave.

If the doors were any indication, it looked as if the cave were large enough to drive trucks inside.

The house was situated farther up a hill and looked down upon rows of neatly planted grapevines. Intermittent moonlight revealed the trellis system employed to support the vines.

If this were Claudia's new place, she had to hire workers to tend the vineyard. If she didn't, she'd eventually be surrounded by an overgrown vineyard and rotting fruit.

Although I hadn't paid much attention to moon phases, I now realized the moon was waxing toward full, which meant Watson and every other werewolf and shifter would be turning on that night.

In fact, they were already feeling the effects of the moon's pull, since we were two or three days away. At least Watson hadn't been growly or upset when I spoke to him earlier; some werewolves were— a full week before and after—a full moon.

"Here's a good place to turn around," Kory pointed to a small side road on the property. The road was fenced and gated, with a lock on the metal gate. It didn't matter; we had enough room to turn in and back around to go out the way we came.

The moment we passed the main gate leading to the house, however, vehicle lights blinked on and a van pulled out behind us.

I think all of us realized it wasn't a good thing.

Mason hit the gas, causing the wheels to spit gravel at the vehicle behind us. If they'd been out on a normal errand, we'd have left them behind.

Instead, they sped up, too, until they were almost on our bumper. I screamed when our back window shattered—they'd fired weapons at us, spraying chunks of glass everywhere. Yes, I should have considered going to mist, but I was so terrified I couldn't think for a few seconds as more bullets hit the back of our vehicle.

Those same few seconds happened differently for Kory.

He disappeared from the front seat.

The loud crunch and subsequent screech of brakes behind us made me turn my head immediately. With the window shot out, I had an unimpeded view of a High Demon in his smaller Thifilathi punching right through the windshield of the van tailing us.

When the van squealed to a fishtailing stop in the middle of the road, Mason jerked the wheel of our vehicle and pulled over.

He and I were out of the car swiftly, but by that time, the full Thifilathi had made his presence known.

At seventeen feet or so, neither the van nor its inhabitants were any match for him. The van and everything in it was ablaze when the High Demon Thifilathi lifted the vehicle in large hands and casually tossed it into the vineyard. Some of the vines caught fire quickly.

Blowing clouds of smoke before emitting a terrible roar, the Thifilathi threw back his head and beat his chest.

By any standards, he was a perfect specimen of black-scaled High Demon maleness. Massive wings unfurled at his back. Large, curved horns, much like a ram's only black as jet, curled about his ears. Eyes, mere slits of burning red, gazed upon the wreckage he'd carelessly pitched thirty feet.

Snorting more smoke, he turned his gaze upon us.

Then, just as I feared, he became humanoid.

Kory, his clothes missing because they had burned from his body in the change, walked toward me.

My mind, as frozen as it had been, now worked furiously.

Kory.

Kordevik.

I kept my eyes on Kordevik Weth as he stalked toward me.

Whatdoldo? Whatdoldo?

Fuck.

Suddenly, I was pissed.

"Why didn't you tell me?" I shouted at him. I dropped to my knees and buried my face in my hands.

"Why didn't you tell me?" I wept.

CHAPTER 16

*K*ordevik

When she stopped crying, I attempted to talk to her.

She wasn't having it. I couldn't determine whether she was too angry, or merely confused and angry.

Either way, it didn't look good for me. Mason stayed behind to drive the car back to the safe house; I'd skipped back with Lexsi in my arms.

At least I was dressed, now. Normally I wasn't embarrassed by nudity, but Lexsi wasn't used to it. I dressed quickly after settling her on the sofa and wrapping her in a blanket.

"Lexsi, baby, stop shivering," I coaxed. Her eyes met mine for a moment before she turned her head away. "I can hold you and get you warm," I offered.

No response.

"Come on," I whispered. "Let me hold you. I'm not going to hurt you, I promise." It took a bit of effort because she wasn't completely cooperative, but eventually I held her, blanket and all, in my arms.

"Want me to take you back to your place?" I whispered against her

230

hair. She huddled closer against me. "Baby, tell me what you're thinking," I coaxed.

"Difik," she smacked her palm against my chest. I couldn't help but chuckle.

"Everything all right?" Mason walked in and dropped the car keys on the coffee table.

"I think we're fine," I said. "I just need some alone time with Miss Lexsi."

"I can go," Mason offered.

"No. I'll take her somewhere else. Come on, onion, let's go."

Lexsi

I was mad at Kory. And I wasn't. Mixed emotions ran through me, which alternately caused me to feel nauseated and furious. Neither of those things meant I never wanted to see him again, or talk to him again; it just ended up confusing me.

Be gentle with Kory when you discover his secret. He loves you.

Aunt Bree's words came back to me. I wanted to yell at her, too, because she knew who he was and didn't tell me, either. Instead, I was a shivering mess as I considered how Kory's revelation forced my perception of him to change so dramatically.

Uncle Kevis would say that my shivering was caused by the aftereffects of an Adrenalin surge, which resulted in unsteadiness when Kory placed me on my feet. I understood now what Kevis always said could happen if I found myself in such a tense, dangerous situation.

The bullet that shattered the SUV's back window could have killed me in human form. Kory, realizing the same thing, had leapt to my rescue. I'd watched firsthand as he'd destroyed the ones who'd followed us; they'd tried to kill us, first.

"Where are we going?" My voice wobbled as I tugged the blanket tighter about me. I felt cold. Perhaps it was the natural drop in blood sugar and blood pressure after the Adrenalin rush.

"How about coffee at your place, baby?" Kory pulled me against him again. "With lots of sugar and cream?"

"All right."

So many things lay between us. What would he say about me leaving him at the altar and running away? How had he ended up here, too? It couldn't be a coincidence. Suddenly, I felt like weeping.

"It's natural," Kory wiped a tear off my cheek. "Come on, I'll skip us over."

"Decaf," Kory told Anita as he settled me on a barstool at the island. She was in the kitchen, waiting for us to arrive.

Kory had mindspeech.

"Oh, my God," I mumbled and covered my face with both hands.

"Hey, what's wrong?" Kory attempted to pull my hands away.

"You have mindspeech," I burbled between fingers.

"Yeah. That. I had to take a cold shower after one of your recent sendings," he said.

Anita had no idea what we were talking about while I, in my utter stupidity, had confessed to Kordevik Weth that I wanted to sleep with him.

"I thought you were human," I dropped my hands and my gaze. "Or shifter. Not," I waved an unsteady hand.

"I know."

"You're like two people. I think of you as Kory, when you're really," I breathed a heavy sigh.

"Kordevik Weth, former fiancé," he admitted.

"Former?" Anita huffed. "When did that happen? When were you engaged? This is completely confusing." She thumped a mug of decaf in front of me.

"We were engaged when she was a baby," Kory admitted.

"Oh. Now I see the light," Anita said. "Here. Your decaf, demon of the high persuasion."

"More like seeing the fire and not the light," I huffed. After a moment, I realized Kory was attempting to suppress a laugh.

"So, what happened?" Anita asked, taking a seat on the opposite side of the island and lifting a cup of decaf to her lips.

"I taught some of Claudia's minions a lesson after they shot at us earlier," Kory rubbed the back of his neck uncomfortably.

"In other words," I supplied, "they're toast. In a very real sense. Their van, too. Maybe some of Claudia's grapevines on top of that."

"Well done, you," Anita grinned at Kory.

"I'm concerned about retaliation," Kory admitted. "I followed my instincts when I did what I did, but I figure they'll know who to blame for it."

"That means we need to keep Watson away from Claudia," Anita said. "Or we could have a hostage situation on our hands."

"Fuck," Kory shook his head. "You're right. Fuck."

Listening to Kory and Anita discuss the possibilities and methods of retaliation by Claudia and Granger helped me to calm down. Eventually the shaking stopped, too, and I was grateful.

It didn't keep me from feeling embarrassment every time I recalled my mindspeech to Kory, though. When I let the blanket slip off my shoulders, Kory reached over and ran a hand down my back and up my ribs.

I had no idea that would kindle a different kind of fire. I wanted to complain when he took his hand away.

"Anita, will you excuse us?" Kory asked.

"Sure," she shrugged. I watched her mouth, she'd hidden a frown.

Something passed between them, then, because she nodded and slipped off her barstool.

"Huh?" I turned to Kory as Anita shuffled through the hall toward her bedroom.

"It's all right," Kory held up a hand. "I just wanted to say that we need to give this some time, onion. You know what happens if I kiss you. I want you to ask for my kiss, and be sure that you mean it, before we go any further."

With that, he skipped away, leaving me alone in the kitchen.

~

Monday morning, I was furious with the world. Furious with Kory, furious with Anita and furious with Lee's replacement, who hadn't even arrived yet. Barry was in charge for the moment, until self-important and probable aggrandizer Milton Landreth arrived to take over Lee's office.

The only good news that morning was that George sent an e-mail, saying that he'd gotten a call to interview with Lee at News Eighty-Two.

In the interim, while I and every other employee in the building had growing anxiety, I settled in to do more research on DSG Enterprises.

I also received an e-mail from Marine Animal Sanctuary, saying that the problem of dead seals had cleared up in the Bay area, but now dead animals were washing up on a beach in Colombia.

Colombia wasn't their problem, though, so they were exhibiting signs of relief. I didn't know what to make of the information, so I tabled it for the moment.

That resolved one of the items Hannah eliminated from Vann's list of investigations. The other one she'd dropped—Abe and Donna Raven's murders—was still there waiting, as long as I continued looking into it on the sly.

DSG Enterprises commanded most of my attention, however. The *G* could stand for Granger, but the *D* and *S* stumped me. After all, if the Romes were in this with Claudia and Granger, the other two letters didn't match at all. That led me to believe that Granger wouldn't be so obvious with his involvement.

That's when it hit me.

Why hadn't I considered talking to other guests who'd gone to the Rome's anniversary party? Some of them had to know that the Ravens attended.

Like Mike, had they seen or heard something they shouldn't, resulting in a death plot carried out by the Romes or Granger?

I also recalled that the Ravens' supposed murderer, Reece Channing, had moved from the LA area shortly before the murders.

Perhaps I should talk to the Ravens' daughters, too. Everybody else had dropped the case, including the police. They considered Reece to be the murderer, and she'd conveniently offed herself after killing the Ravens.

I considered that the Ravens may have become something of an inconvenience to the Romes, who arranged to off them using someone who'd had no connections but had likely been obsessed.

The Romes appeared to be master manipulators—they'd killed the Ravens, then engineered the scenario where Jeremy Rollins was murdered by Hannah, who was then killed by Fiona, who subsequently died from gunshot wounds after being shot by the police. I still believed the real Hannah to be alive and hidden away, however.

Anita, I sent. *See if you can bribe away the guest list for the Romes' anniversary party.*

You're speaking to me now?

Only because I want something.

Fine. I'll see what I can do. Have you heard from Kory?

You mean my ex?

He's your ex, now?

He pushed me away last night. You tell me.

Yes, I was still upset and angry.

I'll get the list. Anything else?

No.

New boss there yet?

No.

Let me know how it goes. If you're still speaking to me.

I'll consider it.

"Lexsi?" Barry appeared at my cubicle.

"Hi Barry, what's up?" I asked, shutting down my mental conversation with Anita.

"Mr. Landreth's here. He wants to see you."

"Sure."

Barry looked guilty, in my estimation. That meant Mr. Landreth didn't have good news. That was fine with me. If he wanted to fire or demote me, well, Aunt Bree said to take the Romes down. I would do it, whether I was employed by them or not.

"Come in, Ms. Silver," Milton Landreth answered my knock. He had reddish-blond hair, ruddy good looks for a man in his fifties and I didn't trust the smile he wore. "Please, sit," he invited.

I sat, although I'd have preferred to remain standing. Forcing myself not to fidget, I waited for him to announce his intentions.

"I have good news," he grinned. "The Romes want to move you to the LA station. You'll have a bigger market and you'll be reporting there on weekends."

~

"I told him I'd think about it," I slammed my coffee cup on the breakroom counter and reached for the coffeepot. Farin, biting her lip in shock, stood nearby, hoping I'd give her a better answer than that.

I imagined that the Romes wanted to start manipulating me, just as they were manipulating so many others. Did they imagine that their pet Sirenali could lay an obsession and I'd do whatever they wanted, like Hannah had?

Or—did they intend to lay a trap? Would they pull me away from Aunt Bree's house, which was evidently protected in some way, and move me to an unprotected home in the LA area, where they could attack at will?

I considered telling Kory, but recalled that I was pissed at him.

"Want to talk about it over lunch? I'm meeting Tibby for pizza at one," Farin said.

"I need to make some calls," I said. It was an excuse, but I did want to contact the Raven's daughters. I could skip home and call from there, so I'd have privacy. I suspected Milton was watching me already; I didn't trust his smile and friendly attitude for a moment.

So far, nothing he'd said was a lie, but there was more beneath his words and I hadn't had the courage to demand answers.

Kordevik

I considered that I may have been too abrupt with Lexsi. I hadn't heard from her. Anita let me know that Lexsi was short with her, too. I'd laid down an ultimatum, which, in retrospect, wasn't the smartest thing I'd ever done.

Weth, you should have said you'd take it slow so she wouldn't feel pressured, I mentally chastised myself. *Instead, you let your cock do the talking and now she's not speaking to you.*

After all, what woman doesn't want to jump somebody, knowing the male will put his teeth in her neck, marking her for life? Yes, my mental conversation was filled with sarcasm.

She didn't know it wouldn't be a painful memory; Li'Neruh Rath had seen to that. She'd only known me for a short time, too. Claiming marks meant forever.

Lexsi was barely twenty-three, and descended from a race where the women weren't fully mature until twenty-two. I was more than a thousand years old. I should have better sense.

You've never been engaged before, a small voice reminded me. *Never been in love like this, either.*

Perhaps I should apologize.

Better yet, apologize and send flowers. My hand was on my cell phone before I could talk myself out of it.

Lexsi

The house was quiet when I skipped into the kitchen; Klancy would be asleep in one of the bedrooms, but no matter how much noise I made, he wouldn't wake.

I still didn't intend to make much noise. Pulling out my cell phone, I scrolled through my contacts until I found Maya Raven's number. I'd added her and her sister Nela's numbers only that morning.

Punching the number, I listened to it ring three times.

"Maya Raven's office, how may I help you," she said, sounding completely professional. She should, she was a popular realtor, whose clients' homes were worth millions.

"Hello, Ms. Raven. This is Lexsi Silver from News Seventy-Four," I identified myself. "Is it all right if I ask a few questions about your parents?"

"I'm surprised you called," she said, assuming a less formal tone. "The police have given up on the case."

"So you don't think Reece Channing is responsible?"

"My father wasn't having an affair. That's ludicrous," Maya huffed. "I have no idea who Reece Channing was, and I doubt my father knew her, either."

"I think so, too," I agreed. "Did you talk to your parents before their murder?"

"I talked to them three days before," Maya said. "They'd just gotten back from a trip to Peru."

"Peru? Was it a vacation?"

"No. Dad said it was to check out an investment property. When I spoke with him after they got back, he said something sounded fishy about the whole thing and he'd decided not to invest."

"Do you know who the investment was with? Did he say?"

"No, he just said some friends told him about it. I didn't ask questions because I really wasn't curious. I only wanted to know how they were doing."

"I understand that," I said. "I'm merely concerned that the investment thing may be more important than you thought."

I did think that. The moment Maya said Peru and investment, my skin tingled. Something was going on, and I hoped I could put things together before more bodies piled up.

"I'll ask Nela," Maya offered. "Can she call you back at this number?"

"Of course. I'd be happy to speak with her, if she has more information."

"Thank you for calling, Ms. Silver. I was beginning to think the world had forgotten my parents' murders."

"I didn't forget, and I intend to get to the bottom of this," I said. "Thank you for taking my call."

~

I had no way of researching investment properties or sales of such in Peru, at least not through normal channels. That's why my next call was to Davis Stone, werewolf agent for the Joint NSA/Homeland Security Department.

"I hate to ask this," I began after he barked a hello. "But is there some way to find out if a corporation called DSG Enterprises has recently made a purchase of a business or land in Peru?"

"The same DSG that currently owns Tooth and Nail?" he asked.

"Yeah. That one," I agreed. I attributed Davis's shortness to the approaching full moon, which was two days away.

"I'll check into it," he said and hung up.

"Well, as short conversations go," I stared at my cell phone. The screen went black after only a few seconds.

Feeling somewhat defeated, I made a sandwich and ate quickly, so I could go back to work.

~

Kordevik

"Yes, delivered this afternoon, if possible," I said. I'd found a florist near News Seventy-Four's station, so the delivery wouldn't take very long. Lexsi would have two dozen red roses and an apology before the day was over.

~

Lexsi

When I got back to the station, I had an e-mail waiting from Dan Logan. He wanted to see me in his office before he went home late that afternoon.

On my way, I e-mailed back and left my cubicle.

"Hey, Lexsi," Dan offered a grin when I knocked on his open door. "Come in and have a seat. Oh, and close the door, if you wouldn't mind."

"Sure." I shut the door and moved to sit on one of Dan's guest chairs.

"I got this earlier today," he said and turned his computer monitor around so I could see. The e-mail was from someone at a Sausalito police station, who said they'd discovered a body inside a rent house. The man had been dead for a while.

"Who?" I blinked at Dan after reading the e-mail.

"Private detective," Dan said. "Everything has been removed from his downtown Sausalito office. Friends thought he was out of the country, working on a case. Turns out, he was dead and not far away the whole time. A neighbor reported the smell yesterday, at the empty rent house. Somebody went to check and they found the body inside. Had to ID using fingerprints and dental records."

"Wow. So he was working on something and somebody took offense?"

"Looks that way. His files, cell phone and anything else that may have been important were taken. Thing was, the office was locked up the whole time and a hall camera outside didn't show anybody going in or out of there. Windows still locked, too, and the camera from a business across the street shows nothing."

"You think this is worth reporting?" I asked.

"I'd do it, but you know what the edict is on high—or was," Dan shook his head. "Feed everything to Hannah, except Hannah broke the law and now she's dead for being a spiteful bitch."

"Yes, and Fiona is dead along with her," I sighed. Dan pulled the monitor back around and minimized the e-mail.

"Very true," he agreed. "This is a mess, no matter how you look at it. I don't know about you, but Milton Landreth gives me hives."

"I feel the same way," I said. "You heard he wants to move me to LA?"

"You gonna take it?"

"I don't think so, but I said I'd consider it and I will."

"I'll present this to Milton," Dan said. "I'll see what, if anything, he wants to do about reporting this death. Police are asking for information, and we have the jump on the other stations for now. If Milton drags his feet we'll be left behind, because my source will go to the other stations later today."

"Yeah, I get that," I said. "Thanks for the info. One more thing," I said as I stood. "Do you have any information on who owned the rent house?"

"Nothing yet; my source says they're still investigating. I'll let you know if I hear anything."

"Thanks."

"Lexsi," Farin's head appeared over my cubicle wall.

"How was lunch?" I asked. "Isn't it time you went home?" I'd been doing research after I left Dan's office. Dead ends appeared to be my constant destination.

"Lunch was good, and yes, I'm leaving in a minute. Tibby's picking me up," she smiled. "But you had a flower delivery earlier. Milton said he'd see you got them. Where are they?" She surveyed my cubicle with an analytical eye.

"I didn't get any flowers," I said.

"Oh. Maybe Milton forgot. He took them to his office."

"Yeah? Who were they from?"

"Kory, who else?" Farin said brightly.

"I didn't get any flowers," I repeated, feeling numb. Something troubled me about the fact that Milton had taken my flowers to his office, when everyone at the station knew they were from Kory, and also knew who Kory was.

Granger had a price on Kory's head.

Granger knew the Romes.

Kory sent me flowers.

"I have to go," I said. "Make sure Tibby is careful driving you home."

"Huh?" Farin expressed her confusion as I slipped off my chair and headed for Lee's old office. For me, Milton hadn't earned it and never would.

Just before I reached the office door, Milton walked out of it, my vase of flowers in his hands. A smile crossed his face as he held the vase out for me, then pulled the door shut the moment I accepted the flowers.

He didn't think I'd seen them—the people in his office. They hadn't come in the usual way, either, because I'd have seen them.

Somebody Milton knew could fold space or skip.

"Thank you," I said, pretending to sniff one of the roses. "Aren't they gorgeous?" I turned and strode back to my cubicle. A worry nagged at me as I set the flowers down on my desk.

There were two possibilities. The first, of course, was that somewhere, hidden in two dozen roses, was a tiny electronic bug that would track the vase wherever it went. I suspected that once it entered the perimeter Aunt Bree set around the house, it would no longer work.

The second was this, and it was ultimately worse. If the Romes had a wizard or warlock in their employ, whatever spell they'd placed on the vase hadn't worked the moment it came close to me.

Only one race in all those I'd studied had that ability, unless you were counted among the gods. High Demons nullified spells. At all times, a sixteen-foot diameter of spell-nullifying space surrounded me.

All a spell-wielder had to do was attempt to set off a spell around me to know what they were dealing with.

Yes, all this was conjecture on my part, but any wizard or warlock would run this test if they suspected anything.

I also worried that the spell would become active, once I left the sixteen-foot perimeter behind. It could explode in someone's face, as a worst-case scenario. At best, it could be a simple listening spell, meant to capture friends' conversations.

It broke my heart to consider it, but I'd have to get rid of Kory's flowers.

That's why I called Farin, and told her I was coming to her office for a conversation about weather.

"I need you to cover for me," I whispered, clutching the vase as tightly as I could. "Start talking about tornadoes, and explain in detail how they happen, okay? I'll be back in a couple of minutes."

Farin, her eyes wide in alarm, nodded, before opening with the standard about unstable weather in spring, fed by cold air from the north, which met with warmer, moist air from the gulf.

I skipped away.

Somewhere between LA and Las Vegas, there are empty stretches of desert. I landed there first, before searching for a suitable mountaintop. Somewhere I wouldn't be seen, and if the vase exploded, it wouldn't be seen, either.

Yes, the spell maker would be alerted that his intended target could also skip or fold space, but at this point, he was already aware.

If that's what this was.

A part of me worried that I was destroying Kory's beautiful flowers because I was paranoid. Another part chastised me for thinking it. If there were any chance of danger to someone else hidden in those lovely buds, then I had to get rid of them.

I gazed over the edge of the small space I stood upon, at the crevice far below. Setting the vase down carefully, I pulled the note off to read it.

Lexsi, I'm sorry for being such a troglodyte, Kory wrote. *We'll work through this, I promise—Love, Kory.*

I wept as I set the card among the roses again, before lifting the vase over the edge and letting it go. I skipped away the moment the vase exploded, sixteen feet down.

CHAPTER 17

Lexsi

It took another ten minutes to get a replacement bouquet from the same florist, with one of their cards. When I skipped back to Farin's office with the flowers, she looked as if she'd gone through a shredder.

By that time, she was talking about wind speeds and levels of destruction.

"Wow, that's really fascinating, Farin," I said.

"You've been crying," she hissed softly.

"I'll tell you why, later," I whispered. "Do you have facts and figures on some of the worst tornadoes?" I asked aloud. "I think I'd like to do a piece on that, sometime. I'd like your help to do it, too."

"Anytime," Farin agreed. "Thanks for bringing the flowers down to show me. They're awesome."

"The vase Kory sent exploded," I shook my head at Anita and fingered a replacement bud. Anita was at home already when I skipped in with vase of roses number two.

"Have you told Kory?"

"I haven't. How am I going to tell him this?"

"By opening your mouth and saying the words?"

"It'll make me cry," I admitted. "I cried when I dropped them off the mountain."

"He still needs to know," Anita pointed out.

"Yeah. I know. I just feel stupid, and I never want to go back to that station again. Somebody I didn't know was in Milton's office, and they didn't get there in traditional human fashion."

"They want to trap you, one way or another," Anita agreed. "Kory, too. That spells Granger to me."

"This makes me wish I were my mother. Or even Great Aunt Glinda," I said. "Both of them have experience taking down some of the worst people ever."

"Like who?"

"Well, the San Gerxon brothers, to name two," I shrugged. "Know about them?"

"Hmmph. Anybody from either Alliance knows about them," Anita huffed. "Quite the family, there."

"Yeah."

"Ask Kory to dinner. I'll help cook—you look worn out," Anita said.

"Yeah." I hunched my shoulders and made myself smaller on the barstool I occupied.

"Then I'll do it," she said.

"Wait," I held out a hand. It was already too late; Kory stood in my kitchen.

"Boy, do we have a story for you," Anita announced. "Have a seat. This could take a while."

Kordevik

"So they know."

"About me, at least." Lexsi hugged herself.

"Then that's that," I said. "You're not going back there. Send them your resignation by e-mail or go to the downtown office and turn it in. You're not going back to that station." I didn't stop the cloud of smoke that blew from my nostrils. This was more than upsetting; they'd tried to kill Lexsi or draw her out.

"But," Lexsi said. "Farin still has to go back there. George has put in his two weeks' notice because Lee hired him at Eighty-Two, but he's there, too. Anita works downtown. Officially, you still work for them."

"That will end shortly," I fumed.

"They'll go after somebody we know if they can't get to us," Lexsi wiped tears away. "The worst part? We still don't know what they're up to."

"Then let's make sandwiches and go take a look at Lexsi's corkboard in the study," Anita suggested quietly.

I sat on the edge of the desk, Lexsi in the crook of my arm as we walked through the points Lexsi had on her board. She'd added the news about a dead private investigator, too—off to the side with a question mark beside his photograph.

"I really need to talk to some of those people on the Romes' guest list," Lexsi shook her head. "Maya Raven said her parents had recently returned from a trip to Peru before going to the Rome party. She said that they'd gone there to check on a potential investment, but decided it wasn't their thing."

"What sort of investment?" I pulled her tighter and placed a kiss on her temple.

"She didn't know, all she said was her dad, Abe Raven, said it sounded fishy."

"Fishy as in suspect, or fishy like the seals getting bitten in the Bay?" Anita asked.

"Surely he'd have said something if it was seal-biting fishy," Lexsi replied.

"We don't know that, onion," I breathed against her hair. "Has there been any connection made between Abe Raven and the private investigator? Was he having the investment thing investigated—quietly? Did somebody find out and have them both killed?"

"I don't think I can hack into financial records, but I know somebody who can," Lexsi said. "Should we call Davis and Thomas and let them know what's happening? I mean, if the private investigator was involved somehow, then somebody had to pay him, right?"

I called Davis.

"We've hit a dead end," Davis admitted. "We'll come by and take a look."

"If you tell me where you are, I'll come get you," I offered.

"Yeah—best if this happens tonight; tomorrow is the full moon," Davis agreed. "We'll be at the coffee shop near your condo."

"I'll be there in five," I said and ended the call.

Lexsi

I missed the warmth of Kory's embrace the moment he skipped away. The corkboard on the wall taunted me, too, while he was gone. I watched as Anita went through the whole thing, which looked to be random bits and pieces put together by an amateur.

There, in the center, was the piece of red paper with *DSG Enterprises* written in broad strokes with a felt-tip pen.

Peru, land of the Incas, was off to the side and near the private investigator's image.

At the top left, at the beginning, was *Abe and Donna Raven.*

Hannah and Fiona were at the bottom center, although I'd placed another question mark beside Hannah's name. I still doubted she was dead.

"Look who I found." Kory had not only brought Davis and Thomas, but Mason, too. That meant Klancy was up and guarding the house.

"Anita, will you bring Klancy in?" I asked. "He may have some insights we don't. Watson, too, if he's home."

"I'll look for him, but I didn't see him come in earlier," she said. "He didn't leave a note, either, telling me where he was going."

"That's not good," Kory blew a smoky breath.

I wanted to tell him I could do that, too, but it didn't seem ladylike at the moment. He'd guess I could become Thifilatha, and that didn't sound ladylike either.

Fuck ladylike, Gran always said. Just the thought of her made me sigh. She'd have made mincemeat of these assholes already, while I felt less than adequate on the best of days.

Davis brought a tablet and his cell phone. He was on the phone with someone quickly, asking them to research financial records belonging to Abe Raven and the private investigator, Steve Parker.

"Ten thousand?" Davis asked after several seconds ticked by. "When? All right, that matches. Anything else?"

"Plane ticket?" Davis began tapping on the tablet while holding the cell phone to his ear with his shoulder. "To?"

"Yeah. That matches, too. Any chance of getting an itinerary from credit-card purchases?"

"No, that's all right. Look, see if there's been a sale of property anywhere near that. Call me back with the information, okay?"

Davis let the phone slide down his chest, where he caught it neatly in his left hand while still gripping the tablet with his right. "Your hunch is correct—Abe Raven paid the private investigator ten grand and bought him a plane ticket to Peru. He didn't get back until after Raven's murder, so he wasn't killed until then."

"We need to find out what this investment is," Kory said, leaning against me on the desk.

"Credit-card receipts show Parker's visit took him toward the Amazon, in the lower Andean region," Davis said. "That area has a lot of farming—coffee, oranges, that sort of thing."

"Drugs, too," Anita observed. "Lots of cocaine grown in Peru and Colombia. Any idea why you guys can't seem to shut those operations down?"

"We locked up ten drug lords a year ago," Thomas snapped, pointing a finger at Anita. Yeah, it wasn't a good idea to bait a werewolf the night before a full moon.

"Ten drug lords?" Anita didn't sound impressed.

"Worst of the lot," Davis claimed. "They're in the federal prison in Colorado, right now. They'll be there until they die."

"Did you say ten?" My words wobbled, I was suddenly so scared. "Did they all speak Spanish as a native language?"

"Yeah, why?"

"Did they come from Peru?"

"Six of them, yeah."

"May the Mighty save us," I whispered.

Kordevik

"You have no idea how much red tape is involved in getting DNA samples from ten convicted drug lords," Davis growled. He was so close to turning wolf, even Thomas wore a worried frown.

Lexsi, Anita, Mason, Klancy and I were in the kitchen, waiting until Davis finished a phone conversation with his superiors, which led to a conference call between them and federal authorities at the Denver prison.

Even with modern (by present-day Earth's definition) equipment and procedures, it could still take days to discern whether the DNA of the prisoners matched that of the men originally convicted.

That's when the doorbell rang.

"It won't be anybody who's not allowed," Lexsi's hand covered mine as I half-rose from my seat at the island.

"I will answer," Klancy nodded and almost glided from his seat toward the front door.

In moments, he and Tibby were back in the kitchen. Tiburon was terrified. "Farin is missing," he hissed. "I cannot find her anywhere."

Lexsi

Watson was also missing. He no longer had the TinyCar to protect him, and somehow, he was gone, too. Phone calls to him and Farin went unanswered. Anita, normally not inclined to worry or fidget, was now doing both.

"We have to find where they are," she said. I worried she'd turn right in my kitchen and scare the bejeezus out of everybody. She was thinking the same thing I and everybody else in the kitchen were; that Farin and Watson had been kidnapped.

Anita was a deadly fighter, but it concerned me that we could be facing kidnappers nobody from Earth had ever seen before. Not least among them were warlocks or wizards. Either could go bad, I knew that much.

I'd seen the evidence of one of their spells earlier in the day. I berated myself, too, for not telling Farin that I'd take her home.

"Fuck," I hissed my grandmother's favorite word.

"I'll bet money that Claudia has Watson somewhere at her vineyard," Kory said. "Probably in that wine cave that you could drive a truck through."

"If he's still alive," Anita snapped.

"I have to believe that he is," Kory said. "What good are dead hostages?"

"I think so, too," Davis agreed. "This is a potential hostage situation until we learn otherwise. After all, we have no proof that they're in Claudia's or Granger's hands."

"If there are hostages, there will also be a ransom or other demands," Klancy's words were even and filled with the weight of lives.

Farin, I wish you could hear me, I sent. *I wish you could send mindspeech back, to tell me where you are.*

Unlike my words to Kory, there was nobody on the other end who was able to reply.

While Davis and Thomas made dozens of calls and employed every resource they had (which was considerable), the rest of us spent the worst night of our lives.

Tomorrow was the full moon, we still didn't have sufficient information and continued attempts to contact Farin and Watson proved futile.

My hunch about the ten imprisoned drug lords was still on the table, but we couldn't verify anything. All we had was ten missing migrant workers from a bus, all young men, to offset ten drug lords from Peru and Colombia.

DNA on the prisoners wouldn't be verified for days or weeks.

As it turned out, we didn't have to wait for DNA. Shortly before dawn, when all except the vampires were exhausted from lack of sleep, word came that a simple blood-typing test was all we needed.

Of the ten drug lords imprisoned, six didn't have the proper blood type for the prisoner originally incarcerated. The others appeared to be matches, down to the fingerprints, but I wasn't willing to bet that their DNA would also match. I felt it was merely coincidence that the blood types were the same.

I wanted to yell at Davis, then, about Loftin Qualls, who was probably enjoying his murderous freedom while a double created for that purpose had died in his place.

Davis had enough on his plate, however, and looked like a werewolf who'd been dragged behind a truck for several miles when he heard the news.

"The fucking fingerprints match," he hissed and tossed his cell phone onto the kitchen island. "We have six to ten drug lords who could be in Peru by now, starting up their cocaine operations again. Can we get some coffee?"

"Yeah." I scrambled from my place at the island and slid toward the coffeemaker.

While Davis and Thomas had their third cup, they learned that the kidnap victim who'd shown up in Dallas had a different blood type than the original college student had. At the time, they'd chalked it up to faulty records.

At least we knew more about why he'd disappeared a second time.

Somewhere, other criminals were probably walking free while all those young men were imprisoned in their place.

My guess was that most of them were obsessed or had compulsion placed—our enemies had a Sirenali and plenty of vampires at their backs.

"How can this be done?" Thomas accepted more coffee and a plate of food Anita and I had prepared.

"I told you if there were wizards or warlocks involved, they can do this if they've gone rogue. My guess is a warlock or warlocks, because a duplication spell would be right at any third-to-fifth-level's talents," Kory said.

"You call that a duplication spell? What about the fingerprints?" Davis snarled.

"As long as they have the original, and in this case, they did," Kory explained patiently, "then it would be easy enough. It takes a day or two, last I heard, to get the complete outside to look like the other."

"They were running out of time, in Loftin Qualls' case," I breathed. "That's why the victim who was put to death recalled that he wasn't Loftin Qualls."

Davis' cell phone rang again. "Stone, here," he barked.

"Houses are on fire at the bottom of the hill," he announced after ending the call and setting the phone on the island again. "No cause listed," he added. "Firefighters are on the scene."

"Should I go to work as if nothing's happened? Farin will already be late to work," I said. It was nearly five; I could get there on time if I dressed quickly and skipped to my usual landing place.

I looked from Kory, who was breathing smoke, to Davis, who was considering the idea.

"If I were going to be awake during the day, I would vote no," Klancy said. "I shall retire now, as must Mason. I hope to see you when I awake," he added.

"Thank you," I nodded at Klancy. We watched as both vampires disappeared down the hall toward their shared bedroom.

"I say yes," Davis said. "We need somebody to act normally and without suspicion. That means you, Lexsi. I assume you'll know whether the concern over Farin's absence is real or genuine."

"I don't like this," Kory snarled.

"I can get out of there fast if it doesn't look good," I said.

"Lexsi, you don't have combat experience," Kory said. "I know you can take down three humans in a parking lot," he held up a hand. "But when you're met by those who may not be human?" His dark eyes were slits and his forehead wrinkled as he frowned at me.

"Who else do we have?" I whispered. "I have to go soon, or I'll be late."

"If they ask, tell them you thought Farin spent the night with Tiburon," Davis instructed as I headed for my bedroom and clean clothing.

You'd better keep me informed every step of the way, Kory's voice sounded in my head.

Don't place yourself in danger; skip away if you have to, Anita's voice followed Kory's.

I'll do what I can, I sent to both of them.

I found the note on my bed when I walked into my bedroom.

I blinked at the short message.

Da'quon the'lat vic nacca.

The words were from the Falchani language—the warrior's motto.

First, kill your fear.

My breaths were shaky as I struggled to clear my mind. Uncle Sal would be disappointed in me—that I allowed my emotions to rule my abilities and my actions.

After all, I was High Demon and not susceptible to compulsion, obsession and any spell, unless the spell was meant to help and not hurt. I could skip from one place to another in a blink. I could also turn to mist, thanks to my grandmother.

Lastly, I had a Thifilatha. I hoped it would come when I needed it.

Kory hung his head when I rushed into the kitchen, dressed for work. For any other couple, this is where they'd kiss. He—we—couldn't.

"I have to go," I said, shoving terror down for the hundredth time.

Kory lifted his head; dark eyes locked with mine.

I love you, he said simply. *I will kill anyone who attempts to harm you.*

Yeah, I replied. *Same here.*

Before he could reach out to hug me, I skipped away. I didn't want to cry in front of him and the others. In the coming moments, cold anger could become my staunchest ally. Somebody had Farin and Watson. My guess is that my new boss knew all about that.

I could tell when he was lying. I wondered if Milton understood that yet. Straightening my clothing after landing in the alcove, I marched away, determined to make it to work on time.

~

Kordevik

My father always says that shifters become restless and angry the day of the full moon. I watched those things bloom around me, in werewolves and a rat who hadn't slept the night before.

Should we send them to bed? Anita asked.

I'm not suggesting anything, I jerked my head to emphasize my refusal.

When do you think we'll hear from Lexsi? She asked. I could tell she was just as frightened as I was.

We know where she went, I said, attempting to soothe Anita's fears as well as my own.

I'm here, Lexsi sent, startling Anita and me. *They have Gerald doing the weather reports. He doesn't look happy. Turn on the news. Buildings are on fire near downtown. I have a meeting scheduled with Barry. I'll let you know what I find out.*

~

Lexsi

Barry was now obsessed. I knew it the moment he handed me a contract, freshly concocted by the legal department at the downtown office.

The person who'd written it was also obsessed, because it spelled things out specifically.

Either I accepted the promotion offered by Rome Enterprises, transferred to the LA station and agreed to move into a rather expensive home there (photographs were included), or Farin Armstrong and I were subject to immediate termination.

My breath stopped at the word *termination*.

They didn't mean losing our jobs. They meant losing our lives.

"I told you she'd understand immediately," Milton walked into Barry's office with another man. I blinked at both. "Deris Arden," the stranger introduced himself. "We'd have come in by folding space, but your peculiar talents prevented it."

"Because you employ spells to do it," my lips felt numb as I spoke. "Only those who have the talent naturally are unaffected by my nullification." I didn't add that I knew he could have, if he'd meant me no harm.

This one meant harm. Somehow, the Thifilatha in me understood that better than I did.

"Ah, well educated, too," Deris crowed. "Granger will be most happy to have her, I think."

I wanted to curse—I held it back. I recalled my meeting with Granger at Hannah's dinner party. He'd seen something he wanted. I had no intention of giving it to him.

They have Farin and Watson, a small voice reminded me.

First, kill your fear.

"You get nothing from me until Farin and Watson are safely returned," I said. "Without obsession or compulsion."

"She wants to bargain," Deris smiled at Milton. "How's this for a bargain? We leave both alive and discontinue setting San Francisco on fire?" His subsequent grin betrayed the joy he'd taken in setting homes and businesses on fire already.

"I can seal the buildings, you know, before setting them on fire," Deris added. "So many lives to be lost." His grin faded and he glared at me.

"I'm not the only one you should worry about," I snapped.

"Oh, we have plans for him, too. We think that a threat sent his way involving you will ensure that he'll either obey or leave us alone."

I wanted to ask how we were so dangerous to him and his associates.

I already knew the answer. We could fuck up everything that he, the Romes, Granger and Claudia planned to do with spells as the impetus.

He also knew we had to be in close proximity to prevent the spells from working. "Did you lose a warlock inside a van, recently?" I asked.

Kory had destroyed everything inside the van, then destroyed the van that followed us from Claudia's vineyard.

They considered me the weak link. *They think I can't turn. They think I'm all but human, except for my nullification talent.*

First, kill your fear.

"I want to see Farin and Watson," I said. "So I know they're safe. Then I'll sign this stupid contract." I pointed the papers in my hand toward Milton.

"Ah, she can see reason," Deris chuckled. "Barry, have George bring a van around. We'll make this trip together."

Kordevik

We're heading for Sonoma, Lexsi informed me. She'd already read me the important points in the contract they'd shoved in her hands at work.

I understood, too, that they wanted to blackmail both of us, because we presented a problem for them.

If they don't let you see Farin and Watson, get the hell out of there, I instructed.

I will, but we're still stuck with the asshole warlock, who wants to burn down San Francisco and kill people inside their homes and businesses.

Baby, I'll take care of that problem; you just tell me where you are when the van stops.

But what if it gets Farin killed? I could almost hear the terror in her voice. *She's human,* Lexsi continued. *At least Watson can go down fighting. I doubt Farin knows to knee an attacker in the crotch.*

That's provided they're not under compulsion or obsessed, I reminded her. I realized too late that my observation would only frighten her more.

Kory, I get the idea that Deris isn't the only warlock involved in this, Lexsi said.

Davis strode into the kitchen while I was having my mental conversation with Lexsi.

"Peru just resigned from the Union of South American Nations," he said. "Their borders are now closed and calls from the State Department to the President and Prime Minister have gone unanswered. Guess who filed a flight plan two days ago to take their private jet to Peru? If you say anyone besides James and Laurel Rome, then you're denser than I thought."

"What the hell is that supposed to mean?" I demanded.

"It means that the league of assholes we're dealing with are more serious than I thought about producing cocaine."

"Dude," I snorted a cloud of smoke without attempting to stop it, "cocaine won't be what they're growing. With an outside alliance and local funding, it'll be a lot worse, I assure you. Right now, they have Lexsi, and they're supposed to be taking her to Farin and Watson. That's the only reason I'm still here at the moment. If they threaten her or I find out Farin and Watson are dead, I'm going after them. Lexsi and I pose a major threat to their newly formed kingdom, and they want us out of the way."

"What the hell are you, man?" Davis demanded.

"High Demon. They have Karathian warlocks at their command. If you don't understand how much trouble that can be, then I suggest you learn how to read Alliance common. Entire libraries are dedicated to how much trouble can come from Karathia."

Lexsi

I didn't tell Milton and Deris that I'd already been to this area once before. In fact, I saw the shallow crater and burned grapevines left by Kory's destruction of the van as we drove past. My captors didn't say a word as that section of Claudia's vineyard disappeared behind us.

Yes, I thought of them as my captors, because they considered themselves as such. I intended to get Farin and Watson away when I saw them, while praying to whoever might listen that they were still alive.

The company van, driven by an obsessed George, turned into the long drive that led toward Claudia's home on the hill overlooking acres of grapevines. We took a left, however, before we reached the house.

Just as Kory imagined, the wine cave that eventually came into view was large enough to drive a vehicle into. The double doors opened automatically to allow us inside, then closed behind us.

It would have been very dark inside the man-made cave, had it not been for the fluorescent lighting overhead. I couldn't see where the end of the cave was—farther ahead, that part was still in darkness.

Two smaller caves branched off from the main one on either side; those had been added recently, I could tell.

"If you want to see your friends, step out of the vehicle," Milton ordered.

Without a word, I opened my door and slid off the seat. Only bare walls surrounded me as my shoes touched the concrete floor of the cave.

"They're in the smaller cave on the left," Milton pointed and flashed his teeth in a grin. I wanted to snatch his neck in my hands and see how long it took to kill him. A thin stream of smoke escaped my nostrils as I considered that.

Milton had turned away; he'd missed seeing my cloudy breath.

We're in Claudia's wine cave, I sent to Kory. *I haven't seen Farin or Watson, yet.*

I'm standing by, he responded. *Anita took Davis and Thomas to gather more troops.*

Wait until I see them, I said. *I have no idea what I'll find.*

Understood.

Milton walked ahead of me, Deris behind as we made our way into the smaller cave on the left. My breath stopped for a moment.

Watson's cage was on one side of the cave, Farin's on the other. Both were pressed against the back walls of their cages while a lion snake shapeshifter in snake mode guarded the front. Both cages were small enough that the snakes were within striking distance.

If either hostage were bitten, they'd die within seconds.

Kory, they brought lion snake shapeshifters with them to Earth, I said. *If we manage to save one of ours, the other will die.*

CHAPTER 18

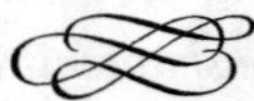

*K**ordevik*

"We have a problem." I scanned the ten werewolf agents currently occupying Lexsi's kitchen, in addition to Davis, Thomas, Anita and Tiburon. I considered the best way to describe lion snake shapeshifters to a crowd of werewolves, a Sirenali and a rat shapeshifter.

Thankfully, Anita knew exactly what I was talking about. Getting the others to believe me took a bit longer.

Meanwhile, Lexsi informed me that another cage had been brought for her. Unlike the others, hers had a chair and no snake inside it.

I wondered if this were merely a concession, or whether the warlock knew that High Demons weren't susceptible to poisons. Perhaps they only had two lion snake shapeshifters and placed them where they'd do the most good to keep Lexsi under control.

Either way, it didn't look good for one of our friends.

What do you think they're waiting for? I sent to Lexsi.

Granger wants me, came the reply. *I think they're waiting for nightfall.*

I cursed at length in the High Demon language before explaining Lexsi's conversation to Davis.

260

"Better for us to wait for nightfall," he shrugged. "We have vamps who can go in with us."

"Not if it gets Farin or Watson killed," Anita snapped. I understood, then, that Anita cared more for Watson than she—or anyone else —thought.

"You know what will happen at nightfall," Tibby said. "It is the full moon, tonight. We cannot handle weapons; we will only have our animals. These snake shapeshifters you describe—they will also become quite dangerous. When the wolf turns, he may be bitten, just from the act of turning. It will be automatic, you understand, and will likely mean his death."

I could hear several growls from werewolf throats. They didn't like that assessment at all. They knew Tibby spoke the truth, however. Our enemy had planned this carefully. The Romes were in Peru, which had now closed its borders. In all probability, the government now in charge of the country would sever all ties with other countries.

The Romes had extremely wealthy friends across the globe. They'd asked for investment funds so they could control an entire country.

The Romes and their partners needed to get Lexsi and me out of the way, probably because we could interfere with the spells their warlocks cast. If they were keeping count, too, on our skirmishes, the scoreboard would read *Enemy—0, Kordevik—3*.

For them, even one High Demon could destroy what they'd built. They had two to contend with, although Lexsi wasn't as great a threat as I was.

This was what we were made for in the beginning, I reminded myself. *To keep the dark worlds in line and prevent them from interfering in the worlds of light.*

In the here and now, Kifirin, our homeworld, was still responsible for those things. That would change in the future, but for now, I felt obligated. My father, Nedevik Weth, would expect nothing less.

We'll work this out, I sent to Lexsi. *Hang on; we have to devise a plan.*

Lexsi

I felt awful that I had a chair to sit on while Farin and Watson could only stand at the back of their cage, watching in horror as the large snakes inside their small prisons studied them as if they were a meal.

I'd also been warned by Deris that skipping away would result in the deaths of both hostages. I wanted to kill him for that; he'd offered a nasty smile when I glared at him. I held back a scathing retort, too.

I wanted to apologize to Farin and Watson; so many others would have figured this mess out already. Instead, they were stuck with a neophyte who'd only turned Thifilatha once and merely practiced going to mist in the safety of her own bathroom.

I had no field combat experience. The most I'd done was punch a woolly mammoth of a vampire in the face before skipping away like a coward.

We may have a solution, thanks to Tiburon, Kory's mental sending interrupted my thoughts. *You'll have to tell me exactly where the three of you are and then keep me updated on the progress our first wave makes. If they're successful, Anita and I will bring the rest in and take care of business.*

When? I asked. *Farin and Watson are forced to stand, and her legs are getting shaky. If she moves, I'm afraid she'll be bitten.*

It has to be near nightfall, so the snakes feel the effects of the moon and are more animal than usual, Kory replied.

Who's coming in first?

Tibby and two of his cousins. I hope you're not afraid of rats.

How are they getting in? I asked, after pausing to consider what Tibby's animal was.

Are you kidding? Rats can get in just about anywhere.

But what if they're bitten?

It's a chance they're willing to take, Kory said, including a mental sigh in his mindspeech. *The good part of this, of course, is that fool of a warlock can't do anything while you're close by—it'll take normal measures to chase down rats. I've already told Tibby not to wander too far away from you.*

If he can get the snakes' attention, that's all I'll need, I said.

Let me handle this, he said, his mental voice stiff.

You handle Watson, I snapped back. *I'll get Farin.*

Kordevik

"She may be better than you think," Anita pointed out.

"Two lives hang in the balance," I fumed.

"You doubt her capacity to understand that?"

"I think you're giving her more credit than is due," I blew a cloud of smoke to emphasize my point.

"I think you consider her less than she is, merely because she's female," Anita informed me. "How do you think I survived when the bomb went off in my apartment? Lexsi's Thifilatha saved me, that's how. I hoped she'd tell you herself, but it's obvious she didn't."

"What the bloody fuck are you talking about?" I shouted.

"Don't shout at me. She feels unworthy enough next to big, strong, Thifilathi man," Anita retorted.

"Please, no fighting," Davis held up one hand while using the other to rub his forehead. It was clear he had a headache, likely due to lack of sleep.

All of us were in the same boat, or nearly so. None of us had rested. Tibby was back to pacing after speaking to his cousins on the phone.

I worried we'd have an exhausted army to lead into a wine cave we might not escape. At least Anita's information regarding Lexsi's Thifilatha was welcome news—if I had to turn up the heat, it would protect her. The rest—they'd burn just like anything else. Employing my fire had to be a last resort, because for most involved, it would be the final resort.

Yes, I realized how selfish that act could be—that I'd save Lexsi and leave the others to die, but some things are worse than death. A terrible obsession by a less than virtuous Sirenali could make someone do things they'd rather die than commit.

"Lexsi, baby, you'd better be as good as Anita thinks you are," I breathed. "And hope they don't have ranos weapons," I added.

A ranos rifle, from close range, could kill a High Demon. I could survive a shot from a ranos pistol, but it could still injure me; that's how effective they were. My fire could cancel the blast of a ranos weapon, but it had to be timed properly, before it reached me. That meant a fraction of a second.

Almost futile, when you applied logic to the scenario.

Fuck.

"I think we should eat and have a planning session," Anita suggested. "Then rest as much as we can before we go in."

~

Lexsi

Deris and Milton had left our branch of the cave; probably to get far enough away from me so Deris' spells would work. I didn't intend to let the opportunity slip past. Farin's legs were shaking; it was obvious to me that she could drop to the floor at any moment.

Farin, can you hear me? I sent.

She closed her eyes as I carefully studied her; I almost didn't catch the tiny nod as she opened her eyes to watch the snake again.

Don't react when I speak, I said. *Watson, can you hear me?*

The werewolf wasn't as bad off as Farin—at least his legs weren't trembling so much I feared he'd fall.

Another small nod came from him.

Good. Don't react when I speak, then. All right?

I was rewarded with a second slight nod.

"Ai, grz-gitch," I announced aloud.

Both snakes' heads whipped in my direction.

Yeah, they understood me, all right. I'd just called them bastards in their own snake language.

I suppose it helped if two of your uncles were lion snake shapeshifters. That's how I'd recognized these so easily. Uncle Farzi would be proud of me for learning his language.

I also understood something else—these probably didn't know English—or knew so little it didn't matter.

They would, in all probability, understand Alliance Common, however.

"When I get my hands on both of you," I said in Alliance Common while I had their attention, "I'm gonna have belts and boots made from both of you."

Farzi always said that was the worst—for a humanoid to wear the skin of a lion snake shapeshifter. It infuriated them, for some reason.

Probably because it would infuriate me if somebody made boots or a belt out of my skin.

Farin's snake slithered out of her cage before he became humanoid.

As tall as I, he glared at me with eyes going strange with the approach of a full moon.

Watson's snake also slithered out of his cage before becoming humanoid next to his brother.

Twin lion snakes. I'd never seen that before.

Farin collapsed in her cage and began weeping. The shifters barely paid attention to her—I'd insulted both of them. Now I was going to pay.

"What the hell is going on in here?" Milton was back—with a gun. It wasn't just any gun, either. I knew a ranos pistol when I saw one.

Sit down, I barked mentally at Watson, who was now at the front of his cage, gripping the bars tightly.

"You two, get back in those cages," Milton waved the pistol at the shifters. Yeah, they knew what the pistol was, too, even if they didn't understand Milton's English.

Both turned back to snake and crawled into a cage. Yes, they'd stood before me naked.

I was used to that—shapeshifters not having clothing when they returned to their humanoid selves. Thifilathis and Thifilathas didn't either—theirs burned off them. Shapeshifters either burst through their clothing or crawled out of it, depending on their size.

All I'd accomplished was allowing Farin and Watson to sit instead of standing, but at least that was something.

Perhaps I should have skipped out of my cage and took on both snakes, but I didn't. Milton, satisfied that things were back to what they should be, dragged in a chair for himself and sat near the entrance while he held the gun loosely in his hands.

Uncle Lendill would have snatched the weapon away and pistol-whipped him with it.

I didn't have to remind myself that I wasn't Uncle Lendill.

They have ranos weapons, I sent to Kory and Anita.

What kind? Came the prompt reply.

So far, I've only seen a pistol, but if there's one, there are probably more where it came from.

True. Another half hour, onion. Tibby and his cousins will come in, then. We may have reinforcements, too; Davis has been on the phone, calling in favors.

Please don't do anything to get Farin and Watson killed, I begged. I felt I'd done as much as I could, calling the snakes out of their cages once. With Milton on guard, who knew what could happen if I opened my mouth again?

I didn't want to wait another half hour, but I had to. Lives depended on it.

~

Kordevik

I explained carefully to Tibby how dangerous a ranos weapon was. Hell, a normal pistol would blow a rat apart. I think he understood that much, but there wouldn't be a toenail left to bury if he were hit by a ranos pistol. He and the wall behind him would be obliterated.

He only had Farin's safety on his mind, I think. His cousins, Martin and Diego, listened better than Tibby. What concerned me most was that like their cousin Tibby, neither appeared worried.

How would I explain those three deaths to their families? Rubbing my forehead, I nodded to Anita, who'd fold space with them in her arms, then set them down near the wine cave's entrance before folding space to a designated spot at another vineyard across the road.

Davis had set that up for us; we could use the neighboring

vineyard to launch an attack, provided we paid for any damages afterward.

The rest of Davis' plans involved things I'd never considered, but I was used to fighting battles with other High Demons at my side, not werewolves or vampires. His expertise involved using only werewolves, vampires and shapeshifters. He'd never had the opportunity to work with a High Demon before.

"We're going in," Anita announced, pulling me out of my mental wandering. Tibby, Martin and Diego changed, leaving their clothing in a puddle on the floor. Anita gathered them into her arms; I was grateful she didn't appear troubled about holding rats.

They were big rats, too.

It made sense—most shapeshifters were larger than their animal counterparts. I could tell which one was Tibby; he wore an angry expression—more so than his cousins. With no idea how they would survive this experience, I nodded to Anita, who disappeared with her passengers.

The first part of the plan was in motion.

Lexsi

Tibby and his cousins are in the vineyard, near the cave entrance, Anita informed me. I drew a deep breath as softly as I could.

In the past half hour, I'd heard the sounds of electric carts driving back and forth in the main cave, voices farther down and other noises, as if things were either being loaded or unloaded onto the carts.

All three cages were placed in our branch of the cave so we couldn't see what was happening in the main cave.

By design, no doubt. Still, I relayed what I heard to Kory, who informed Davis. Surely, Deris knew I had mindspeech.

Surely.

If he didn't, so much the worse for him.

Don't react if you see rats come in, I informed Watson and Farin. *They're on our side.*

Farin's eyes locked on mine. She was crying again. Neither she nor Watson had been given anything to eat or drink the whole time I'd been there. That concerned me; anyone interested in keeping hostages alive would have attended to that.

They intended to get rid of anyone who knew anything about them or their operation. The Ravens had been killed for the same reason—I was suddenly sure of that. Abe Raven's private investigator was killed too, because he'd gathered information.

Too bad his office had been looted; I suspected that any information he'd gathered regarding the investigation was already destroyed.

After all this time, everything went back to those first two murders. Something had bothered me about it in the beginning, but I hadn't kept on it as I should have. The Raven's daughters should have been contacted in the beginning. At least that would have led us toward Peru.

I realized I was letting my mind wander; Farin squeaked, causing the snake shifter in her cage to turn sharply in her direction.

I blinked—three large rats had gathered beneath Milton's chair. Milton, who was now scrolling through his cell phone while holding onto the gun, had no idea there were rats at his feet.

The snake in Watson's cage, however, had scented them.

Farin, who couldn't stop staring at the rats, made her snake turn in their direction, too.

What followed would have made a good bedtime story for children, if it hadn't been so deadly serious.

When the snakes slipped out of their cages for the second time, both headed for the rats beneath Milton's chair, I waited for a moment, just to make sure they were out of range of both Farin and Watson.

The rats are here, I sent to Kory.

That's when one of the rats locked his teeth on Milton's calf, causing him to scream, leap from his chair and attempt to knock the small rodent shifter off his leg. It resulted in a comical dance while

Milton alternately cursed and shouted, which caused both snakes to back up.

Neither of them wanted anywhere near the ranos pistol that Milton used in his attempts to hit the rat.

Two other rats waited beneath Milton's chair while this went on for seconds—until Milton started shooting. The first shot blew a hole in the cave wall. Milton's second shot obliterated his own leg and part of the floor, but by that time, his rat attacker was already on the other side of the cave.

The rat's companions went to work, then, biting snake tails and dodging out of the way whenever the snakes struck at them.

Wake up, Lexsi, I shouted mentally. This was my opportunity and I was letting it get away.

Mist. I needed to be mist. *Get in here now,* I shouted at Kory. He and a small army of werewolves, led by Davis and Thomas, appeared inside our branch of the cave.

Kory's smaller Thifilathi ripped Watson's cage apart, freeing the werewolf. I, however, misted toward Farin and gathered her into my mist. Her mental shriek at her sudden transformation distracted me for a moment.

Milton, with one foot and part of his right leg missing, attempted to crawl out of the cave.

The snakes had abandoned the rats and scuttled out of our cave as quickly as they could.

Trap.

They'd laid a trap for us.

I could hear running outside the cave—our captors were getting away.

"It's packed with explosives," Watson shouted.

Now I understood.

We were going to die.

Unless—I had no idea how much time I had. Gathering everyone inside the smaller cave into my mist, I flew toward the cave entrance when the entire hillside exploded around us.

CHAPTER 19

K ordevik

As traps went, it was one of the best I'd ever seen.

I barely recalled being weightless for uncounted seconds, while we tumbled so high into the night sky we wouldn't have survived had we still been ourselves.

Still, I attempted to quiet the ringing in my ears from the explosion. I was the only one on his feet, too, when we spilled into the vineyard across the road.

Lexsi was out cold—she'd gotten us safely back to solid ground before passing out. I considered it a miracle that she'd lasted that long.

Unconscious werewolves, rats and one human were also scattered about me, where they'd dropped after Lexsi rematerialized.

Lexsi, somehow, had inherited that talent from her grandmother. I wasn't about to quibble about the amount of vampire in Lexsi's blood —it had just saved our lives.

Turning, I gazed on the smoking ruin of the wine cave. From six hundred yards, I could make out the swarm of werewolves and others, sniffing and digging in the rubble where the smaller cave had been.

They were searching for our remains, to determine whether they'd killed all of us.

"That was rough," Anita sat up with difficulty.

"We're alive," I growled the reminder.

"Yeah. I hope Lexsi gets better at her landings."

"Lexsi's unconscious," I snapped. "She isn't broken, just out. I've already checked."

"Oh. Where is Farin, then? I'll check on her."

The sound of a plane in the distance drew my attention. "Take Farin back to the house, then wake Davis and Thomas," I said. "Our reinforcements are almost here."

Lexsi

When I regained consciousness, I was lying flat on my back with Anita bending over me.

Around us, vampires dangling from parachutes, each holding an unhappy werewolf in their arms, dropped out of the sky, hitting the ground softly. Werewolves were released immediately, and all of them hopped away from the vampire holding them as if they'd been caught in a compromising position.

Yes, I thought I was dreaming at first. Vamps and werewolves seldom got that chummy, even when it wasn't during a full moon. I eventually understood that a changed werewolf couldn't pull the cord to release a parachute, but I was disoriented when I awoke.

Davis had arranged to have his small army delivered to the vineyard across the road from Claudia's.

"What happened?" I croaked while attempting to sit up.

"I think you passed out when we—uh—hit the ground," Anita said. She helped me sit up, then pulled me to my feet.

"Sorry." I wobbled for a moment, searching for balance between rows of grapevines.

"Kory says that Claudia's wolves are digging through the rubble of the cave. They're looking for us. I don't know what they'll do when they don't find anybody."

"They'll find Milton," I suppressed a hysterical giggle. "He shot his own leg off, trying to get Tibby away from him."

"Smart," Anita mumbled. "We'll save that story for later. You okay to join the others?"

"I think so. Is there any water?"

"We have problems," Mason appeared behind Anita. "All the werewolves have changed, including Davis and Thomas. I have messages coming from agents and police near downtown San Francisco. An entire city block is on fire and the firefighters can't put a dent in it. Nothing they've thrown at it does any good."

"Spelled fire," Anita said. "From our friendly, neighborhood warlocks."

"Yeah. I was beginning to think they had more than one," I agreed.

"What can stop it?" Mason asked.

"Either a counter spell, which we don't have, or a High Demon going building to building, to nullify the spell," Anita explained.

A wolf howled across the road.

"I think they've discovered we're not dead," Anita mumbled.

"Somebody has to help with the fires," Mason pointed out. "The entire city could burn if we don't."

"The war is about to start here," Kory walked up in his smaller Thifilathi, breathing clouds of smoke.

"Mason and I are going with Lexsi to put out fires in the city," Anita said. "I trust you can handle things here?"

"Yeah." The word was a growl. Kory didn't look happy.

It didn't take anyone with tendencies toward genius to realize that they'd planned this carefully. Without my mist, we'd have died in the cave explosion. Since they'd failed in their first volley, they intended to split our forces by setting downtown San Francisco ablaze with spelled fires.

What did they plan to do here? I wasn't naïve enough to think this battle would be close to an even match. I suspected they had other tricks up their sleeves, but had no idea what they could be.

Either way, Kory and I were in for a long night. Our enemy wanted us out of the way; that was certain. Their attacks would be geared toward killing us. The rest they could handle with their pet Sirenali and rogue warlocks.

Don't get killed, I sent to Kory.

Blinding clouds of smoke formed his reply.

The unrelenting screech of sirens filled the air, nearly deafening us as Anita set us down at the perimeter of the most recent outbreak of fires.

At least it was night and most of the workers had gone home. Only a few, late-night bars and restaurants were still open; their occupants spilling into the streets as the businesses they'd exited burned behind them.

A few screams could be heard amid the blaring sirens. Firetrucks were everywhere, blasting water at flames that were never meant to be quenched.

"You need to go to Thifilatha," Anita shouted over the din.

What if they mistake me for the one causing all this? I swept out a hand.

Will your nullification work if you're mist?

There's one way to find out.

Then take Mason and me with you.

Fine.

Kordevik

They fired at us, first—a normal shot from a rocket launcher. That meant they had humanoids on their side—werewolves can't fire weapons while they're wolf. Klancy, in Mason's absence, had to take over phone duty with Davis' contacts.

That's when the line of enemy werewolves broke through Claudia's fence and charged us.

Granger's vampires were right behind them. More deafening

blasts hit the ground around me, tossing gouts of earth and twisted grapevines far into the sky. When they fell, we were pelted heavily with vines, rock and debris.

A werewolf was knocked into me by a vampire; whether from our side or the other, I couldn't tell. I'd barely had time to hold back my heat to keep the werewolf from incinerating against my scales. Smaller wars, with participants fighting to the death, were waged all about me.

Time for me to stop worrying about Lexsi and what else might happen. With a roar, I became full, smoking Thifilathi and stomped through the vineyard, heading for the other side.

~

Lexsi

I wanted to weep.

Every time I nullified the spell feeding one fire, another broke out nearby. I could feel Mason cringe every time we flew through a fire, too; Anita refused to give in to her fear.

This isn't working. Anita verified what I already knew.

The buildings are firing in a line, Mason said.

I almost jerked at his mindspeech.

I should have expected it, though. He was a King Vampire. It made sense that he'd have at least one gift.

I'll get ahead of it, then, I replied.

Flying swiftly, I settled in position beside the next building.

The Warlock who'd set the spells was probably laughing at me; the fire moved to the building beyond, which was outside my diameter of effectiveness.

Set us down, Anita sounded weary.

Yeah. I became solid next to the building I'd saved while Mason and Anita tumbled into corporeality beside me. The sidewalk around us was deserted but not quiet—fire has a loud voice all its own. It rejoices with every boom and flurry of sparks as it finds something new to destroy. I wanted to slide down the side of the building, cover my face with both hands and let the tears come.

I, a High Demon who could not only turn Thifilatha but could also become mist, could do nothing against this carefully laid spell.

"At least this one isn't burning," Anita sighed.

"I don't know what to do," I shook my head at her as tears began to fall. The heat from the fires around us dried them on my cheeks.

Somewhere, news crews positioned on the perimeter of this disaster, were recording and reporting while a nation—a world—fed hungrily on their words.

Had this been caused by normal means, I would be reporting next to them.

My mother would have sorted this out—I had no doubt of that. She'd done so many heroic things during her time with the ASD. She'd even forced a volcano to burn—*wait.*

"I think I know what to do," I turned to Anita. "Get Mason back to Kory's army and pray what I'm about to do works."

Kordevik

We were losing. Every time I skipped toward the humanoids firing rockets at us, they relocated instantly. I found myself tiring; stress and lack of sleep ensured that.

The one who'd planned this battle was a genius; I understood now that he—or she—had realized early on what a High Demon's talents were and took measures to combat us most effectively.

The road and the vineyards on both sides was littered with vampire ash and dead or dying werewolves. I had no idea how to sort them, even had I the time to do so.

We're here, Anita announced in my head. *Mason and I*, she clarified.

Lexsi? I skipped toward a nearby hill, where rockets and bullets had been sent flying in our direction.

She says she thinks she knows how to deal with the fires. She sent us back to you, Anita replied.

You need us, Mason added. My addled brain didn't process his mindspeech for a moment.

Yeah. I need you and a hundred more like you, I said. The roar escaped me involuntarily—my quarry had vanished, only to reappear on another small hill to my right.

They were circling me, while allies and enemies died in private battles of their own. I wasn't helping them; I was playing Whack-A-Mole with a talented warlock and losing badly.

Anita and Mason fought somewhere behind me; more rockets fired from another small hill.

Except this time, they weren't ordinary rockets.

By the time the ranos blast tore a hole in one of my wings, I was already shouting mindspeech at Anita to get everyone away. We were doomed and I knew it.

Not many to save, will do what I can, Anita sent back. I understood she was fighting an enemy while making a reply.

I'll hold them off as long as I can, I said. *Let me know when you're past this ring of hills.*

Will do, she grunted.

I'll help, Mason joined the conversation.

Good. Do it now, I'm about done for.

Don't get killed, Mason echoed Lexsi's words.

Lexsi.

I love you, I sent to her and waded into the blasts sent in my direction.

Lexsi

I heard the desperation in Kory's mental voice and understood he expected to die.

Hold on, and get everybody away from those vineyards, I responded.

There was no reply.

Yes, I wanted to scream my fury and grief as I hurled myself toward Claudia's vineyard.

My larger Thifilatha thumped to the ground near the road. In the distance, I could see the rubble of the wine cave. When I'd landed, someone still fired ranos blasts from a nearby hill, causing enormous gouts of rock and earth to fly upward with a resounding boom.

Whatever they aimed in my direction, however, was useless against me. Suddenly, the firing stopped. Suddenly, things had gone still. Quiet. The only sound that could be heard was the fire licking my body.

It's as if I'd pulled the fire from the buildings in the city and clothed myself in it.

A Thifilathi—or Thifilatha—will never be harmed by fire.

Release it, a small voice instructed. *Before they get away.*

Anita

Kordevik hadn't gotten away.

Lexsi, when she appeared at the center of the battle, burned so brightly nobody could look at her.

When she released the fire that surrounded her, a meteor striking Earth would have caused less damage. Light bloomed; the ensuing explosion rocked the ground beneath our feet and knocked us down from a half mile away.

My guess as to the damage proved correct; nothing but a huge crater remained of Claudia's vineyard.

"Are you well?" Klancy, who'd sunk his lengthy claws into the ground to keep from being thrown farther back, ended up beside me.

"I'm okay," I sighed before dropping my forehead onto the grass. "How many did we lose?" At that moment, I prayed that Watson was still alive.

"Many," Klancy replied. "I must go and see who survived; that will be an easier task than counting the dead."

"Kory and Lexsi?" I mumbled.

"No sign of them."

"Fuck."

"Agreed."

I had no energy left, but found some well of strength to hold me upright. It took three trips to transport the living back to Lexsi's house; Watson wasn't among those I hauled.

Davis was wounded; Thomas better off. Mason tended Davis while two other vampires assisted Klancy in setting a few broken bones.

One of Tibby's cousins didn't make it back, either.

"What happened?" Farin wandered into the kitchen, which had become a temporary hospital. She was dressed in a robe and pajamas —somehow, she'd been exhausted enough to sleep. I was grateful for even that small miracle.

The full moon still held sway over every shifter in the house; that's why Tibby's rat squeaked once and leapt into Farin's arms. I'd never seen anyone kiss a rat before, but Farin had her mouth all over Tibby's head. Somehow, with the other events of the night, it seemed perfectly normal.

Watson is gone.

I sighed.

I'd lost three good friends during the night, but now wasn't the time to grieve. I had to help Klancy and the others put wounded werewolves back together. Common sense demanded it. I'd never felt less like doing anything of the kind in my life.

The early-morning news was filled with images of the fires in San Francisco, burning out of control until the miracle happened. I knew it was Lexsi's work, and still didn't understand how she'd done it.

The fires went out, one by one, as if set to a timer. Blink, blink, blink. That's how they died.

Some news stations claimed to have footage of a fifteen-foot, winged creature rising from a city street after the last fire died. Nothing could be proven, however—their cameras only recorded a huge fireball, because it burned too brightly for their equipment to record properly.

I knew it was Lexsi, who held all the fire from all the buildings about her, or possibly *in* her as well. As I said, I didn't understand how she'd done it.

The news then switched to the crater in Sonoma County, where authorities claimed a meteorite had struck Earth, destroying one vineyard and part of another. Authorities had blocked the area from unauthorized visitors, so there were no images on the news.

That crater had also been caused by Lexsi.

Had she known that Kory was taken down? Is that why she'd done it?

I had no answers and holes in my heart.

CHAPTER 20

*L*exsi

Kory's unconscious body covered mine at the center of the crater I'd created. Overhead, a few stars winked in a brightening sky.

Dawn was coming.

If I could muster the strength, there was one more thing I wanted to do. Perhaps I'd dreamed it while unconscious.

I only knew I had to do something or he'd die—the real James Rome, Jr., who didn't look like the real James Rome, Jr.

"Kory?" I brushed dark hair off his face. Like me, he was naked. Our fires had seen to that. Mine, though, had been more intense than any Thifilathi could ever lay claim to.

The ranos cannon blast meant to kill Kory had almost reached his Thifilathi when I sent the fire I held flying. Thankfully, it had kept him from dying.

"Mmmm?" Kory buried his face against my breast.

"We have to go to LA," I said. "To Rescue Jamie Rome. The real one."

"Don't want to."

"I know." I traced his left ear with a finger.

"God, Lexsi, you smell good."

"I smell like fire," I sighed.

"My favorite." He snuggled closer.

"Come on, let's get this done, then we can go to bed."

"Your bed?"

"If that's what you want."

"Yeah. Where are we going again?" He still hadn't opened his eyes.

"To LA."

"Okay. Will you take us?"

"Yes. You can sleep on the way."

"That'll take two seconds."

"You can sleep for two seconds. Then you have to help me get Jamie Rome back to Aunt Bree's house."

"Okay."

James Rome, Jr., looking emaciated and in his late twenties, was chained and gagged in Laurel's closet. We'd walked right through the spell a warlock created to keep him hidden from the authorities who'd searched the house.

I had no idea how long Jamie had been there, but Kory was awake enough by then to allow his smaller Thifilathi to break the chains and toss Jamie Rome over his shoulder.

"I'm burning the house," I told Kory. "Go ahead and take him. He needs food and water."

Kory nodded and skipped away with his burden.

I studied Laurel's closet for a few moments. She'd left designer shoes and gowns behind, in addition to jewelry and who knew what else.

After all, if you have a warlock in your employ, it would be nothing to get in and out whenever you wanted something. The police stationed outside would never know.

Becoming Thifilatha, I blasted the closet with fire. Fine dresses and scarves burned quickly. Skipping to other rooms in the house, I set fires in those, too. I didn't intend for anything to survive.

Fuck you, Laurel Rome, I sent to her. *Fuck you, your warlock and that pretender you say is your husband. Pray now that I never get my hands on you, because you will surely regret it.*

Sirens were sounding at the foot of the hill by the time I skipped away. Behind me, the roof of the Rome mansion caved in with a thunderous crash.

The house was dark and quiet when I arrived. Jamie Rome, after getting water and a sandwich, had been put to bed on a living-room sofa. On the floor nearby, two werewolves snored softly.

The house was full and sleeping.

"Here." Kory, still naked, held out a glass of milk and a sandwich. His plate of food was sitting on the island.

"We can eat this in bed, then go to sleep," I suggested.

"I'm all for it," he agreed. "Should we wake Anita and let her know we're back?"

"No—let her sleep. We'll tell her in the morning."

"It is morning."

"Tomorrow morning."

"Oh. That morning."

"Yeah."

"Come on, onion, let's go to bed."

EPILOGUE

PERU

*L*aurel Rome

"She's still alive," I shouted.

"I agree," Deris said, casually examining his fingernails. "And so are you. I assure you, we'll get around her. Daris confirmed the hit on the Thifilathi, so he's gone."

"What caused the blast at the end?" I demanded. I was incensed that the warlock wasn't taking me seriously. The threat that bitch had placed in my mind—I wanted to blast her with the weapon his sister, Daris, had given me.

She'd said it would kill anything. I wanted Lexsi Silver dead for threatening me. I no longer cared that Granger wanted her for himself.

"A mundane weapon caused that blast, what else could it be?" Deris sighed. "I'm sure it was something they carried in with them—you saw the ball of fire appear at the center, didn't you? I'm sure it was a weapon of last resort, when they saw they were losing the battle."

"We were only watching the live feed, which was cut off when everything exploded," I argued. "We weren't there."

"Look, we're going to make you rich beyond your wildest imaginings, Dervil and I," Deris' eyes narrowed as he glared at me. "All you have to do is sit back and look beautiful. Our business is about to take off."

"That's fine, but I warn you," I shook a finger at him. "If I see her, she's dead."

The End

Lexsi and Kory's tale will continue in *A Demon's Work is Never Done*.